ELEPHANTS

WITH

HEADLIGHTS

BEM LE HUNTE

transit lounge

MELBOURNE, AUSTRALIA
www.transitlounge.com.au

Copyright © 2020 Bem Le Hunte
First published 2019
Transit Lounge Publishing

Cover design: Josh Durham/Design by Committee
Typeset in LTC Kaatskill by Cannon Typesetting

Printed in Australia by McPherson's Printing Group

A pre-publication-entry is available from
the National Library of Australia
ISBN: 978-1-925760-48-4

To the women of the world — the eternal flame of the sacred feminine,
To the transformational hopes of our mothers, and to my mother, who
inspired in me the love of literature.

PROLOGUE:
A CALL FROM THE FUTURE

NONE OF IT would have ever happened if Siddharth hadn't received that call from the future. It came disguised as the usual ringtone from his smart phone — a time machine pulsing with numbers and people and deals and connections yet to be made. It was his business colleague who had bought the house in Golf Links from their family and helped him finance his outsourcing company — a motor trade mogul with a pot belly like Ganesh and an appetite for disruption like the Vedic messenger Narad.

'You heard of this driverless car, yah? We're going to see about getting it out to India, Siddharth, and we could be the first — just imagine.'

Imagination was something that Siddharth had in fountains — especially when the pragmatics were handled by underlings. All they had to do was to go to Goa, where the science fiction stories he'd dreamed about as a kid were waiting, along with some people from Google who had come out from Silicon Valley to paint a picture of an India catapulted into an unrecognisable new era.

This new India was a place where the entire history and forecast of the Earth existed in the same time capsule simultaneously — from the ancient world to a future still waiting to be articulated. And what fun it would be to open that time capsule when the story was told!

'Want to come as part of the investment team?'

Siddharth was known as a shrewd futurist — someone with demonic insight in his capacity as an angel investor. A businessman who could both move and shake and, even more importantly, 'smooth the way' for the momentous changes ahead — a fearless oiler of wheels for the juggernauts of business pushing their way into his country. The pandits (the new ones, that is — not the priestly kind) claimed it was the Asian Century, and Siddharth had no problem at all being a part of the success. Maybe one day when the future called he would no longer be able to answer because he no longer inhabited it, but for now he was part of the invincible subcontinent that was answering the call.

But driverless cars?

In India?

What kind of algorithm or sensor would account for the cow that decided to give birth in front of the Toyota three cars ahead in the traffic jam on the MG Road? Or the cartwheeling, kajalled child beggars by the side of the road? Or the elephants that returned home down the side streets after attending one of those grand Delhi weddings? Why, they'd only fairly recently passed a law that these elephants would have to wear headlights at night — would they equip the prehistoric beasts with sensors next?

'So, you coming to Goa?'

'Why not?'

Siddharth was not one to regret decisions. He never regretted a business deal that failed, never regretted leaving behind his girlfriend in England when he returned from his studies, and never regretted marrying his wife, although there may have been more than the odd occasion for regret. He did, however, regret his decision to ask his son Neel to come with him to Goa as a reward for finishing his High School Matriculation — and yes, he regretted encouraging him to 'have a bit of fun on the beaches' before planning a university education overseas. For if Neel hadn't seen Mae dancing through the fire that night, he could have kept him at home — and he would never have met the Australian girl who had caused all the trouble in the first place, bringing together two continents that hadn't been joined since the beginning of time.

Neel was sitting on a mat, looking at the slow waves lap the shore through a tall fire on a Goan beach — the waves probably slow because he had smoked a lot of *bhang*. He saw Mae first as an apparition dancing in the flames of the fire, which hovered over the inky sea: she was like a goddess who could survive any torture or affliction (how wrong he was about that), and he kept on staring at the goddess in her dress of flames and dancing hands that reached up to the bonfire's golden tips. She came into his life like the miracle of fire on water — the sea in the distance — as she danced towards him to sit down on the beach mat opposite his.

They began a conversation, if you could call it that, even though he barely understood her, perhaps because of the *bhang* or perhaps because her accent seemed somehow less than English, a slur of syllables and unrecognisable cadences. Still, the words weren't as important as the kind of electricity that wakes you up in a dream, hard and ready for your evolutionary purpose.

She sat closer to him, a hallucination: a talking goddess, trying to speak the human language. He mumbled something about being there as a prize for having finished school.

'I've just finished school, too,' she said. 'But Carrie and I decided we wanted to do schoolies in India.'

'Schoolies?'

Neel only found out later about the strange traditions of her distant land, where the beaches of her hometown filled up with vomiting teenagers, on account of the fact that they had just finished their Grade Twelve matriculation exams.

'And we wanted to get away from the toolies.'

He found out, too, about the toolies — the guys who 'cracked onto' the girl schoolies who were too inebriated to object. It was as if he was being introduced to a new tongue — this language of 'schoolies' and 'toolies', together with a world where ladies could go alone to a beach and be groped by unknown men. Not even in the festive rampage of *holi* would such allowances be made in his world. Why, he and his friends always had to work so hard to get a girl to even look at them, yet here was this foreign goddess who had arrived, absolutely without any propitiation, as if his stare alone (together with some *bhang*) had the magnetic force required to summon her.

'Your parents don't mind you travelling together, just two ladies?' he'd asked. The word 'lady' sat well with her. Yes, she could be one of those, she thought. She was far enough from home for it not to sound embarrassing.

'My parents wanted me to go overseas and get some life experience. You know, do a gap year,' she replied.

Through his *bhang*-filled thoughts he tried to imagine such brave parents who would want to send their daughters off to dance on beaches in front of a thousand eyes — to accept the gap in their lives as a natural chasm and wave goodbye to their daughters' virginities. Yet no matter how hard he tried, he couldn't quite picture them. His smoky imagination tried to summon an English gentleman in a pinstriped suit, but the man didn't look like this Australian girl's father. Then he tried to imagine his parents meeting hers and felt sick. No, their parents had to be absent — the centrifugal force of authority had to be circumvented. The two young ones had to be re-imagined like two colonies granted their independence, unattached now from their colonial umbilicus, free to explore each other's continents directly.

And what should they do with such freedom?

Neel held Mae's hand and without words he pulled her down onto a mat, which was only large enough for one person and so required the good patchouli-scented lady to lie down on top of him so that he could protect her hair from the sand. (And this was the pleasure enjoyed by toolies? What gods they were.) For a few minutes he enjoyed the spoils of those toolies, but when he tried to find some words in her language he could only articulate these.

'Do you like India?'

He said this as he ran his hand under a *kalamkari* dress of crimped cotton that Mae had purchased only that day from the local bazaar.

'I like you,' she replied.

He was Rahu now, a creature planet — the rascal god who stole the sun and ruled at his birth, according to their family astrologer.

It took him a few seconds only to feel the skin of her legs — to reach up and find that she was wearing no underpants beneath that *kalamkari* dress.

All that was required was that first brush of his hand against the warm, trimmed, thoroughly modern triangle. A finger slipping into a damp cave that led to another country. One very long seaside kiss and he knew he would do better overseas than in the country of his birth, as is the same for all those with Rahu exalted in their charts. His fate was sealed. But his overseas education would have to take place in Australia now, not at an English university like Oxford or Cambridge, or at a last resort Babson College in the United States, as his father had once hoped, because the new world he was entering had new rules. And women, it seemed, were in command of it.

THE DANCE CLASS

ARUNJI, THE FAMILY astrologer, had once told Savitri that they were entering the age of the goddess rising — and that being named after a goddess would serve her well. 'You have powers that you will discover,' he'd told her once. But on that particular day when Dadi told her to call Arunji, there was no such encouraging prediction.

'Do one thing — make sure you *do not* go to your dance rehearsal today.'

The prosaic nature of this advice stalled her. It held none of the profound or prophetic wisdom of seers long gone, nor the visionary poetry of those uttering wisdom from the depths of consciousness. Savitri held the phone away from her face and whispered to her grandmother, withered by her multiple sclerosis, who was clutching her arm in panic. 'Dadi — don't worry, it's nothing serious.'

'Do you hear me?' Arunji's voice continued. 'Under no circumstances are you to go to your dance rehearsal!'

'Okay, okay, Arunji, I will be certain not to go ...' She felt a mixture of disappointment and rebellion. All of the family and a few friends were rehearsing for a Bollywood dance they were going to perform for her brother's wedding reception. 'You're just talking about today, yah? I can go next week?'

'Just today.'

Odd.

Savitri was inclined to ignore the request, just as she'd ignored other predictions Arunji had made. Like the time he told her that she'd get married before her brother. What nonsense! His wedding was less than a month away — as if she was going to pick someone off the street and marry him to beat her brother to the finish line. She was tempted to go to the rehearsal anyway — what the hell.

Dadi amplified the family astrologer's concerns. 'But how can you go, darling *beti*? Remember what happened to Papa when he went to the golf course against Arunji's advice.'

Oh, that incident! It had been replayed on the ancient cassette of family mythology for as long as she could remember. Arunji had told her father that he had to avoid the golf course and he'd blindly ignored the prophecy. The fact that he'd been knocked out cold by a golf ball hitting him between the eyes was all the evidence required to confirm Arunji's sibylline divinatory powers.

'Please, *beti*. Arunji is our family. He has our best interests at heart.'

Dadi had known Arunji since he was a little boy who accompanied his father to wash Dadi's clothes, squatting on the courtyard floor by a square brick sink and cleaning saris and kurta pyjamas and petticoats and tablecloths under many steaming suns. But as Arunji was to later find out, destiny can pivot in a day. Almost forty years earlier, Dadi was walking past this small *dhobi* as he squatted next to his father, vigorously slapping clothes and swaying to the rhythmic sound of cotton pounding brick. The sun was full glare on white walls and his prospects in life were fully illuminated.

'Why aren't you at school?' she asked.

Dadi didn't need to wait for the answer. Here was a tiny boy — far smaller than her own son but the same age, and his only life choices were between squeezing out cotton or letting it drip.

'But who will help my papa?'

Doubtless, the clothes needed ironing after they'd been washed, and of course Gandhi had announced that caste was a sin against humanity and God — and of course she knew the answer to her next question, too.

'What job do you think you'll have if you don't go to school?'

She was interfering with this sin against God and humanity — she knew full well she was meddling with something that was embedded in the circuitry of culture. She knew she was about to handle live electrical wires in an attempt to reroute the forces that be, but what choice did she have? She was a Gandhian and a housewife — the only action she could take towards equality would have to occur within her household.

'Why don't we send little Arun to school?' she asked her husband that night all those years ago. It was a contest against fate and history combined with culture. The fact that the *dhobi's* father's father's father had also been a *dhobi* didn't even need mentioning. 'He is a naturally intelligent and hardworking boy.'

She was seeing to a rebirth of a kind now — the mother in her knew this much.

'Just let's see if he does well until tenth grade.'

This cosmic intervention was nothing short of electrifying. The fact that Arunji went on to become a professor of mathematics at

Delhi University was astounding, but it was hardly surprising that he should also become interested in the mathematics of destiny, given the cosmic numbers that had devised this plan to redeem his future all those years ago.

Dadi remained fearful after Arunji's latest advice. Not for herself, but for her granddaughter — going off to a dance rehearsal where the dancing Shiva himself could be present, tapping his toes on skulls and laying the world to waste. Her body was tortured with multiple sclerosis and there was nothing she could do physically to stop Savitri except use a little cunning — which she still had command of, thankfully.

Savitri had hesitated at first to go to the dance class — fighting her inherited sense of rebellion, her refusal to do the bidding of men, as fostered over generations of strong-headed women who resisted permission-seeking and sought to lead. Yet Arunji's prediction had made her feel as if she was holding on to both ends of a rope in a tug-of-war competition, as she called the 'spare' driver to pull up in front of the farmhouse. Together, she and the driver headed down the MG Road, with Savitri in the back listening to the dance track on her headphones, oblivious to her grandmother's concerns now that they were travelling away from home. Only when the driver pulled over to the side of the road and opened the bonnet did she think to pull out her earbuds and ask what the hell was going on.

'So sorry, madam. *Garhi toot gayee.*'

Oh shit!

He told her that they would be taking a detour to see 'Sahib' in Chattarpur Farms.

'No way — you've got to be kidding! Fuck, fuck, fuck!'

The 'Sahib' they were going to see was Uncle Hari, her father's best friend from his university days in England. *It's a ploy.* This much was clear to Savitri. Whenever her parents decided to 'drop round' to Hari and Susheila's it was always with the intention of marrying her off to their son.

Mohan would have been the most convenient and suitable match of all time. But what a disaster their last 'encounter' had been! She'd been skilfully avoiding Mohan ever since the night he'd given her too much whisky, disguised in Coca-Cola. The night she'd put her feet in his lap and her head down on a cushion, and she'd felt a crunch. She'd lifted his cushion and found his porno magazine, with the horrible sight of a defiled goddess on the front cover — a toy, not a woman, with parted plastic legs. Being a literary scholar, she'd tried to remind herself that even in celebrations of Durga Puja, when nine days of the goddess were celebrated, women of faith were depicted collecting earth from the *haveli* of a prostitute. So why not collect the 'earth' from this depiction?

She started to read the text out loud to Mohan.

'Give it to me, yah. I didn't buy it. This guy left it here.'

'So you didn't even look at it?' Savitri asked.

'No.'

He stretched down next to her, as if trying to read the magazine for the first time.

'Yah, that position would be so uncomfortable in real life,' Mohan said, his hand reaching slowly up to one of her breasts as the other reached for the page, to turn it. He was leaning over her.

The whisky must have been to blame, because she let him — this man of the world with his libido under a cushion. She let him do what he wanted ...

And now we are going to Mohan's house! It was a detour to hell. The car pulled off the main road and traversed the lush roads to luxury homes in Chattarpur Farms. Savitri found her spine straightening. Authority has a posture. This much she knew from her work at Kamala Nehru College. She could take on the world if she had a straight back. When the car pulled up she strode confidently up to Hari's house to knock on the door. Nobody was there. Brilliant! She waited for a maidservant to appear. 'Mohan Sahib is here,' she told them, 'I'll just call him.' *Oh Shit!* Served with a capital S.

'Don't disturb him. We only want to borrow some tools from your driver.'

But disturbed he was — the male *purusha* energy of the universe was awakened. Mohan arrived down the stairs looking dishevelled. He'd been unemployed since his return from Babson College, mostly because he'd been turning down jobs with the same frequency that Savitri had been turning down the boys who were introduced to her with a view to marriage. He walked over to her, his singlet covering muscles that had clearly been developed in the family gym, pulling on his longish hair, his thin legs and tight pants tucked into oversized Doc Martens. They hugged, amicably enough.

'You been well?' Mohan asked. 'Still teaching, yah?'

'Yes. And what are you going to do with your life, Mohan?'

'I'm going to take a look at your car,' he answered, striding past her.

Savitri was taken off guard. She watched him as he took a look underneath, back down, tummy and chest up, nothing but boots and skinny legs emerging elegantly from under the dark metal. She said nothing, but watched as he stooped over the open bonnet, pulling at meaningless, mindless cords as if he knew what he was doing. Was he the only Indian male in her circle who knew more about mechanics than banking?

'Where'd you learn about cars?' she asked.

'In the US. We took road trips all over. I taught myself.'

'Mmm.'

'You know there's nothing wrong with your car,' he said after a while. 'It works just fine. Maybe it was just an excuse for you to come and visit me?'

'Are you joking?'

'Come on, yah — we should go for a drink together some time.'

'You know I don't drink ...' She realised the irony, given the whisky he'd plied her with last time.

Mohan seemed apologetic. Respectful, even. Different from before. But Savitri got back into her car and instructed the driver to continue on to the dance class.

'Come back any time,' Mohan called after her.

When they arrived back at the MG Road they were held up by a major collision ahead. People lay bleeding by the side of the road, and crowds were using any tools they had to prise open cars. Their driver jumped out to inspect the action. Savitri stayed in the car and tried to look away as she saw a vision of a soul trying to escape its body, possibly a male body, but too covered with blood for her to be sure.

There were enough people around that person. Nothing she could do.

'Take me home,' Savitri instructed when the driver returned to the car, calmly, even though every cell of her body was shocked at the happenstance. She felt her entire body steeped in awakened gratitude: even for Mohan, for her grandmother, the driver. She knew nothing. There was so much to learn. Hamlet came to her mind: *There are more things in heaven and earth, Horatio, than are dreamt of in your philosophy.*

ॐ

Siddharth was just about ready to go for his monthly facial and manicure when his driver announced that his wife, Tota, had just rung and he had to go for lessons with the dance master instead. He looked at the perfect face of his Patek Philippe watch — something he usually did with pleasure, because it was the one piece of jewellery that a man could wear. Yet even the miraculous Patek couldn't squeeze the hours up close enough to fit in his trip to Venus Beauty Parlour (the men's floor, of course) as well as a dance class with the choreographer hired for his son's wedding. Where was he going to find the time to make an appearance at the office to make sure the good-for-nothings were working?

Even though Siddharth's wife had her own driver, Tota commanded Siddharth's driver as if she owned the world — which of course she did. 'Memsahib told me to take you straight to dance class,' he announced, and in their familiar silent submission to all things female, driver and master made their way towards a room at the Taj Hotel, where a dozen or more family members were set to rehearse a dance routine that in Siddharth's mind was promising to turn the wedding into a circus.

'What a *tamasha* there would have been if my father were forced to dance for our wedding,' Siddharth announced crossly as he reached for a copy of the *Hindustan Times* and went straight to the 'Delhi Times' section to see if he knew anyone on page three. If the future had to belong to his son's generation, they'd be better off preparing with their brains, not their *bhangra*.

'Yes, sahib, what a *tamasha* there would have been if they'd forced your father to dance at your wedding,' the driver lamented, repeating, as always, exactly what his master said with a 'sir' for emphasis and implicit agreement. Siddharth always took great comfort in his reflection as given to him by his driver: the one and only person in the entirety of India who never had an opinion on anything of importance — or any opinion at all, for that matter.

The driver turned off the cricket, knowing that sahib liked to read the paper in silence, and turned on the air filter of the Mercedes as the engine began to puff smoke over the perfectly trimmed lawn. There was so much pollution you couldn't get from the farmhouse to central Delhi anymore without the air filter. It was the artificial lung that made this city liveable, the only way of cutting out the air that one had to breathe in between the farm, the office, the club and proper homes.

Siddharth's hesitation to dance was more complex than a mere case of lead feet. It was the heaviness in his heart that slowed him down, and turned what would have been a proper, traditional, Punjabi *shaadi* into a 'wedding'. His son, Neel, was marrying that Australian girl he'd met in Goa.

Mae.

When his son had told him about the 'girlfriend' on the phone, Siddharth said, 'Why did they name her after a calendar month?'

It was his way of pretending that the news was of no significance, and like the month of May she would pass. But somehow the name stuck: it spelled trouble, disruption, distraction and disloyalty, right from its first utterance.

'We named you after a god,' Siddharth said, to accentuate the chasm between the girlfriend and his son.

'Yes, and why the hell?' Neel replied. It was Neelkanth in full, a name for the blue-necked Lord Shiva that completely lost its sacred colour in translation.

At the airport, both parents, both drivers and Buddhi Ayah, Savitri and Neel's ayah, who had looked after them ever since they dribbled breastmilk, were waiting for his flight to arrive at Indira Gandhi International Airport, inside the terminal where it was air-conditioned. And in that same cool air, that girl, Mae, appeared next to Neel, pushing their shared luggage. She was wearing a dress down to the ground like Tota used to wear when she was back in college, and she had the kind of blonde hair that made foreigners look anaemic.

'You must be June,' Tota spurted out quickly.

'Wrong month,' Neel replied, hugging his mother, and began to make introductions that seemed strangely formal.

Tota gave her an outsider's hug — a brief and distracted formal embrace that was a simple recognition of existence, nothing more.

Siddharth noticed that it was Buddhi Ayah, frail and wizened, with two missing teeth, and soft, loose skin under the layers of her white sari, who took Mae's hand, kissed it, stroked her face, teased out her blonde hair, muttered something in her native Bihari and then burst into tears of joy. Mae gave her boyfriend's elderly nanny a patchouli-scented hug and allowed herself to cry.

'I've heard so much about you,' she told Buddhi Ayah, who kept murmuring meaningful vowels and consonants, and touching her hair again, examining it like she might have examined the bright yellow tresses of the Barbie dolls that Savitri used to play with as a child.

As soon as they arrived back at the farmhouse, Neel announced privately to Siddharth and Tota that he intended to marry Mae.

'What are you saying?' his mother asked. 'You hardly know the girl!'

'Err, Mummy, we live together,' Neel replied, 'so I know her a *lot* better than you knew Papa before you got married.'

'Is she pregnant?' Tota asked, direct as a bullet.

'Mae wants an Indian wedding, so no, she's not pregnant,' Neel responded emphatically, as if to ward off the premature assassination of his heirs. Then he added with a hint of cruelty, 'And we have every intention of returning to Australia to settle after the wedding.'

'What for does she want an Indian wedding, then?'

'You'll get to know her,' Neel added. 'You'll see. She's not what you expect from a *firangi*.'

It was true that Mae had a passion for all things Indian, which was why Siddharth now found himself on his way to a dance rehearsal for their wedding — she had more passion for Indian dance than he ever could. Siddharth was far more comfortable pulling out his credit card to pay the wedding organisers than he was putting on his dancing shoes, but for now the dance was his 'duty', and if there was something that Siddharth had absorbed since he was a child, it was his obligation to 'do the needful' in the delivery of duty.

The car pulled up at a detour due to a horrific incident on the road, which triggered Siddharth's heart to go into one of its familiar involuntary spasms. But nothing to worry about. He turned on his GPS and navigated along an alternative road until they pulled up smoothly in front of the pillared lobby of the Taj — a grand entrance of the whitest marble with every square inch defying the Delhi dust. The doorman opened the passenger door for Siddharth to get out. He asked the concierge for the hall where the dance practice had been organised and was promptly shown to a room where some loud filmy music was playing.

Tota glared at Siddharth as he entered, and Neel and his cousins started complaining that this was no time to arrive, halfway through the class.

The 'master' was a young boy, lithe and, most importantly, accommodating. After Tota whispered something in his ear the dance master said, 'Madam, no problem, we will be giving him a separate dance to perform so we won't have to be starting from the very *bigning*. Sir, you can come here and please start making this step like this like this like this.'

Rolling his eyes, Siddharth joined the others at the front of the line. It was clear that the joke was on him. He was the klutzy-footed father of the groom and somehow that meant that he was the perfect foil and centrepiece.

The master showed him some awkward moves, which Siddharth mimicked, making them more awkward still. His was a different routine, but he couldn't see what the others were doing because they were all behind him, and tittering — probably at him rather than each other.

'Now, I want you to be putting your foot out and turning it like this like this. Backwards, left side, right side' ... Siddharth's foot twisted from left to right, taking off in any direction, like a deserter, while the rest of him jiggled from side to side, his body inside his jacket almost as still as a mannequin.

Siddharth couldn't see the gyrations of the small family group behind him, but he could hear their giggles and the way their feet tapped to the rhythm of the song, intoxicated by the dreadful beat.

'Perfect,' the master shouted out. 'There's only one problem, sir. You are forgetting to smile!'

Siddharth squinted and let one corner of his mouth rise to the occasion, reproducing the exact smile of Amitabh Bachchan in an early performance as *Don* — an arch gangster's undecipherable, undecided smile.

'Yes, we are all happy now,' the master concluded. 'We will make everyone dance with us for the *shaadi*. Everyone will be happy!'

THE USE-BY DATE

S AVITRI'S GRANDMOTHER HAD felt it was almost improper to cross over the chalk line that separated 'her' century from the new millennium. The future, however, was shamelessly waiting. Slowly it encroached on her life, presenting an endless track of noughts. Sometimes it felt as if she'd be using those noughts as stepping stones for the next thousand years — if only she could take steps. As it was, she was pushed into the twenty-first century on wheels, thanks to the damned multiple sclerosis.

Everything about her room remained as it had always been. She had a display cabinet with exquisite glasses from a business trip to Czechoslovakia she'd taken with her husband as a younger woman. In those glasses the Iron Curtain still hung, and she still told stories of the guards at the country's borders. In her room, Gandhi was still alive in a statue carved out of sandalwood, even though it had long ago lost its fragrance and had half lost a hand, which now dangled loose, holding a book. Even so, with his head stooped, Gandhi had travelled with Dadi into the Asian century.

She also had a broken cuckoo clock from her trip to Switzerland, where as a young woman she'd spent a month at the famous Bircher Institute, trying to solve her digestion problems. Unlike Dadi, the cuckoo had long ago transcended time, giving up on the precision of the coil fashioned by its makers. If anyone asked why it had stopped working, she would tell them about how Siddharth, aged six, had stood on a chair to take the bird from its perch and tucked it under his pillow. Then she would move on quickly to stories about the Bircher Institute, especially the one about the discovery of amoebas in her stool. So rare was the discovery in the alpine purity of Switzerland that everyone in the institute was invited to look through the microscope at the squirming splodge, with its pseudopodic dance of rearranging endoplasm.

There was nothing about the twenty-first century that ever entered her room, except her grandchildren, and they continually tried to drag the new century in with them, brandishing its temptations.

'Dadi, why don't you stop using that landline? We can give you full wireless access, no problem.'

Dadi didn't need a phone that could slip out of her hands and find a new home in her bedsheets. She liked being able to reach out to the Bakelite receiver by her bedside, neatly connected with curling wire, and let her fingers dial the numbers of her beloved ageing cohort with ritual accuracy. Every morning she'd do what Savitri called 'the rellie rounds', ringing each of them up to ask them how they felt on that particular God-given day.

'*Aapka tabiat kasa hai?*' she'd ask again and again, as if the ailments of her cohort were the social glue that kept them all here in the twenty-first century. 'And did you have a bowel movement today?'

She was always happy to discuss bowel movements with the ancient ones — indeed, they could all pontificate on them for hours, and you didn't need a Blackberry or an Apple for that.

Her deepest wish, the one that she would never articulate in public or in private on the phone to her contemporaries, was to be no longer held for trial in God's waiting room. Her only constant companion in this whole business of ageing was Buddhi Ayah, the grandchildren's nanny, who had long ago stopped spoon-feeding Savitri and Neel and begun to look after Dadi's ablutions instead. Buddhi Ayah was getting old herself, though, and it wouldn't be too long before she would need someone to be doing the same for her.

You could say that it was a mistake to have come this far, but it was more than that. Dadi had been pulled into the future by a prediction that Arunji once made: a prediction that she would only be able to rest in peace once Savitri was married and the future was secured, and that this in turn would secure a spiritual destiny for her heirs — all of them — for the millennia to come. A transformation of sorts. A legacy.

When Arunji had first come up with these words, Savitri was a literature student specialising in feminist writing and sacred texts written by celibate seers from the Vedic era — two fields of study that didn't lend themselves to marriage. Nor did her *Manglik* status, an astrological curse that stated no man could marry her without some threat of death in doing so. She adored her granddaughter, but she seemed to 'suffer' from too much education. What to do about her stubborn nature and her refusal to get married?

Dadi decided to call Arunji over to see if there was anything she could do to help the girl, especially with the whole problem of ...

the problem of ... she didn't like to say the word *Manglik*. She didn't like to think of her granddaughter as someone with a curse — not now that they'd entered the twenty-first century. She didn't like to think of her granddaughter as anything but a goddess.

ॐ

Arunji had failed to report the exact troubles around Savitri's chart, even though his own destiny was bound to the Kailash family's in a cosmic collusion of the most outrageous proportions, and you could even say he was obliged to tell them about the upcoming incidents. He had never offered to explain how Savitri's mathematics of destiny and Dadi's commitment to seeing Savitri married could be untwined. Yet Dadi remembered every prediction her 'son' had delivered, including his promise that she would live to see her granddaughter married — and yet Savitri's marriage was not even on the distant horizon. What was he thinking?

'Arunji, tell me more about my tryst with destiny?' she asked when he came to see her.

Arunji understood this euphemism — taken, as it was, from Nehru's Freedom at Midnight speech.

'Mataji, I am not knowing what kind of independence you are seeking,' he replied.

Dadi made it clearer still. 'All right. No tryst with destiny. Tell me one thing: what is my use-by date?' She was not one to have a tantrum, but she was getting impatient.

There was no escaping her question this time. What Arunji's spiritual mother meant was that she wondered when Savitri's date with destiny would arrive, given the fact that she had rejected every eligible bachelor her parents had introduced to her and was in no hurry to find herself a suitable boy.

Arunji began to randomly write some numbers and rewrite a few more.

'Tell me, is there some kind of problem with Savitri? Apart from the *Manglik*, which we can of course manage.'

He didn't respond. Instead, his comb-over fell off the top of his head, which was otherwise boiled-egg bald. He recognised the hair falling down as a sign that he was lying. It always happened when he refused to speak the truth of his numbers. The hair fell, and his bald head was revealed like a brown crystal ball that spoke only the truth. There must have been a hunch in the back or a twitch in the neck that made this happen whenever Arunji had to present the future as if it were unknown and adopt the innocent ignorance of events that were either too obvious to highlight or too disastrous to unveil. Yes, the hair always fell, and the bald patch was always exposed, yet it was invisible to anyone else as a sign. What's more, this sign occurred regularly with the Kailash family, because just as they had triggered an intervention in his destiny, he had conspired to intervene in theirs, with love and compassion, whenever there were issues that simply needed to be concealed. It was a sacred duty, he believed, this whole business of concealment, and by some strange twist, an act of cleansing not too different from the original role he had played as their washerboy in the old house when he was a child. There were so many secrets in those stars that needed to be wiped clean of significance before he could possibly present them to his patrons as predictions. He readjusted his comb-over and continued to draw some signs and circles and tokenistic gestures in honour of the science of Jyotish.

'You haven't told me. You're hiding something.'

Arunji felt a terrible burden of responsibility. He had tried to demonstrate his gratitude to Dadi in every way possible, because she was a mother to him — she hadn't given birth to him, but she was responsible for his rebirth, and he had honored the gift with regular visits, not to mention attention to her laundry needs, for many, many years after the obligation should have ceased to exist. Even when he was a junior academic at Delhi University, Arunji used to come every Sunday to personally hand-wash Dadi's clothes, as he had promised his father he would always do. Dadi used to beg him to stop, but she loved seeing him. She loved hearing the stories of good fortune and the gratitude that accompanied these tales.

'You must stop thinking about when you'll be going to your heavenly abode, Mataji,' Arunji insisted. 'It's not healthy.'

Besides, he'd never before issued any terminal numbers, even when his most famous clients had asked for them. Whenever they appeared in his calculations he skipped over them — looked away and instantly forgot the figures — because in his mind the date of death was only a single point on an ongoing journey. A turning point in a story.

But Dadi applied the same persistence to her interrogation as she had to Arunji's education.

'Why won't Savitri get married?' she asked again. 'She's never been interested in a single boy we've introduced to her.'

Arunji thought about his professional duty. Like journalism, his art demanded a semblance of truth. Yet, like a doctor who has taken the Hippocratic oath, he still had an obligation to 'first do no harm'. So how should he tell her of the hurdles that lay ahead? Instead he repeated a prediction that he could stand by.

'You will live to see your granddaughter as a married woman. And how!'

Dadi began to weep. '*Hai Ram*, if only Neel could help Savitri find someone!'

Now those noughts of the new millennium stretched across a thousand more years till the end of time. What hope was there for Savitri?

'Maybe Neel *will* help Savitri!' Arunji responded.

'Neel will be walking around the fire and Savitri will have nobody. How will it look?'

What Dadi meant was that the Bedis and the Jains and the Kapoors would wonder why they'd let Neel get married before his sister, even though he was three years younger. By birthright and order of descent, she deserved to be married first.

Seeing Dadi's distress, Arunji began afresh with his prediction. 'You will live to see this miracle of Savitri as a married woman and you will see it in all its splendour, so please don't be getting anxious, Mataji.'

Dadi tried to think about Savitri and a potential husband. She tried to remember the exact chemical formula that such an attraction required, but nowhere in her physical memory could she detect the place in the human body where one can accommodate such desire. It had disappeared long ago, when she had lost her legs and all sensation from them. Her only wish now was for a departure, and that seemed like many, many millennia away, due to Savitri's reticence to even look at a potential suitor, let alone agree to marry one.

INVITATIONS AND INTRODUCTIONS

QUITE SOON AFTER the nine hundred invitations to the wedding of Neel and Mae had been sent out, a murmuration of gossip began to fill the airways alongside the Nokia ringtones, and Siddharth was at just the place to hear them, drinking whisky and snacking on pakoras with a group of business colleagues at the Gymkhana Club.

Meena, an elderly regular at the bridge club who was always impeccably decorated with a string of gobstopper-sized pearls around her thick neck, came to give Siddharth a Chanel-scented hug.

'So exciting to hear about Neel's wedding. We're so happy for you, but you never would have guessed — I thought it was an invitation for Savitri's wedding, would you believe? I didn't have my glasses on!' Meena smiled through layers of make-up, fully expecting Siddharth to share her sense of surprise that it was Neel getting married, not the older daughter who should rightfully be pushing past him to the front of the matrimonial queue.

'We haven't found anyone good enough for Savitri yet.' He tried to laugh as he added, 'Even though they'd all be good enough for us!'

'Oh, don't worry, she's a darling. It will happen.' And with these words she went back to playing bridge, leaving behind a saccharine-scented haze of superior fragrance. Sure, it would happen — but when?

Pran Aggarwal, who was sitting with Siddharth, had never thought of Siddharth as a potential in-law, but found himself sizing up his old colleague as the proverbial two and two came together.

'You know, we're looking for Gokul. He's just come back from studying for his MBA at Babson College.' Ah, Babson. The place where all the good boys studied. Pran immediately pulled out his phone and started flicking through pictures of his son. There he was, with a graduation cap on his head, smiling with satisfaction — perhaps even at his future father-in-law?

'What a handsome boy!' Siddharth responded, and he was telling the truth, but at the same time searching for flaws that Savitri might pick up. Damn it, he had begun to think like the girl. He had to cast these thoughts aside. Gokul was from a known family, so he would be perfect — but what would happen to his reputation if Savitri turned down Pran's son? He felt obliged to issue a warning.

'Savitri won't be married unless she agrees to the match,' he said, adding tactfully, 'even though I would give the marriage my blessing this very day if it were in my power.'

'Don't worry, let us just introduce the young people — have dinner, yah? That is all that we will be doing.'

'And you can meet Mae, Neel's fiancée,' Siddharth added. It was the one certainty he could offer. Perhaps the soon-to-be-weds could encourage the hope-to-be-weds. Perhaps this marriage business was contagious. Perhaps Neel and Mae could be the spring that makes everyone's thoughts turn to love and nesting. But by way of another warning, Siddharth added, 'My son's fiancée is from Australia.'

Pran wasn't going to say it, but he didn't like Australia. He'd gone on a business trip to Sydney once and had been knocked down by a car while crossing the road. He did make one concession, though. The hospitals over there were very good.

'Sure, sure. Let's make a date.'

Tota had spent an entire afternoon getting the house ready for the imminent visit. She told the *mali* to turn on the fountain, which gushed a river into motion around the garden path, culminating in a synthetic waterfall. She instructed Ram Lal, the cook, to create all the Punjabi classic delicacies and spent a full hour working out which sari she should wear to welcome the Aggarwals to her home.

Dadi got out of her dressing gown for the first time in two months and had Buddhi Ayah iron one of her finest Banarasi saris. Putting it on was a struggle, because she had to be lifted to wrap the six yards of silk around her frail body and make the pleats neatly, and only then could the feather-light bones be lifted into her wheelchair, but it was an effort worth making if it meant that Savitri would finally find a nice boy. Siddharth had told her that the boy was very handsome. In her mind the whole business would be settled, and in fixing the date for the wedding her own date with destiny could be realised. The groom-to-be, Gokul, hadn't even set foot in the house, but as far as Dadi was concerned, the gods and goddesses were having a celebration in advance, such was her eagerness for the match.

As for Savitri, she decided to play along only because she was beginning to feel the pressure of letting down her brother if she didn't go ahead and at least look at the boy. The evening drew closer, and with Gokul's imminent arrival came a flutter of activity around Savitri, which she found mildly irritating. She was receiving far too many instructions. She'd planned to meet Gokul in a Fab India kurta with a who-gives-a-damn attitude, but she was told to wear a dress in her wardrobe designed by Gauri and Nainika, as Gokul had been educated overseas and perhaps would want a more modern girl. The dress had a neckline that swooped low enough to be sexy for Gokul yet retreated just in time for it to be respectable enough for his parents.

I'm being paraded like a cow in silk chiffon, she thought. *Why am I even agreeing to this?* But then she caught Dadi's proud eyes — and saw the expectation etched into the brackets that widened on either side of her smile. The kurta-clad Cinderella had been banished and Savitri was ready to meet her prince.

Savitri was told to wear some lipstick. NO. *I want to be who I am.* She began to paint some black *surma* around her lips but washed it off when she thought of Dadi, waiting for her to emerge from her bedroom looking even more like a princess — not like a witch. She put on some of the doll-red glimmering stuff instead and stared at another woman in the mirror. She could have been stuffed.

A large Toyota pulled up and Savitri watched from her bedroom window: Gokul was checking his reflection in the passenger-seat mirror, adjusting his hair. He wasn't nearly as bad as she'd imagined. Perhaps she could even go through this marriage business, for everyone's sake?

She ran downstairs to the garden. Siddharth was there to welcome the much-anticipated potential in-laws: Pran, his wife, Amrita, and their son, Gokul. He shook Gokul's hand with the firm confidence of a man with means.

'I'm so glad you could come and meet all of us, and our new daughter-in-law,' Siddharth said before ordering drinks and securing comforts, trying not to look in the direction of either Gokul or his daughter, who nonetheless were the focus of the show.

'Aren't you going to introduce Savitri?' Dadi asked. She'd been waiting for this moment all day and she knew she wouldn't be able to last the night. Everything was working out. Why, the girl had even put on lipstick!

Savitri and Gokul were introduced, casually, as if they weren't really the reason for this important gathering of clans, ready to converge, to mingle juices and bloodlines. Nonchalant, hospitable, unattached.

Savitri found herself watching herself smiling back at him — watching herself because everyone else was watching her smiling at him. She was a spectacle in her own eyes. She put on a Mona Lisa half-smile, then committed her lips to a more docile smile, like the one you're supposed to put on as you cover your head with your sari *palla* and touch your mother-in-law's feet. She felt her lips quaver at the edges from the show. The dress was beginning to feel too racy. It didn't go with the sari *palla* smile. What's more, she didn't dare to smile at Gokul in case he misread it as desire, because there was none of that, but she did notice once more that he was good-looking, and this was the first good-looking son that any of Papa's colleagues had managed to squire.

'Go and call Neel and Mae,' Tota instructed the sweeper, Adarsh. 'You have to meet our happy couple,' she enthused, ordering Adarsh to call the soon-to-be-weds, who would surely prompt the hope-to-be-weds into action.

Adarsh was a timid young boy from Bihar who spoke mostly with his kind eyes. He hurried upstairs to the mezzanine level, where he hovered outside Neel's door, not wanting to knock because he felt sure that he could hear some breathless foreign language being spoken inside. He put his ear against the wood and heard that the foreign language was actually the familiar international language of lovemaking. *What daring*, he thought, *all while memsahib is trying to make a match downstairs!* He boldly knocked on the door, at the command of his mistress, and exactly as he expected, the sound dulled.

'Memsahib wants you to come and meet the guests.'

'*Bhago*,' Neel replied — Get lost. 'I'll be there in a minute.'

The soon-to-be-weds came downstairs and Neel made a discovery that he really didn't want to make.

'Hello, everyone,' he said, and his eyes landed on Gokul. *My God. HIM!* The instant Neel saw 'the boy' who had been brought along to meet Savitri he felt a sinking disappointment, knowing what he knew.

'Gokul — we've met before, but I don't quite know where.' He was testing him — Neel knew exactly where.

'You look familiar too, but I can't place you.'

Neel felt pleased that Gokul didn't remember. They'd both been very drunk at the time.

'What a handsome boy,' Gokul's mother offered. And to Neel she said: 'This must be your beautiful fiancée we've heard so much about.'

'Nice to meet you.' Mae nodded to everyone gathered around the living room, wondering what exactly they'd heard about her. 'Savitri, you look beautiful.'

Buddhi Ayah wheeled Dadi a little closer to Gokul so she could ask 'the boy', who she already thought of as Savitri's husband, if he could step closer so that she could have a proper look. Neel watched Gokul touch Dadi's feet; as he rose, she took his head in her hands and looked deeply into his eyes, making no attempt to disguise the fact that she was examining the virtues of her granddaughter's future husband.

No, no, Dadi — hold those hopes! Neel thought.

So the formalities continued, and Neel witnessed them all as if his sister were a princess and he her bodyguard, allowing all the pleasantries to float past his ears — alert to the dangers that only he knew about.

After dinner was served, the Aggarwals upped and went, as one does after eating, and it was time to talk business.

Dadi was the first to ask the question, as soon as the doors of the Toyota were shut. 'He was such a nice boy, *hey nah,* Savitri?'

'Yes, he was really nice,' Savitri replied.

Silence.

This was a first.

Almost too much to believe.

Did she say he was nice?

'So should we talk to Pran and Amrita?' Siddharth asked.

This was too much for Neel. He had to say something.

'What if they back off when we tell them she's a *Manglik*?'

He knew he had brought up the unmentionable — the tainted star that had hung over the hospital the day that Savitri was born. The star that so many feared would mean the death of any spouse who agreed to marry her.

'*Chup*, what nonsense,' Dadi said.

'It's true, though — they'll find out and then they'll back out. They'll find some excuse.'

'Nobody believes in this nonsense anymore,' said Tota, smirking.

'Then why are there still columns in the newspaper of *Mangliks* seeking partners?'

'What's *Manglik*?' Mae asked. She was intrigued.

'It's dumb shit,' Savitri replied.

'Totally dumb,' Tota echoed.

'If you're born under this star then you'll kill your spouse — it's unlucky for you unless you marry someone who is also *Manglik*.'

Neel could see that Mae simply wouldn't get it. For her, this family secret must have seemed like a bizarre dragon, trapped under their castle and fed by ancient, irrational beliefs.

'Weird. So it's like a curse — that means there must be some way to lift it?'

'Yah, yah — they still make the poor girls marry a Peepal tree before they marry their husbands, to trick the planets and save the lives of innocent men,' Neel explained.

Mae seemed utterly fascinated, clearly wondering what kind of a marriage you could have with a tree. He tried to see it from his fiancée's perspective and it looked very odd indeed — this idea of a tree entwining you with its draping roots and feeding you its figs.

'I'm not marrying a bloody tree,' Savitri announced.

'What nonsense,' Tota said. 'Let's just speak to his parents.'

'Forget it,' Savitri said. 'He's ugly. You can arrange anything you want, but I'll lock myself in the bathroom rather than turn up to any wedding you put on. I'm taking up *sannyas*. I told you all before.'

'They're not going to ask for your birth details,' Siddharth replied.

'Bullshit. They always ask in the end. They can't stop themselves,' Neel said, heated up well beyond his usual temperature. 'How about we change her birth certificate?' He was laughing now. 'We'll all have to remember her new birthday, but she'll be married off in no time! And finally we'll all be rid of our responsibilities!'

Neel was willing the marriage plans to fail before they all got too excited — hating his own repulsive performance.

'Forget it — I'm not bloody marrying anyone if they're from your gender. I'm not some kind of cow you can put in a field with a prize bullock. You can get lost, all of you!'

Neel hadn't meant to be so cruel. Like the rest of the family he had tiptoed around the whole *Manglik* business and pretended that the curse didn't exist. He hadn't intended to bring up the issue of Savitri's astrological status, so he decided to speak with his father to tell him the truth — that Gokul had made a pass at him in a Delhi nightclub a couple of years earlier. They'd been waiting to use the bathroom and Gokul had offered to share it with Neel, trying to take his hand and lead him inside. Neel had politely declined, but Gokul had been persistent and Neel had found a hand reaching for his pants. He needed to explain all this to his father — to somehow mitigate his behavior.

'Nothing against Gokul,' Neel told Siddharth, 'but would it be fair on Savitri to let the marriage go ahead?'

'Savitri would be better off married to a Peepal tree,' Siddharth replied.

If it hadn't been for her waterproof make-up, Savitri would have had black tears falling from her heavy eyelashes as she started to take off her jewellery. Mae reached out to hug her.

'It's bullshit that you're going to kill your husband,' she consoled Savitri. 'Unless you're going to kill him with your good looks.'

'I was only going to do it to help out my arse of a brother, because I'm meant to be married before him.'

'I've never seen him be so awful to anyone,' Mae said. 'Let's go down and ask him why the hell he did that.'

Savitri didn't want to go back downstairs, but Mae persuaded her to confront Neel. They found Neel holding Siddharth's pulse and Ram Lal wiping his forehead with a cold cloth.

'Papa's having a turn,' Neel said.

'He suffers from arrhythmia,' Savitri explained to Mae. It was clearly no time to talk about Neel's unacceptable behaviour. And so the unspeakable curse had its tongue sliced off once more, and it seemed that the world would simply have to continue hurtling into the future, tolerating its ancient, invisible presence.

Dadi had already been wheeled back to her room, to rest and recover from the disappointment of wedding vows that would never be made. She lay on her bed and felt cross not only with Savitri but her entire generation. In her day, girls were willing to oblige their families and their husbands and even nature. And what on earth was wrong with marrying a tree, anyway, if it would appease the sky and trick the fates and make your in-laws happy? What was it about the young people today? Why were they so fearful for their futures?

As she lay on her bed, watching the fan make the shape of more and more noughts, she dozed off, not knowing if she'd ever see Savitri as a married woman, not knowing if she'd ever be released from this mortal coil. And then dreaming ... in and out of thought forms. She remembered the nuns from her convent school days. Hadn't they taken vows of marriage? Yes ... yes ... they had married God. Would that be good enough for Arunji? Hadn't Savitri said that she would rather take *sannyas* than get married? And hadn't Arunji once said that Savitri's chart glowed with spiritual light? So this was what he'd had in mind when he'd drawn up the chart ... it all made sense ... and it fitted with the story that she knew about her granddaughter, unwritten as it was. She would marry God ... yes!

TWO HUNDRED YEARS AND COUNTING

WHEN THEY FIRST moved out of central Delhi to get some fresher air, Savitri noticed that the farm at number thirty-three was different from the others — outside this farm there were women waiting in groups at four in the afternoon, tying their dupattas into makeshift cotton bags and balancing baskets of grass on their heads.

The 'spare' driver (she liked to think of him as her driver) had been found locally, so she asked him what they were doing. 'Memsahib, they are coming to collect the cut grass,' he said. 'The big people are cutting it every day and these women are using it to feed their cows.' She later enquired what happened to the grass that came off the lawns at their farmhouse and learned that it was left to dry and burn. No such altruism.

Later, Savitri began to notice that an hour or so after the women had collected their grass each day, young children would gather outside the house, dancing, pushing and throwing stones, unable to sit down in the dust and wait for free grass like their mothers.

Her driver told her, 'They are very good people in this mansion, memsahib. They feed these children so they don't go without their *khana*.'

Curious now, she began looking at number thirty-three whenever the driver brought her back from college. One day as her car was passing, she saw that the gates had been flung wide open. An entire world expanded in front of her, layer after layer of it, and something of a future unfolded. Inside she saw workmen erecting white tents, a dais, loudspeakers, microphones and red carpets; they busied themselves placing garlands of marigolds and tuberoses on the podium and at the gates. When she asked the driver what was going on, he told her they'd invited a two-hundred-year-old guru down from the hills to come and give discourses at their farmhouse.

Who were these people at number thirty-three and who on earth was this two-hundred-year-old guru? And more to the point, was this her opportunity to turn her paper-based study of ancient sages and their wisdom into a real, embodied study?

The driver told her that Ram Avtar, the owner of the house, was a local farmer who had owned all of the land around Ghitorni, where her family's farmhouse was built. For most of his early life he'd milked his buffalo by hand and sold this milk to locals, but as New Delhi expanded and the inner-city time bomb exploded into the mushroom cloud it was now, growing upwards and outwards, the city *wallahs* had come looking for 'rural' land. Encroachments started on the Mehrauli—Gurgaon road and businesses started building illegal constructions by the roadsides. A flower seller brought out a few buckets, then built a shack, which turned to a shop, which somehow attracted the furniture makers, who needed tea, which meant the *namkeen wallah* arrived, and so the march to the call centres and garment factories and malls of Gurgaon became flagged with opportunities and delights to entice the pilgrimage to the shrine of the future, which was moving ever closer to Rajasthan.

And then the cars came — and how! The Commonwealth Games, and the light rail too, to demonstrate the patriotism resurrected by the new century.

It didn't take long for the developers and builders to start arriving at Ram Avtar's farm. To be honest, he only sold his first block of land to them because he was worried that they'd build there regardless, willy-nilly, brick by clumsy unqualified brick, saving money on the cement in between them. His land was close to the road, after all — a road that had once been a track in the time of his great-great-grandfathers, a track lined with the shadow of Ashoka trees to shelter the people who travelled between Delhi and Jaipur.

The first piece of land he sold to these developers brought in more money than he had ever imagined he could earn in a hundred lifetimes. He replaced his hut with what he thought was a lavish house and carried on milking his buffalos.

Some time passed, and the next piece of land came up for sale; it was much smaller, yet he earned three times as much for it. Of course, he'd worked out by now that this land was only going to get more valuable, because he'd met his new neighbours. They'd started building their farmhouses — not the mere farmkeepers' cottages the law permitted them to build on these blocks that weren't really farms in any real sense of the word, but rather walled gardens with massive constructions for homes: divided plots of farmland with swimming pools, fake hillocks, fountains, follies, stages, cloisters, verandahs, columns, Greek statues and even the odd rushing waterfall and garden nymph. Ram Avtar still milked his buffalo by hand every day, but he was no longer beholden to his beasts for a livelihood — they'd become his lucky charms and he was a disguised king in a cowherder's costume, just like Lord Krishna. Instead he started to milk the new lust for rural land on the outskirts of Delhi — land where the air was less polluted and guests could be invited for parties. Oh yes, and what parties they had. How they entertained their imaginations as well as their guests! There were weddings where once there had been milkmaids: weddings where guests could walk down long paths lined with garlands; weddings where uniformed guards were interspersed between the garlands to protect the ladies who came in yards and yards of elegant silk, jewels gushing more than any waterfall that flowed in the new farmhouse gardens that lined the MG Road. Truly, from the time he was a boy until when he was married he'd thought of Delhi as a distant opportunity. Now he *was* Delhi. The New Delhi. And the so-called rural land that had been his duty had become his boon.

Eventually Ram Avtar knocked down the house he'd once thought was grand and built himself a fantasy mansion in keeping with all the neighbours' homes. His newfound friends, the developers, gave him architects and carpenters who worked in teams on his lawn. Stables lit with a single light bulb became a quaint memory. Now electricians came to connect him up to the brave new cosmos where airwaves and wires linked his world of buffalos to the towers of New York, London and Paris. The electricians came with the shrines and tools that they worshipped and they prayed that the gods would protect them from the shock of satellites and 4G and force fields beyond even Krishna's imagination.

And from then on everything was an intoxicating electric rush. There was a single sizzling charge between Ram Avtar's farm in Ghitorni and the world.

Realising that he was not only able to sell his own land, but also help his people sell theirs and profit from the hard work of their ancestors, he began to work as a go-between, then a real estate agent and then a developer, who had his own *babus* and *mistris* and *wallahs*. Before long he had his own fountain, his own cobbled pathway, ten bedrooms for the great-grandchildren of his great-great-grandfather's. He had inlaid marble floors with paisley twirls, and even a statue of a koala in the garden, a bit like the Greek statues in some of the other houses he'd helped to build. He bought three new Mercedes and sent his children to good schools and they learned English, which he'd never learned, and he even considered sending his eldest daughter to the University of Middlesex in England, but then thought better of it. What would she do there, anyway? Why would anybody ever need to go to England? India was surely the future global centre.

Ram Avtar and his family came into Savitri's life at the same time as Guruji, at the same time as she went past number thirty-three and saw the gates flung open and the marigolds welcoming the world to share the spiritual bounty of a rush of good fortune that the new India and New Delhi had laid at their feet. Savitri asked her driver to stop the minute he said that there would be a two-hundred-year-old guru about to visit her neighbourhood. This she just could not miss.

'Madam, you must be coming to the discourse,' said the girl standing inside the gates. The girl was Ram Avtar's eldest granddaughter, Sweetie.

'Please be coming at five p.m., *pukka*,' she told Savitri. 'Guruji likes to start with *aarti* exactly at this time, and only after this, then he is talking.'

'And can I bring Dadi?' she asked.

'You *must* bring her' came Sweetie's reply.

And so the time was set for Savitri and her grandmother to meet the man who was to become their guru — five o'clock that day, English time, not Indian, just as Guruji had requested.

They'd never had a guru until this watershed moment. They'd had a family priest with an office in a dark marble room next to the Ganga at Haridwar — a man from a lineage of priests who kept the books that recorded each and every birth, death and marriage of their ancestors, who had long since gone. The book had generations of signatures and dates that marked the continuation of their bloodline over centuries — forebears who had come to pay their respects to the holy mother Ganga, the liquid goddess. Long before Savitri was born, these pandits had waded down the sacred steps and knee-deep into the Ganga's chilly Himalayan water, their oil lamps reflected in the ripples they made in time. Over the years, these same pandits had overseen every urn of ashes that had been brought to throw into the holy river; the pandits had helped ancestors long forgotten to launch floating leaf boats with dying flames downstream, and they'd blessed every child that had ever been born into the family with vermilion powder and dried rice on their foreheads. And yet, in spite of it all, they were more like holy accountants than wise gurus, or so it seemed after Savitri and Dadi met Guruji.

The man who was soon to become their guru looked to be in his fifties, with only a little grey in his hair and a few flecks of grey in his beard, eyes of glistening depth and thick eyebrows for shade. His voice was low and warm and educated, and he wore a modern-looking orange robe, not the dirty robes worn by the mendicants with begging bowls by the roadside. No glasses, either. He'd obviously been smearing his eyes with some secret Ayurvedic camphor and soot mixture that maintains eyesight for a thousand years or more, should his mere two hundred years extend that long.

Absolutely nothing about this man appeared ancient or decrepit. He was a miracle, a modern miracle of India — and yet he would have been there before the British traders turned into conquerors. He was born in the time of kingdoms, maharajahs and stolen treasure chests. He'd lived in Punjab before partition, where he travelled the North-West Frontier by camel, and he'd seen the riots in the wake of Churchill's quaking hand as partition boundaries were drawn. He'd been alive when there was no New Delhi, only Old Delhi. When there were only bullock carts in its streets, not cars, let alone autorickshaws that played 'Where's the Party Tonight?' He was alive when you could still see the stars twinkling over Delhi. When you had the time to lie down on a straw mat on your roof and look at those stars that had now gone into *purdah* behind a thick veil of fog. When there were no sounds of horns, just the calling of crows, the bleating of goats, the sigh of cows and the clicking wings of crickets in these parts. He was born when a cow herder would always be a cow herder. When you would have to tie a sari around your loved one and jump into the village tank together if she wasn't of the right caste. When there were no high heels or miniskirts or tattoos or movies where ladies undressed and let their lovers, not their husbands (if you please), press down on them as they sighed with pleasure. Forget even that — there were no movies at all. He was born in a time when there were no air conditioners — when dozing servants pulled a piece of string with their toes to mobilise their masters' fans ... And my God that was old!

'We have reached a stage in our evolution where we can no longer trust ourselves as a species,' spoke Guruji from his podium, decorated with marigolds, stroking the fragrant *mala* that hung from his neck. 'We can no longer rely upon our ability to solve the complex problems of the world today that we have created from our limited, disconnected, short-sighted thinking as individuals seeking only the best for ourselves. If we are to progress, and it is my purpose to ensure that we all do, then we must all become a little "touched" by the divine, no matter how we conceive of it. Inspired to embody goodness and be its witness in the world. We are going to have to rely on forces that require our fullest capabilities and our finest hour of collaboration — forces that we have not yet witnessed ourselves wielding.

'We are going into a future that requires not only ancient wisdom, but a new kind of wisdom: a state of consciousness that doesn't leave the thinking to the mind or the feeling to the heart, but requires our whole being to work together, transformed in the way it receives infinity. We have arrived at a moment that requires us to seek the most purposeful, in all its luminous geometry and poetry. A time when our inner lives will be validated as integral to all that our outer lives achieve ... And as we go into the future with this gift, there will be nothing in the cosmos, either in the material plane or the spiritual plane, that cannot be directly cognised.'

Dadi gripped Savitri's hand and brought it up to her heart as Guruji continued telling them of the more practical boons of a meditator's life. 'Silence permeates that layer of consciousness below thought or speech. Its functions are intuitive and spontaneous and evolutionary. It knows where to give life, to give healing. It powers the world whether you know it or not, just in the same way that you are breathing whether you're aware of it or not.'

Oh honeyed words, dripping like sacred nectar over the two of them!

Both Dadi and Savitri learned to meditate that same day in the surging exultation of their many hilltop epiphanies, and they continued their practice every morning and evening till the end of their days.

For Dadi, meditation became one of those routines you added to all the other daily routines to pass the time, like brushing your teeth or having your hair oiled. Nobody needed to know that she'd been following the advice of a man in orange robes who spoke of kingdoms of consciousness. She didn't like to boast about it or even tell people that she was meditating. Indeed, Buddhi Ayah mostly thought she was taking a doze, as she usually did her practice in a horizontal position.

Savitri, on the other hand, decided that everyone needed to have their lives changed — and nobody more than her father, who she felt should meditate for health reasons if nothing else. What better way to reduce his blood pressure and manage his heart condition, after all?

'I don't have time to meditate,' Siddharth said. 'I have a business to run. I have mouths to feed.' It was funny how Papa always talked about feeding mouths, when in reality his business was more about putting a Mercedes on the front lawn and an empire in his son's hands — and even naming that enterprise Neelkanth Enterprises after his son, to ensure that the empire was passed on to the correct male beneficiary.

'There are many other busy businesspeople who make the time to listen to Guruji,' Savitri told him.

'Of course,' he said, without adding that it was in the guru's interests for businesspeople to visit him and pay for his wisdom. What use were grandmothers or dependent unmarried daughters, after all?

'If you go and see Guruji and learn to meditate, then I'll go on a date with Mohan.'

Now this was no ordinary offer. This was the *über alles* bid to end all bids in the history of marriage negotiations. Savitri had thrown it into the conversation oh so casually, fully knowing that it answered Siddharth's most persistent question: the *What the hell am I going to do with Savitri if she carries on refusing every boy I introduce to her?* question. It balanced the eternal equation on every father's mind and did so with superb symmetry. Why, if she were to marry Siddharth's best friend's son, he would be able to die in peace, his responsibilities complete. Or at least he wouldn't have to embarrass himself with yet another business colleague when his daughter turned down one more darling *raja beta* — a king child, pampered with excessive masala-rich love.

This enticement was followed by an interstitial silence that was enough time for the deal to seal and those present to feel the force of it.

Hari and Susheila, as well as Siddharth and Tota, had been encouraging the two of them to 'see some more of each other' ever since Mohan had returned from America with a degree in economics.

'You'll really go on a date with Mohan? You mean a serious date?'

Savitri knew what this meant. A serious date meant one thing — that they could start fixing a date for the wedding.

'I'll go to dinner with him if you learn how to meditate.' She knew this wasn't quite enough. 'Maybe Mohan and I could talk about possibilities ...'

Siddharth reverted, just when she thought she had him convinced. 'But how can I believe in anybody who claims to be two hundred years old?'

And how can I date a guy who has touched me while looking at pictures of somebody else? she thought. *No, Papa, I'm the one who is making the sacrifice here. I'm doing it for you.* What had happened with Mohan was tame, according to her friends who were willing to talk about such things. They had to put up with their uncles and cousins doing such things to them, quietly, while pretending to be their chaperones and mentors — the same men who propitiated the goddess without knowing of her powers.

'Okay, forget about Mohan — you obviously don't need to learn to meditate if you're so worried about the evil Guruji,' Savitri snapped. 'Mohan's hideous, anyway.'

'He is not. He's very handsome and very qualified and he'll look after you so well. Everyone has said this all along, no? And won't it be so much better to have someone who is known?'

Of course. It was always better to have someone in your house who was known. They always said the same thing about the servants.

'So you'll go and learn to meditate?'

'Yes, yes, I'll go and see your Guruji ... And the meditation will be so good for my health.'

Incredible — he almost sounded like he meant it.

'But you've got to do the practice, too, yah? You can't just learn to meditate and forget about it.'

'Yes, yes,' Siddharth replied convincingly. 'You fix a time and I'll come and learn. I promise. I would love to learn!' His old heart was a-rush with young love. Was this all it was going to take to get his daughter to fulfil one of his dearest wishes, a wish shared and cherished by Mohan's father, his childhood best friend, Hari? For Siddharth this had all the potential of that first business deal, which allowed him to buy his digital publishing company a few seconds before the whole world (not to mention his important overseas clients) started hanging their hats on a digital future. This was the auspicious watershed moment in their family's future. If he could have poured milk on that moment as a libation, he would have requested gallons of it from the old cow herder who passed as a neighbour at number thirty-three.

And the gods? How they must have laughed as they made their own plans to shift the earth's axis to make way for the coming events.

STUMBLING ON THE 'REAL' INDIA?

NEEL HAD SPENT the past half-hour in his parents' bedroom discussing the wedding without Mae, so Mae, sick of waiting for him, decided to take a walk around the grounds of her fiancée's family home, which she'd been so keen to explore since Neel first described his farmhouse.

'A farm? You live on a farm? In the middle of the city?' She couldn't imagine how — even the farms in Byron Shire didn't seem real by Aussie standards. The real farms were thousands and thousands of hectares wide, with a few lonely gums reaching out to the cockatoos for company, the odd sheep or cow snuffling around in the scrub, and a creek or dam, usually dried up for most of the year. Naturally, Neel's farm couldn't have been like this because it was in a major Asian metropolis, but she still couldn't picture what kind of a farm could exist in a city until she arrived and set eyes on what passed for a farm in Delhi — Neel's farm — without cattle or crops. 'Of course we grow vegetables,' he'd told her back in Sydney. 'But mostly these are eaten by the servants.' Only later did Mae discover that the family's vegetables were harvested from Spencer's, the European food store in nearby Gurgaon.

Mae put on her shorts and her runners, slipped a camera into her pocket and began her rounds of the 'farm', first running up the red earth on the driveway, past the perfectly pruned palms and the lush abundant Queen of the Night, the Flame of the Forest, the sunflowers and seedlings in pots that lined the driveway. She waved to a gardener who was squatting as he picked weeds off the ground and to another who was sweeping the beautifully mown lawns as if they were living carpets. The staff waved back self-consciously and looked the other way. She continued running up the pathway, past the fountain to the front gates, where she waved at the guard, who immediately leapt off his seat and saluted.

'Good morning, sir,' he said.

'Er ... good morning,' she replied, feeling embarrassed to be a 'sir' rather than a 'madam' — although to be either felt a little uncomfortable, to be honest.

At the gate she found her way to the wall and decided that she would do a few circuits of the grounds to work up a sweat. She continued running, past a creature that looked a bit like a ferret (a mongoose, she would later find out), which triggered a reflexive urge to reach for her camera. It wouldn't stand still so she followed it as it made its way towards the back of the property into a patch of guava trees. She couldn't call it a guava orchard; it was more of a small gathering of trees, a few guava trees and some star fruit trees as well as some other trees that were totally unrecognisable. There was a monkey in one of the trees, so the camera came out again, and as she took a photo of the monkey baring its teeth she heard some children laughing to her left.

'Namaste,' she called out.

'Hello' came the giggling voices.

The wild-eyed little boy was beautifully dressed in a fake Nike *Just Do It* T-shirt and the girl wore a skirt and a shirt with puffed sleeves.

'Can I take your photo?' Mae asked, gesturing towards her camera.

The two children put their arms around each other and produced two perfectly painted smiles under the guava trees.

'Thank you,' they said in the cutest voices imaginable. Mae showed them the photos she'd taken, and the boy asked if he could take a photo. Mae put her arm around the skinny little girl and smiled for the shot.

'Do you live there?' she asked them, pointing to the small hut nearby.

They giggled some more and pointed to a similar hut on the periphery of the property, behind an enormous mound of earth at the edge of the large vegetable garden.

The children started walking to their quarters and Mae gesticulated, pointing to herself and then at the house, hoping she could follow them and see inside a genuine Indian home — at last she'd arrived in the real India, here on the periphery of a farm that wasn't really a farm. *But would I be welcome?* The girl in the puffed sleeves smiled as she nodded towards their hut, and Mae took it as an invitation, although it was probably more of a gesture that they'd be off now. Just as she thought this, little Just Do It charged ahead, like an omen and an invitation combined. *What the hell, life's too short to sit around waiting for permission. They're just kids — how could they mind?*

The kids darted inside and hid behind the door. Mae went over to the hut, and seeing that the kids had taken off their sandals, she took off her runners, knocked on the door and heard them giggle nervously. She gently pushed the door open. The wild-eyed Just Do It boy and the puffed-sleeve girl began talking loudly and excitedly in Hindi and scrambling over the two single rope beds covered only with a thin mattress. Mae stepped inside. One step was all it took to discover their entire home and a single glance to see everything it revealed. There were two single beds (for the four of them?) plus a little area off to the side for cooking, a few plastic flowers, a cupboard, a mirror, a picture of an Indian cricket player (she had no interest in cricket) and a small shrine — a home within a home for statues of Krishna, Ganesh and Laxmi. No second bedroom, no ensuite, no bathroom.

'What a lovely house you have,' she said, knowing this was disingenuous flattery and knowing too that she might be uttering unintelligible syllables. *And just as well.* She reached for her camera but thought better of it. *But when will I be in a house like this one again?* She hadn't taken a single shot of the big house, where Neel and his parents seemed to be forever locked up in bedrooms in endless dialogues, no doubt over her presence and the urgent need to matchmake for Savitri. They'd hardly left the confines of the 'farm'. For God's sake, it was as if they were living out the back of Bourke, not in one of the world's largest urban centres. But it seemed there was a deadlock that would have to break first, and then the prison doors would be flung open and they could begin to explore the real India. Together. And free from his parents.

Seeing Mae was about to put away her camera, little Just Do It reached for her hand and took it with a hopeful smile. Mae helped turn the camera back on, and the little boy took a lopsided photograph of Mae, one of the single window and another of half his sister's face. Seeing these accidental images of India, Mae decided to set up the camera for a time-delayed shot so they could all be in it together. She asked the children to sit down on either side of her and they sat for their portrait, this time with no smiles as they were too distracted looking at the three lights that flashed before the aperture opened.

The moment was recorded in the silence of anticipation.

And as the kids stared and Mae sat motionless holding unknown children under her arms, the door opened, a woman in a nightie and a head cloth entered, and there was an almighty scream that everyone heard coming from the servants' quarters.

Rani (the children's mother) hadn't expected to scream, but then she hadn't expected to see a foreigner sitting down in her hut holding her two children like she was their mother, and she hadn't expected to have this woman with anaemic hair arrive as her guest, as a god, and have nothing to give her to eat for such a blessing. So without even saying hello, she pushed the door shut and rushed to the back door of the farmhouse and into the kitchen, where she beseeched her husband, Ram Lal the cook, for something to eat.

'The *firangi* memsahib is in our house!' That was enough information for the half-lame cook to jump up from the chair where he sat cutting *bhindi* and bitter gourd. She continued, breathless, 'I have nothing to offer her.'

'Hai Ram Bhagwan!' The cook gave her some Parle-G biscuits from his own collection. He couldn't give the cake, because Tota counted the pieces left after every meal, and he couldn't give the fancy sugar-free biscuits from Spencer's or the chocolates, because they'd been locked up in an *almari* after the sweeper had started absconding with them a couple at a time for his children.

'What in Bhagwan's name is she doing in our home?' Never in the modern history of the farm had anybody from the big house come over to any of the servants' quarters for tea and snacks. Even when a new servant arrived, another servant would be assigned to take them to their quarters. Whenever electricity, water, anything in the servants' quarters needed to be fixed, a workman would be sent. Once, and once only, the architect who designed the farmhouse had walked down to the edge of the property where four of the huts were located, but that was not in the living memory of any of the servants working there on that particular day.

'Bhagwan knows what she is doing there, not me.'

Rani ran back to her house with her Parle-G biscuits just as Mae was leaving, and was so rushed trying to extricate one from the top of the wrapper that she broke it and ended up handing over half a biscuit to her guest, without thinking.

Mae was more touched to be offered half a digestive than she ever was by any banquet at the farmhouse. 'Thank you.' She bowed in a kind of Japanese gesture of gratitude, not knowing exactly what she was meant to do, and ate the biscuit with Rani, Just Do It and the puffed-sleeve girl watching eagerly.

'Thank you,' she said once more, wiping the crumbs from the side of her mouth like an inexperienced geisha. She put her hands together for Rani and patted little Just Do It and his pigtailed sister goodbye. She walked back to the farmhouse, not knowing the speed at which the news had spread, from kitchen to bedroom, from mobile to mobile. The only one who didn't know the 'news' was Neel, who was currently in his room, depressed after speaking to his parents, lying on the single bed staring up at the fan. But Mae was still free of guilt about her innocent excursion, still without knowledge of the invisible boundaries she'd just transgressed or the furies that would now be unleashed.

Tota was the first to see her, and she told the cook to bring some tea as she took Mae into the living room and shut the door.

'Mae, where the hell have you been?'

'I've been in one of the little huts at the back of the property.'

'I know. You've been to the servants' quarters. Everyone knows. Don't make a fool of me.'

'Then why did you ask?' She hadn't meant it to come across so rude, but Tota wasn't speaking too politely either.

'You cannot just walk into these people's homes.'

'I'm sorry. I didn't know.' She decided to stretch the truth, just a little. 'I was invited by the cute little girl who lives in the house.'

'That girl had no business inviting you in.'

Mae still couldn't work out the severity of her crime. Certainly, she couldn't fathom a reason why Tota would say what she said next.

'Mae, if you're going to walk around the place like you own it, I'm afraid that I'm going to have to ask you to leave.'

'But ... but I was only going for a walk.'

'If you want to go for a walk, then go outside. Walk all you want up the road and go into the village, but don't go walking around the property into every home you can find. These are simple people. You'll make them feel so ashamed and so uncomfortable.'

Right then it was Mae who was feeling more ashamed and uncomfortable than anybody else within the farmhouse walls. But even more than the shame and discomfort was a loathing of Neel's mother that could hardly contain itself. *Can you even hear yourself? Or are you too much of a bitch to give a shit?*

'I'm sorry. I won't go wandering around on my own again.' There was a hint of the tip of a sharp instrument in her words, but she thought better of having it out with Tota like she did with her own mother back home. Instead, she walked carefully on the eggshells of cultural difference. *I'll tell Neel and he'll tell her that if someone invites you over in Australia it's rude not to accept. I'll get him to tell the bitch and stand up for me.* She had a sense of her own power as she felt her heart quicken. *You know, if he comes home with me you won't have any control over either of us. I can take him away from you, don't you understand? I deserve some respect.*

Of course, none of these words left her mouth.

'Let's forget about everything we've discussed now,' Tota continued, and Mae felt momentarily ashamed of her internal fury, which bubbled up like a poisonously intoxicating moonshine. 'You like exercising, so let me take you out and we can get to know each other a little better. How about I take you to the ladies' hour at my swimming club? I think you'll really like it.'

Mae started crying with gratitude at the unexpected invitation, and Tota took her dupatta and dried the girl's eyes.

'It's no use crying now,' she said. 'It's done. You weren't to know. This isn't your culture.' And Mae couldn't help feeling that it would never be her culture as long as Neel's mother kept treating her as if she'd have to change where she came from in order to belong.

The folded wheelchair leaning against the door halfway down the corridor was not a sign that Dadi had given up on the world. No, it was a sign that she was still prepared to go out and fight the good fight if she had to, even if it meant giving up her place on God's waiting list.

In the bedroom behind that door, Dadi and Savitri heard the *tamasha*. Dadi took it lying down and Savitri took the news bolt upright when Buddhi Ayah was summoned to elucidate on the quarrel between the bride-to-be and her soon-to-be mother-in-law. It was through gossip that Dadi still had her ear to the world, and it was through her most well established and most reliable chain of rumours that this news of Mae's indiscretion was conveyed.

'Why didn't anyone tell her not to go to the servants' quarters?' Dadi asked, but if truth be told, nobody would have thought to tell Mae, because nobody would have realised that the borders that existed like concrete structures in their lives, bolstered in language, cemented in etiquette, were in fact totally and utterly invisible to those who didn't make the cement.

'Invite her to come and talk with me,' Dadi continued. 'Maybe we can explain.' She felt for the new bride-to-be, coming into a strange home with her heart too open and her eyes still covered by the eye mask she'd worn on the aeroplane. How could she warn the future darling wife, in the most tactful way, of the mother-in-law she was all but marrying? A woman she herself had silently, well ... disliked ... and disliked over many years without anyone having any suspicion of the fact.

When things like this happened, Dadi always lamented the fact that Arunji hadn't been an astrologer at the time of Tota and

Siddharth's marriage, otherwise he would have alerted his patron to the potential nuptial mismatch about to take place. Surely?

Back when Tota and Siddharth were still young and hadn't yet learned the compromises that a marriage entailed, let alone the concessions required in an arranged marriage, they would continually throw insults at each other over family meals. Tota announced over her aloo methi and paneer one day that she could no longer tolerate having to sleep next to a 'dud' and could her in-laws please provide her with another bedroom so that she could awake without seeing his ugly face. Dadi, who was never one to pull on anyone's moustache, simply agreed that she would give her daughter-in-law her own bedroom, and the in-laws would move into a smaller room. She said all this as if she were simply a hotel concierge, compliantly booking another room for a disgruntled guest. She didn't once betray her concerns until she arrived at Arunji's Delhi Development Authority flat and asked him to construct the horoscope she had failed to order when they were looking for a girl for their beloved son.

'Your daughter-in-law did not cook the customary ritual meal when she first arrived at your family home,' he told Dadi, as a way of warning her about the woman who had married her son. 'She simply bribed the cook to make it.' This was the only revelation that Arunji made about the new bride in the household, clearly not wanting to cast any mathematical curses across their path retrospectively.

Tota thought back to that first day when Tota came to the old house as a new bride, with red and white bangles up to her elbows, her hands and feet imprisoned in a filigree henna cage. Even then Dadi recognised the defiance — the refusal to bow her head to her in-laws or touch their feet. Instead, she'd held her head high as she went into the kitchen, and began the way she intended to continue, with instructions to the chef to cook channa bhatura. She stayed in the kitchen, of course, to look as if she were making the customary first meal for her in-laws, but she was above the staff, and so her role was only to poke the batter and look as if she knew its perfect consistency, which of course she didn't, having never really entered the kitchen in her parental home.

It was not as if Dadi felt that it was her daughter-in-law's duty to cook for her. Dadi was always the one who questioned the given order — she was the one who had turned Arunji's universe on its head and shaken it until it produced an education. But there was something about Tota ... there always had been, even when they first went to her family home to see what they could organise for their son.

The tension over marriage distilled and made Dadi's thoughts turn to her graddaughter.

'Savitri, you mustn't be afraid to have a love marriage, just because of this business with Mae,' Dadi confided.

'I'm not having any marriage, Dadi.'

'But what will become of you if you don't marry?'

'I'll be happy,' Savitri replied.

Dadi didn't know how to push past this barrier. Instead she told herself that at least Neel had a good chance — and if she could ensure that his marriage went ahead smoothly, then perhaps she could rest in peace after all.

'Ask Mae to visit me,' she urged Savitri. 'And ask Buddhi Ayah to bring some mithai so I can sweeten her mouth.'

Savitri returned after a few minutes with Mae, red-eyed, and Neel holding her hand as well as a tray of mithai. When he saw his grandmother he bent over her and offered his forehead for a kiss. Mae did the same, and Dadi held her face in her hands and looked closer at her, through her cataracts. 'God bless you both. I am so happy for you.'

At this point Mae's tears erupted all over again. Dadi hoped it wasn't because she was seen as a force of authority. 'I have nothing against a love marriage,' Dadi said. 'You have my heartfelt blessings.'

'Dadi, Mae feels as if she's committed a murder in our house. All she did was visit the servants' quarters.'

'What was it like?' Savitri asked.

'Shut up, Savitri,' said Neel.

Dadi watched Mae press the rewind switch on her camera and look at the images flicking across the screen.

'Let me see.' She reached over for her glasses.

Mae showed the pictures of herself with the puffed-sleeve girl and the cheeky Just Do It boy — three innocents unaware of the drama that would soon unfold. Dadi couldn't see much because the images were so small — indeed, the entire incident was small in her mind.

'Nothing happened,' Dadi said with a *tut-tut*. 'Such sweet children. You mustn't worry about any of it.'

Neel leaned over Dadi again and kissed her forehead.

'But you have to be a bit careful with Mama, darling.' Dadi was looking seriously at Neel now. 'I've spoken to Arunji about this. I think it may be because you've picked an inauspicious date for the wedding.'

'Oh, please! Don't mention the Delhi Golf Club incident again. Papa was playing golf. Golf balls fly! Someone's gonna get hurt sooner or later.'

'*Beta*, please. I want you to go and talk to Arunji and get him to draw Mae's chart.' She added, 'I'm so worried about what he's told me.'

'Who's Aroonjee?' Mae asked, making the astrologer's name sound like an exotic fruit.

'He's the son of a washerman,' Neel replied.

'No, no, darling, don't say that,' said Dadi. 'He's a professor of mathematics at Delhi University.'

'He's a famous astrologer,' Savitri added.

'We're not changing the day of our marriage,' Neel said. 'The pandit is happy with the date. The invitations have all been sent.'

'But I'd love to meet an Indian astrologer ...'

'If you get astrologers to make matches for you, then you end up with these marriages made in heaven like the one set up for my parents.' Neel blurted it out. He hadn't meant to be so nasty and he regretted it the second he saw his grandmother's face, her eyes large and moist and full of love.

'He wasn't an astrologer when we made the match,' Dadi said, her voice quaking.

'Neel will never go and see Arunji ... I'll take you,' Savitri said. And then she added: 'Dadi, didn't you want to give Mae something sweet?'

What was needed in that moment, more than anything else, was something sweet — this much Dadi knew. And if sweetening her new daughter-in-law's mouth was cosmically possible, then it had better be done quickly, before the ensuing events made every one of Arunji's concerns come true.

AN AGREEABLE GRUNT

S AVITRI'S AVERSION TO boys and matchmakers had been inherited in her DNA from Tota, with every X chromosome crossing out the possibility of proposals or marital meddling of any sort. When Dadi had arrived with Siddharth at Tota's childhood house to show her the boy who would become her husband, Tota hadn't looked into his eyes once but instead continued interrogating Dadi. 'Who-all does the cooking in your house?' Translation: *Will I be required to be your slave?* 'Do you mind if your daughter goes to work?' Translation: *Are you going to force me to go on shopping outings or sit at home making small talk with you about how wonderful your son is?* The last question about work was particularly important, as she'd been working with the Delhi Women's Chamber of Commerce as a legal advisor. Her father had organised the job for her because he didn't want his daughter to find herself in one of those dark rabbit-warren gulleys beside the Delhi law courts, crowded with men in sixteenth-century wigs and poorly fitting twentieth-century suits — all of whom had lined their shelves with books they bought by the metre and never read.

Much better for a girl to have a proper office with a window and to work with ladies from good families than have her sliming along the corridors of power to satisfy the avaricious desires of Delhi's *goondas* and crooks.

Tota had embraced her genteel introduction to middle-class feminism. 'The ladies there are as good at getting the needful done as any man,' she told her father, and he smiled, assured that he had found her a suitable job, even if he couldn't satisfy her by presenting her with a suitable boy.

Nobody had expected Tota to agree to marry Siddharth, and perhaps she never did agree, because when she was first asked, and was told that she'd be living in a grand house at Golf Links, she simply grunted, and they took this as approval. There were conditions that followed the grunt (of possible consensus, contrition, who knows) and there were questions that needed to be answered, which she sent through her parents. *Will I be able to continue with my work, even if I have children?* Yes. *Can I go overseas to visit my brother without asking my in-laws for permission?* Yes. *Will I be able to make all decisions involving my children's affairs?* Yes — although if the word 'affairs' was to be interpreted more broadly, Tota was clearly asking for more power than it was within Dadi's authority to grant.

With each question answered, the transaction seemed to stiffen and finally solidify, to the point that neither family could have said no to anything. She could have asked *Can I be given charge of all the family finances, including those of my in-laws?* or even *Can we sleep together before I decide?* The decisions were all but made. Nobody asked Tota if she would agree to the match — they just asked her to make a decision about the wedding date, at which point she said,

'I don't care what date you choose. Go ahead and plan it as you please.' And like her initial grunt, this was taken as agreement to the contract of marriage, unwritten as it was at that time.

Tota's marriage was announced at the Women's Chamber of Commerce morning tea the following day, and everyone clapped. Only her friend Joyce, who worked in the office next to hers, dropped by to ask her if she was happy about her parents' choice.

'You of all people, yah! How did you give in?'

Joyce had been following the slow saga — the wooing that took place around the young ones, through the exchanges of bangles and gifts, sweets and *shahtoosh* shawls, each suggesting a further possible confirmation of future vows yet to be articulated. If Tota's approach was to grunt, Joyce's response was to snarl.

'He's educated in the West — he's at least heard of feminism,' Tota replied.

'Have you told them that you're in love with someone else, or do you want me to tell them?'

'No-o-o!'

Joyce had listened to Tota rave endlessly about the young English doctoral student she'd met at a cafe in Khan Market one day when she was shopping at the Full Circle Bookshop. He'd been studying Lutyens' Delhi alongside the work of Sir Walter Burley Griffin, but his real love was poetry. 'Don't get pregnant.' That was Joyce's best piece of advice. (Joyce had been pregnant herself, so she had the scars of this type of knowledge.) Her next piece of advice was 'Run away with him.'

'Are you mad?' Tota responded. 'Leave my job, leave my parents and my family — leave my motherland?'

'So what are you going to do about the poet?'

'Nothing, yah. Isn't a woman allowed to have some fun before she settles down? Every boy educated overseas has had girlfriends called Gillian and Charlotte — why can't we do the same?'

'But are you going to be happy with this boy ... this Siddharth?'

Happiness had never entered into the discussion between families, being at the pinnacle in the hierarchy of needs and therefore not a necessary aspiration.

'How do I know? How do the village women know *thisthing* when they get married?'

'I'm sure your parents have made a good choice.'

'He's doing very well in business and he's a practical man. I'm sure that he will take care of things very nicely.'

'Yes, but what about his heart? What about his soul? Will you take care of these or will he?'

'We'll see about that,' Tota replied. What else could she do? The wedding invitations had already been sent out — the hearts and souls committed — albeit with a grunt.

FALLING INTO THE SOUP

I T WAS THE first time that Siddharth had gone to number thirty-three since they'd moved from Golf Links to Ghitorni. He'd heard about Ram Avtar but had never met him at any of the Farmhouse Association meetings, where the other owners planned to pave a road or contest the New Delhi Municipal Council conditions that demanded smaller buildings on rural blocks. Ram Avtar was never there to help the new local landowners devise strategies for bribing local officials — never there to share stories on how the new locals were encouraging officials to turn a blind eye to yet another pavilion or Grecian annexe. Why was it that Ram Avtar, the only genuine local, didn't seem the least bit interested in local affairs?

'Namaste.' He spoke in Hindi and folded his hands together to greet Siddharth, who promptly broke into English.

'What a lovely farmhouse you have here,' he said with a flourish. Noticing the lavish proportions, he asked, 'Have you had any problem with the local police for building works?'

Sweetie, who was standing next to her grandfather, answered for him in English. 'Uncle, we are related to all of them, so they have not been causing any difficulties.'

The fact that Ram Avtar could freely flout the rules that Siddharth had paid heavily to break was mildly irritating, but not as much as the two-hundred-year-old guru, who appeared beatific and smiling, and even looked a few years younger than Siddharth himself — the cheek of it!

And so this irritation continued as Guruji began his discourse on the nature of possessions, a lecture that was probably timely given the guest of honour that day.

'We think of our possessions as our right, but real wealth comes from being connected to the whole. When the entirety of nature and being is ours. True ownership can only take place when there is no separation and when nothing can be taken away from you. But this right to the world's entirety — to unified consciousness — also comes with responsibilities. You must become responsible for the whole. *Sub Brahman hai!* Everything is Brahman. Everything is one. But we seem to be the first species on this earth that is able to conceive of itself as separate. We see ourselves as separate from each other and from nature — and therefore we think we have no responsibilities ... Ha! Just imagine!'

Siddharth glanced over to Savitri and saw her unblinking gaze of love, not wanting to miss even a split second of *darshan* — the utterly untranslatable blessing that comes from simultaneously seeing and being blessed by what you see. Siddharth, on the other hand, was looking around, wondering whether he should challenge this not-so-old man on the economic implications of his thesis. And it seemed as if this guru of Savitri's was never going to come up for air: he was used to holding the audience's attention for hours at a time. Didn't anyone else in the audience have jobs to go to?

He didn't mind embarrassing his daughter by putting up his hand, and Guruji stopped, smilingly, to answer his question.

'But what if I don't want wealth?' he asked, hoping to throw the Guruji off his rather material trajectory.

Guruji stopped, and then began to match the heckling with flattery, an altogether unexpected approach.

'I'm sure you have a wonderful car,' he said.

'I do,' came Siddharth's reply.

'I'm sure you have a beautiful house, with comfortable beds and lovely decorations.'

'I do.' Siddharth was beginning to wonder where this was going.

'I'm sure that your servants always make sure you are extremely comfortable at every moment — they anticipate your every need — and your meals are always cooked to perfection.'

'Correct.'

There was a silence, so Siddharth continued the discourse.

'So where then is the need to do this meditation of yours if one already has these things?'

'If this is the case, then maybe you are already enlightened!'

The audience laughed and there was a haze of mischief circling the guru, almost like a halo, but not quite. Siddharth was beginning to regret going along with his daughter's plans.

'And if you are already enlightened, there is only one gift that I can give you.'

Savitri pulled on her father's sleeve to remind him that he had to show respect. Siddharth looked at his Patek Philippe watch to see how much more of his potential-filled future he was going to have to spend with the besotted disciples and cow herders to be lectured.

'If you already have everything and you are already enlightened,' Guruji repeated, 'there is only one more thing you can get, but it is a very powerful gift indeed ...'

And just then, if you listened closely enough, you could hear a drum roll, played by mischievous gods attending the discourse, gleeful at the announcement of this gift.

'An enlightened soul has fully developed awareness, so you will receive this one thing ...'

There was a drumming sound in Siddharth's ears, then a tinkle of cymbals. He was scratching his ears, wondering why they'd suddenly started itching, as he received Guruji's blessing, sitting, as it were, on a plinth.

'I will give you ...' He stalled for a moment. 'I will give you *all* the worries of the world.'

There were no gasps from the audience, no recognition that a cataclysmic event had just occurred. Siddharth simply looked at his watch once more, as if Guruji had announced that he was going to distribute mithai and fruit to everyone in the audience and dismiss them all. He knew he couldn't leave without his meditation instruction. That was part of the deal, but he couldn't spend too long away from the office on account of his spiritually inclined daughter.

Guruji ended the talk early and accepted garlands from disciples who came up to the podium, hands folded, foreheads smeared with white clay and vermilion powder. They touched his feet and he answered their questions as quickly as he could, because he knew that he now had an urgent mission — to explore what he'd just unleashed. After all, everyone knows that a man who has propitiated the gods and practised the correct austerities for an entire lifetime must be careful what he wishes for. Everyone knows that if you've practised your *tapasya* those penances can make oceans stand still, mountains shake and astral bodies sway in confusion. To be blunt, someone who has accumulated such powers is to be feared by the gods, and perhaps even by themselves.

Savitri's guru had never before been compelled to wish so much for a single person. It was a brazen gesture and he was fully aware of the ways the gods played with such hubris — the confidence of the saints to take a heavenly force and cast it in an earthly direction. (Ravan, Vishwamitra, the list went on. Just look at the company he was in now.)

All the worries of the world. It seemed the most obvious offering to make at the time, but was it a little extreme given that the daughter and the mother of the man were such devout followers of his?

Knowing the mantric power of words and knowing that he had used his mantric voice for this blessing or curse (he wasn't quite sure what it was, as yet) Guruji was extremely keen to sit down with Siddharth and discover the inevitable consequences that must follow. He also wanted to communicate to Siddharth everything he knew about attaining peace, because peace would be the only thing that could save the poor man — this much he knew.

So the two men, equally keen to collide and continue on their radically different paths, were ushered into one of the smaller white marble rooms at number thirty-three, where a sculpture of

Krishna was installed between two mirrors, creating an infinity perspective of a black, enameled, flute-bearing cow herder who sang his song to the world through reflected realities. There were two low Gujarati seats placed facing each other for the guru and his disciple (or in this case, his un-discipl-ined, involuntary student) to sit and discuss in depth important issues of the spirit.

'How are you feeling?' Guruji asked Siddharth, genuinely hoping that he hadn't already cooked up a frog.

'Quite frankly, sir, I'm in a hurry. I need to know when we're going to finish with this ... this meditation business, because I have lunch at the Gymkhana Club with one of my most important clients.' Guruji knew immediately that there was no such lunch on the agenda — that Siddharth was simply making it clear that he didn't lead the life of the idle rich: that some people were obliged to put food on the table, a Mercedes on the front lawn and an empire in the hands of their son.

'Hanji,' he replied, respectfully playing the subservient role that everyone played in Siddharth's life except his wife. 'I can give you your mantra and show you how to meditate. Your only responsibility is to tell me exactly what it feels like for you. Exactly what this meditation and blessing bring into your life. And we must talk regularly. Even this day itself, once you have done your first meditation.'

And so Guruji lit his incense and said his prayers to honour the line of saints in a painting he held: a line that hailed back to the invisible force of Narayana himself, who lay horizontal, resplendent in light in restful omniscience. Then he lit an oil lamp, blessed some flowers and fruit and mithai and vermilion powder, before blessing Siddharth and whispering a mantra into his ear.

Oh, and there was so much that Guruji knew about the potency of words that Siddharth didn't.

He knew that entire worlds can be created with a word. He knew that from a single word a holus-bolus new story could emerge, and he knew that this story was ultimately something of great mystery, because every such good story must touch on mystery as it manifests. Yes, he was intrigued and even a little concerned about the potential outcome of this story he had initiated.

Siddharth closed his eyes and Guruji could see that he was quick to descend into the soup of transcendence — the lines on his brow smoothed now; his breath disappeared, undetectable. Guruji, too, closed his eyes to feel something of what Siddharth was experiencing in this non-dual soup in which guru and disciple can merge.

Guruji then left Siddharth, in the soup, and came out of the initiation room. Savitri was standing by the door, clearing her throat.

'Did he learn?'

'Yes.'

'I'm so sorry about the *tamasha* he caused in your lecture,' she whispered.

She was so worried, poor thing, and it really wasn't her fault, any of it. She had wanted the best for her father, that's all — Guruji understood this. How could she have known when she first saw the gates of number thirty-three flung open and a world of marigolds welcoming her inside that any of it would come to this?

'I am worried about your father.'

'Yes, I am too, which is why I wanted him to come and learn.'

'I need him to come back here often. He's going to need to speak to someone about what he's experiencing.'

'I'll do my best,' Savitri said, 'but it might be hard.'

After a few more minutes Guruji went back into the small meditation room with its inlaid marble floors and the infinite Krishnas (enough to marry every single girl in Delhi) and slowly prompted Siddharth to open his eyes and adjust to the new world.

'How do you feel after that?' he asked. 'Any different?'

'No different. I think I fell asleep.'

Guruji could tell that this wasn't the moment to start telling Siddharth about the path to peace. His reluctant student was still waking up to his new world, and if and when he wanted advice he would be there — but until then there would be no way of helping him.

LADIES' HOUR

I T WAS A little too hot at the pool, even in the water, but that wasn't why the ladies who swam at Ladies' Hour were panting. Nor was it their state of fitness, although it may have been, considering the amount of flesh falling out of swimsuits. No, it was the handsome lifeguard who sat on a chair at the top of a ladder, in a cleavage-spotting hero's eyrie. He watched Mae a little too intently as she climbed into the pool, attempting to disguise his appreciative smile. Tota, who was standing between the two of them, noticed his gaze and turned to see that her would-be daughter-in-law had taken off her towel to reveal a blue wing painted onto her white left buttock. Not only that, it was fully exposed in her G-string bikini, and seemed to disappear somewhere between her legs ...

'Mae, Mae, wait ...'

It was too late. Mae had climbed into the pool backwards, blue wing prominently on display, and had started her laps, speeding past every Indian lady splashing in the pool getting 'exercise' during that Ladies' Hour.

Tota ran to the steps as fast as she could, a little breathless. Just below the ladder the swimming caps of a couple of young girls bobbed up and down together and she heard them whisper.

'He's looking at us.'

'What nonsense, he's looking at her!'

The shame of it. Tota decided to wait for Mae to finish a lap, but when she reached the end the girl just changed direction underwater and kept on swimming as if she owned the pool. So Tota waited, and when Mae returned she grabbed her now most unwelcome guest by the hair until she surfaced, spitting water indignantly.

'Get out of the pool immediately,' she shouted, loud enough to turn a few capped heads.

'What?'

'Just get out! You're not dressed properly.'

Mae, who had been head down and tattooed bum up, took a few seconds to realise that there was an emergency at hand: a fire in the pool that she had inadvertently started. Tota felt like slapping the girl, but instead tried to be polite.

'I know you people over there don't mind showing your *thisthing*, but ...'

She sounded too loud so she began again, following Mae as she made her way out of the pool, trying to block the view of her *thisthing* with her larger *thisthing*. 'We'll get a new swimming costume, don't worry. We've done enough exercise now, let's go and have an ice-cream.'

'I'm so sorry. I didn't know ...'

Back in the changing room they dressed in their day clothes, Mae in a long skirt and a short-sleeved shirt, and nobody would have known that she liked to wear strings for undies, or that she had a tattoo where there shouldn't be one.

Out by the poolside, Tota said, 'Come, sit.'

The two of them sat down in cane chairs and Tota called for the bearer with the same instructional tone she used for her daughter-in-law. Just as she spoke, one of the girls in the middle of the pool started gasping. The attendant jumped from his high chair and dived into the pool to save her.

'Poor thing,' Tota said.

The girl was dragged to the side of the pool in the strong arms of the Ladies' Hour lifeguard, a secret, satisfied smile on her lips.

'Get me a Limca,' Tota told the bearer, 'and some finger chips, some cake and some ice-cream.' So much for the exercise. 'What would you like, Mae?'

'Just a cup of tea, thanks.'

Another girl seemed to be choking in the pool now and calling for help, entirely unable to commit to the few strokes it would take to get her to the edge. Barely back in his seat, the lifeguard sprang into action again, it being rush hour for female rescues.

'Goodness, I don't think I've ever seen a single rescue mission in the ocean, but in this tiny swimming pool I've seen two in half an hour!'

'The lifeguard is doing his duty well,' Tota commented. 'He's a good boy.' Watching the handsome lifeguard made her think of her own beautiful son and the inquisition she had planned for Mae. 'Tell me, how do your parents feel about you marrying an Indian boy?' she began.

'They love Neel,' Mae replied.

Tota listened to Mae, wondering how she could bring up the issue of this marriage being unquestionably inappropriate. 'Over here there is a lot more than just love that we must consider when giving our permission for a marriage.'

'That's fair enough.' It was said as a conversation stopper, but Tota took it as an invitation to trespass further.

'It is fair because when you marry somebody you have to understand their traditions and values ...'

'That's what's so exciting about getting to know Neel.'

'But how can you ever be expected to understand him? How could you be expected to know about the pressure to find him a wife and everything we've been through?'

'Well, I guess that pressure may be off a bit now that we're getting married?' Mae looked round at the single girls, dangling their legs in the pool opposite the lifeguard.

'Yes, but think about the embarrassment and shame for poor Chandini, who was meant to marry Neel.'

'Er ... Chandini?'

'He hasn't mentioned her? This is exactly what I'm saying. You cannot be expected to understand him. Even he is not expecting to be understood, otherwise he would be able to speak these things to you!'

'He was probably too embarrassed to tell me, or hoping that he could get out of ... er, meeting this girl ...'

'Chandini. The girl's name is Chandini. His fiancée has a name. Or at least she was going to be his wife until we had to make new arrangements ...'

'It sounds to me that you were trying to force this onto him.'

'There is no forcing a boy to do anything.' What would the girl know about the trouble the children gave with these suggestions nowadays?

'Well, if there's no forcing anyone to do anything, that should be fine, then.'

Mae reached for the cake she'd been avoiding, while Tota planned how she was going to deliver her next move.

'If you're pregnant then I know someone who can help.'

The conversation paused momentarily as Mae held her cake in front of her face.

'But ... but who told you I was pregnant?' She seemed to lose her confidence. It was working. 'And I don't know what kind of help you think I need but ...' She put the cake down. 'Hang on a minute, did Neel tell you I was pregnant?'

'No, but we all guessed that you must be, because of the way he wanted to hurry the marriage along.'

'Well, for your information, I'm not.'

'Then why would he have destroyed Chandini's life?'

'What?'

'You have to understand, Mae, that Neel has obligations beyond those he has to you, and these go very deep.'

'But he's also an adult. And he has the freedom to ...'

'Marry who he wants to marry?'

'I'm not here to come and steal your son. I've been invited by Neel to come and meet my future in-laws and get married. He's spoken so highly about all of you and India, and until now ...'

'Of course — we are his family and Neel loves India. He'd never have the life he wants anywhere else. It's just not possible.'

The pool was still now, and Mae was silent as the ladies made their way to the cane chairs, fully clothed, pool laps completed, lives saved and ready for their next snack. Tota felt that she had earned some ground. No doubt the girl was wondering why Neel hadn't mentioned Chandini.

'I think it may have been a mistake for me to come to India ...'

Of course it was! Neel must have known that he was breaking his country's commandments and stamping on his family's holy books when he first glanced at Mae on that beach in Goa.

Satisfied, Tota realised that she had done enough work for one day. The seed of doubt had to be nurtured. There was still time before the wedding, but all the cards would have to be played in perfect sequence for her gamble to work.

'Darling, it wasn't a mistake coming to India! Don't go on talking like this,' she replied. And with a welcoming smile she continued, 'In our country, guest is God.'

THE SHIT HITS THE PUNKA

SIDDHARTH FELT LIGHT-HEADED as he left the 'cowshed ashram' (as he began calling it) at farm number thirty-three. As Savitri asked him about his meditation, he could feel a deep unease in her heart as she spoke.

'What's wrong, *beti*?'

'Nothing's wrong. I just want to know how your meditation went. You're not talking about it.'

'You're not telling the truth. You're worried about something else.' He knew it. He could feel the worry behind her concerned smile. Feel it as if it were his own. 'If you're worried about me, you don't need to be. I'm always okay.'

'But you haven't told me if you liked the meditation.'

'I loved it,' Siddharth said.

'Now you're not telling me the truth,' she said.

It was true that she worried about her father. His blood pressure was high and his lifestyle was demanding and she didn't know where she would be without Papa should something happen. And if Neel went to live overseas ...

As they approached their farmhouse they passed a sign saying *Dayal weds Savitri*. The sign had been put up to direct people to a wedding in one of the nearby farmhouses, but that had been many many months ago and to this day it remained. It was a different Savitri who was being celebrated as victorious in marriage, of course, but it always made her wonder how that Dayal and Savitri were doing now that the vultures and pigeons had shat on their names and the sign had faded and curled up at the edges; now that they'd made Sanskrit oaths to be with each other and only each other for ten thousand years or more. *Had that Savitri been born under the Manglik star? Had she been forced to marry a tree, or accused of killing her husband on account of her astrology?*

Siddharth marvelled. He could literally hear his daughter's thoughts as if they were his own.

Did Dayal prefer porn to reality? Had he slept with many girls for a night or two before his ten-thousand-year commitment?

Never before had Siddharth stopped to try and understand Savitri's anxiety around marriage. Why, he'd always thought the girl was simply obstinate! Unwilling to comply, like so many of them were nowadays.

He tried to listen in some more. He saw images that Savitri was conjuring, this time of her friend Ankita, who they all thought had done very well for herself when she married a boy from a very big family. He saw images of Ankita, through Savitri's imaginings, sleeping on her own while her husband still slept in his mother's bedroom.

And so it was that Siddharth, for the first time, could see through a crack in matter to understand the inner world of someone in a separate body. The level of empathy it required was discomforting, as he could feel her emotions even more strongly than he could feel his own reactions. He could sense the heat prickle in his daughter's skin. The whimsical flicker of memory or some other thought being entertained. The stain of regret.

'We have to take that sign down,' Siddharth said, interrupting her thoughts, 'before Dayal and Savitri become grandparents.'

They both laughed, and Siddharth remembered the deal they had made, as he now saw a picture of Mohan on top of his daughter.

'And you don't have to keep that promise about meeting up with Mohan,' he continued. 'It would have been a lousy match.'

Savitri was relieved. Her father was well on his way to finding peace (or so she thought) and she had been let off her part of the bargain. Surely a miracle had taken place.

Feeling his daughter's joy, Siddharth continued on his way to the office to make sure that there hadn't been a strike or a stock market crash in the time it had taken him to learn to meditate. He didn't know what to make of the experiences he'd had since visiting farm number thirty-three, but somehow the world seemed a little less certain than it had yesterday.

When the driver was alone in the car with his master he took the opportunity to ask for some leave.

'I need to go and visit my mother, sahib, she's not well.'

'When did you last go and see her?' Siddharth asked. It was such an unexpected question. Siddharth had never asked about the driver's personal life before in the many hours they'd spent together.

'I haven't been home for two years, sir.'

Why on earth hadn't the man asked for leave like the rest of them? Siddharth couldn't understand — or at least he thought he couldn't understand, but then he closed his eyes and the bare truth came out like a heartbreaking internal confession delivered in screaming silence.

I didn't want to take leave, sahib, because I have asked for leave before and you told me twice, without even putting down your newspaper, that you can find another driver at the American embassy if I go home for a holiday. And I know this is true, because I've been there with you when you went to pick up the new guard two years ago, remember? I squatted with the other servants who were waiting to be interviewed. I talked to those other drivers who had been able to study all the way till Class Ten in Christian schools. They owned their own uniforms. They looked so smart and some of them had gone abroad with their masters. How lucky they were. They knew that they would get jobs if they squatted on that lawn for long enough and they knew that they would get Sundays off because the foreign sahibs and memsahibs give them leave. I wished then that I could have one day off every week, but then I am not a Christian, so why would I be given Sundays off? This is what you would have said. How easy it would be for you to find another driver. And they all knew how to speak English and they knew how to use a GPS so they would never get lost in the New Delhi colonies ...

Siddharth wasn't hearing this exactly, but he was witnessing it as an internal dialogue, as if it were his own, and his ears were itching as he strained to eavesdrop on the thoughts.

'What's wrong with your mother?' Siddharth asked.

'She's been very sick, sahib, she hasn't been able to eat since she caught typhoid.' Siddharth could 'read' that his driver didn't know quite how to take this inquisition. He'd spent the past eight years pretending that the only family in the world was his master's, and here he was answering questions about the mother he hardly dared think about during duty hours.

'Why haven't you told us?'

Again Siddharth could hear his driver's thoughts. *But how could I explain to you that it's my fault — if I'd gone back up to the hills and brought down the statue of our goddess and bathed her at Hardwar then none of this would have happened, but I just didn't have the time ...*

Siddharth's ears were itching so violently that he could hardly hear the driver using actual words to say, 'I didn't want to bother you.'

'Do one thing. Take this car and drive up and see her and do all the work you have to do in Hardwar. Take your time — I'll drive myself in the Maruti until you get back.'

The driver got such a shock that he had to turn his head to make sure there wasn't a jinn in his master's place talking this nonsense, and as he did the car swerved to the left and nearly knocked over an entire wedding band who were waking up after an afternoon siesta by the roadside. How on earth could he take the Mercedes to the village? Was Siddharth sahib out of his mind?

'If you prefer the Maruti, take that only,' Siddharth replied. 'You'll feel more comfortable.'

Siddharth witnessed everything. His driver couldn't believe his luck. If this was the boon for his eight years of service, then it was all the reward he could ever want. He would be able to kiss his three children after two years. He would see his wife again, too, and she would hide behind her *palla* and ignore him at first, but he would wait until the children went to sleep in the bed next to theirs. He would stay awake with her and sink into her quietly under the sheet to the sound of the single fan that would soften the sound of their happiness.

'You must promise that you will go and see her ... your mother, that is. And you must go today, or I won't let you have the car.'

What difference does it make if I go tomorrow? I've sent every rupee I can but she still doesn't get better.

It wasn't the joy of the reunion that remained in Siddharth's heart, it was this heaviness of helplessness — something so fundamental, so inevitable, so burdensome that he couldn't dislodge the sadness for the rest of the day as he felt himself missing a woman he'd never known as if he were missing his own mother; as if she had gone, forever out of his life.

MARRIAGE COUNSELLING

'WHY ON EARTH did you tell Mae about Chandini?' Neel asked his mother.

'Why on earth *didn't* you tell her is the more appropriate question,' Tota replied, clearly feeling no reason to defend herself.

'Well, she's really furious with me now.'

Tota didn't seem to mind Mae being furious, but put on a show of caring, regardless. 'You'd better explain it to her, then.'

'I did. But how can I expect her to understand?'

Somewhere, in some grey cells in her cranium that controlled the universe, Tota must have had a feeling that she could still stop Mae and Neel's marriage from going ahead — even though the invitations had gone out, even though the bride-to-be already lived under their roof. However, Tota must have also known that she would have to make some concessions should the nuptials become as real as she feared. It was a problem, and as with most problems, Tota decided to throw money at it. Her solution was a trip to the family jeweller, Bhole Nath, who sold her a ruby and diamond ring, which she casually passed over to Mae the following morning.

'It's so beautiful,' Mae replied, but she couldn't quite get it onto her finger.

'Your finger's a little fat,' Tota said.

'Mummy, Mae's hardly fat! The ring's tight, that's all. I can take her to get it loosened.'

Mae put the ring back in its case, the breakfast arrived and the discussion about future heirlooms was replaced with the morning papers. There were two items of interest in the news demanding attention that morning. The first was a headline, 'Why Australians Hate Us', in *Frontline Magazine*. The second was an obscure article that Mae discovered in *The Times of India* about a woman in Jaipur who ran classes for young girls in 'mother-in-law management'.

The papers rustled at the dining table over *burji* and toast, pomegranate juice and lukewarm tea.

Why Australians Hate Us
After a series of attacks that seemed specifically aimed at Indians, we sent two journalists out to Sydney to discover exactly why Australians hate us.

'Why do *you* think these Australians hate us?' Tota asked, looking directly at Mae. 'Are we so detestable?' It was a rhetorical question but Neel rose to the challenge nonetheless.

'Nobody hates anybody. They must have been short of stories this week.'

Tota tutt-tutted loudly as she sank deeper into the article. 'Is it even safe for you to return?' The question was clearly not directed at the lovely blonde Mae, who would of course have to return, the sooner the better. 'What terrible people they are —' and this seemed to be directed at Mae — 'how could they even think about doing such horrible things to Indians? They're animals!'

'Mummy, we're not all animals.'

'Are you calling yourself Australian now? You want to be like them?' She opened her eyes wider than usual when she flung her gaze at Neel — eyes that looked the same as her son's, only less innocent.

'We must call Uncle Arjun immediately to make sure he's okay,' Tota continued.

'Last time you were worried his house had burned down — do you remember, Mama? Just because you heard there were bushfires outside Sydney.'

'But all it takes is one incident.'

One incident was usually all it took for anything brittle to snap. Mae could feel this incident looming as she reached out for some spare pages of *The Times of India*, where she found an article about workshops in 'mother-in-law management'.

Does your mother-in-law recast your personality? Does she then feed this alternative picture of you to her son? Does she make you feel insecure about your husband's love? Does she try and come between the two of you with an inappropriate sense of timing?

Mae looked up, taking no notice of Tota now, simply trying to apply her X-ray vision to her lover to try and see his heart, hidden as it was under his shirt and his seductive, albeit hairy, brown chest. Did he love her any less now that Australians were supposedly culling Indian students in the streets? She moved her gaze to his eyes, tried to catch a reflection of herself in them. They were fiery and agitated — perhaps a healthy sign of defiance? But on the other hand ... he did have his mother's eyes.

'I wish you'd gone and studied in England or America.' Tota sighed. 'I would have felt far less tension about this ... this whole business of you staying over there.'

'Is it far to Jaipur?' Mae asked.

'It's four hours from here,' Tota replied. 'You can travel on your own as a foreigner and nobody, absolutely, will try and kill you like they do in Australia.'

She had no intention of travelling on her own. Did it say anywhere that partners were required to attend the counselling sessions? What was the point training only herself how to manage her mother-in-law? Surely Neel would have to learn to tame his mother — to stand up to her and protect his wife-to-be — or at least to teach his mother to stop spitting chillis in her direction. Mae continued her investigation.

Should you learn how to take it or should you learn how to leave?

The question came as a thunderbolt, because in that moment they seemed like life's only two options.

Love me, love my mother, or our love must split in two, and my mother will take her rightful share.

No, no, no, there would have to be a better solution. She could steal Neel from Tota, who would then be forced to surrender because she would never follow them to Terra Australis, where the locals skinned evil mothers and skewered their heads over slow camp fires and sizzling she-oaks.

Hah!

She looked at Tota, whose eyes seemed to trail over the blood on the page of her magazine, seizing upon the face of a mother who had lost her son to violence in Australia.

'Oh my God, I'm so worried.'

'No, Mama, please don't worry,' Neel replied.

'But it's my *duty* to worry!' Tota shrieked. 'I'm going to ring Arjun and see. We'll ask him what to do!' She was crying now, perhaps at a future catastrophe she was imagining or perhaps at the current one: the fact that her son didn't seem in the slightest bit interested in moving back to India, in spite of the growing evidence that his life was in severe danger should he ever return to his supposedly beloved home in Australia.

Do not expect to gain your mother-in-law's love, for she can never love you like she loves her son. But you can always work towards gaining her acceptance. And if you cannot gain acceptance, then at least give her no reason for criticism.

Perhaps some marriage counselling with this lady in Jaipur — What was her name? Yes, Rekha Singh — would be just the thing Mae needed if she was going to have to listen to another hysterical sentence spoken by Tota. But would it matter that Tota wasn't actually her mother-in-law? Was it possible to have marriage counselling in India if you weren't even married? Did Rekha Singh take the outlaw experience with the same degree of seriousness? And what would Rekha know about intercultural couplings anyway? Especially given that Mae could never replicate the Indian wife that Rekha Singh was familiar with tutoring.

Tota reached for her sari *palla* to wipe away some tears as she reached for her phone.

Mae read on.

Naturally, your mother-in-law is going to love your children, but the last thing she wants to know is that you've had intercourse with her son to avail yourself of the aforementioned offspring. It is vital, therefore, to hide any signs of intercourse, let alone romance, in order to maintain good relations. When you and your husband have intercourse, therefore, it is better to do the deed in the early hours of the morning, let's say around 3 a.m.

Mae started giggling — uncontrollable guilty giggles that somehow triggered Tota's vicarious grief, turning her tears from a few tasteful sobs squeezed from a news story into a throaty Grecian lament for what could only have been a very real bereavement.

'People have been killed and I have to listen to hee-hee ha-ha,' she moaned. '*Hai Ram Bhagwan!*'

Mae's giggles escalated and she started to choke.

'Are you okay?' Neel asked. 'Shall I get you some water?'

Tears were running down her face as well now, not in sympathy with Tota's cooked-up grief but for the two of them — for their hopeless, sweet, farcical romance that perhaps could never have a happy ending.

'Ram Lal, *pani lao*,' Neel instructed. 'I've called for some water.'

'No, no, I'm fine, I don't need water,' she said, 'I just need to laugh sometimes. It's the only way I know how to cope.'

Tota had got through to her brother in Australia and took the phone into the corridor outside the dining room. 'Arjun Bhaiya, we got the terrible news today ...' It soon became clear that Arjun Bhaiya didn't know a thing about what sort of terrible thing had happened. 'You know, the news about the killings over there. *We-all* are sitting here with Neel and we're sick with worry ... Tell me one thing, are you all right and is the family all right?'

Mae took advantage of her mother-in-law's distraction to whisper into Neel's ear: 'Meet me tonight, in my room, at three in the morning.'

Neel gave her a quizzical look, wondering what treat lay in store, and what had inspired his sweetheart to make such an unexpected proposal. And why had there been such a precise revision to their now established 'freedom at midnight' rendezvous? What's more, how could he possibly wait until three in the morning to make love with Mae?

She smiled at him, and the smile from their previous night's midnight feast lingered. The two touched feet under the table while the cook removed the soiled breakfast dishes. It was worth being in India and tolerating a hysterical outlaw parrot for the promise of those lips. They would never belong to his mother. Not those lips. That was not the dutiful smile of a son who had been educated for the boardroom. That was the smile he reserved for his goddess.

If you always smile at me that beautifully, thought Mae, *I will put up with the world and your mother to stay with you.*

'Arjun Bhaiya and the family are all right, thank God,' Tota chirped as she returned to the table clutching the phone. 'Nobody has been hurt.' She said it as if there had been a miracle. As if war had been declared in a distant nation and somehow her family had survived.

Neel's expression reverted to his innocent boy smile.

'What are we going to do today, Mae?' he asked. 'There's a long time between now and three o'clock.'

'What's happening at three o'clock?' Tota asked.

'Oh, we have an appointment,' Neel replied vaguely, not even looking at his mother as he spoke. 'Mae has some business she has to attend to.'

STORM IN A TEACUP

NEEL AND MAE had spent the day in the city, strolling through the Tibetan traders' stalls in Janpath. On their return Tota wanted to examine the purchases Mae had made, something she had always done with Savitri whenever she went off to any of the Delhi markets. Somehow it was less satisfying doing it with Mae, but she felt obliged to go through the motions and was even slightly curious about what sort of clothes this foreigner would most like to wear.

'Let's have a fashion show!' Tota suggested with great pomp and ordered some tea, which arrived just as Mae was changing into a diaphanous top made of cheap nylon. 'I hope you didn't pay more than a hundred rupees for it,' she quipped, barely casting an eye over it.

'I paid five hundred,' Mae replied. 'Only ten dollars.'

Tota was indignant. 'Neel, darling, why didn't you bargain for her?'

'I did,' he replied, 'only Mae's too blonde.'

After a few more outfits the tea arrived and Mae pulled out the exquisite present she'd bought for her future in-laws, in return for the diamond ring they'd presented her with on arrival: two cushion covers with Aboriginal designs, stitched in the Kashmiri embroidery style.

'Look, I chose these for you. They were designed by Aboriginal women with a start-up in Kashmir,' Mae explained. 'This is the symbol for a women's sacred site, and this here is a sacred river.'

Tota was finding it hard to concentrate. She had to order the evening meal and she decided they would have channa bhatura, the deceitful dish she had supposedly cooked as a first meal for her in-laws. The dish that had given her the upper hand in her husband's family. *But will Mae eat channa bhatura? Probably not. She has a white palate. Maybe I'll order pasta.*

She called for the cook, distractedly. 'You know we have Aboriginals in India, too, and their art is also so simple and lovely like this.'

'Neel wouldn't let me bring you anything when I was in Australia, because he said you had everything you wanted and more ... but nobody has everything, right? You didn't have these, did you?'

Tota made signs that she was warming up. She made a show of examining the cushions further and then, with complete innocence, piped up with a radical question. 'Do Australian Aboriginals make good household help?'

Mae, who was by now balancing a cup and saucer together carefully on her lap, sat paralysed for a second. 'What?' She shook her head, startled. 'Did you just ask me if Australian Aboriginals make good servants?' She looked at Neel. 'Did your mother really just ask me if Aboriginals made good servants?'

'Mama, you can't say that. It's not the same over there ...'

Mae seemed to produce a rash on her chest as she raised her voice now, with more rage than confidence. 'Aboriginal people are not fucking servants, all right?'

Incredible. Had she just heard this chit of a girl fall into a trap that she couldn't possibly crawl out of?

'Excuse me?'

Mae continued, with a red flag raised alongside her Australian one. 'Nobody talks about my people like you just did.' She glared at Neel. 'I can't believe that such a lovely boy like you could have such a heartless bitch of a mother,' she roared, and as she stood up the cup and saucer slipped to the ground, unbroken.

Seeing the perfect porcelain at her feet, she picked up the cup and threw it. 'Your mother has to be just about the rudest fucking —'

'Mae, please ...'

Tota could see that Neel was trying to silence the girl, trying to catch the bullet that flew from her mouth with his bare hands, but with all her heart she was willing Mae to continue, erecting a firewall with her shoulders pressed back, readying herself for this unexpected assault.

'Mama, over there things are different ... What you said was rude.'

Mae started to make her way towards the door, shaking. Anuj, the chef's peon, who had come bearing more biscuits for tea, moved quickly to one side and looked at his feet. Tota could tell that he was deeply embarrassed that the house guest was daring to scream at her future mother-in-law. Watching him gave her the gumption to continue.

'I wasn't being rude.' Tota snorted. 'We've had many Bihari Aboriginals working with us in the past, and I think they make excellent household help. Other people can be so unfair and unkind about Bihari servants, but if you treat them well ...'

'Oh, it's easy enough for you to sit here in your fucking superior home, ordering this and that and paying nothing to the people who work for you, but we don't have the same low standards in Australia. We don't just use people because we can. We wash our own fucking dishes, we cook our own fucking dinner ...'

'I can't speak for Australians,' Tota replied, 'but in our country we respect our elders.'

'Mummy, Mae, can we just stop this right now?'

'Mummy, Mummy,' Mae mimicked. 'In our country boys are expected to grow up to be men and stand up to their mothers if they're out of order.' She was screaming now.

Anuj stood watching like a colonial statue of a slave bearing biscuits, clearly hoping that he was invisible. Neel ordered him to animate and get back to the kitchen. Tota took a split-second summary of the situation: the news would now spread for miles across the kitchens and servants' quarters of Delhi. The servants would tell their bosses and then everyone in Delhi would come to the wedding prepared with bulletproof vests. No harm.

As Anuj left the room he attempted to pick up the broken porcelain, but Neel hurried him through the door with the evidence of the family feud still visible in shards on the floor for all to see. Would the cup even be worth fixing after all this?

'Neel. Tell your mother that she's absolutely out of order,' Mae demanded.

Tota saw Neel's gaze follow Anuj as he left the room, wishing he could be anywhere but in the firing line. Seeing that Mae had no reserve army, Tota summoned the courage to take another line of attack.

'I only asked if Aboriginals made good household help,' she repeated, like the parrot she was named after, delighted to give the offending question some air once again. She saw Mae begin to shake. 'You can't tell me that the British didn't get them to work. We were a British colony for two hundred years ourselves. We were all servants of the British. You can't lie and say that you British Europeans went over to Australia and the Aboriginals politely shared their country as equals! You might not think it, but some Indians are educated. We do know our history.'

'I'm not saying that we didn't do all of that,' Mae started. 'What I'm saying is that you've spent your entire life thinking you can get away with this horrific domination. You walk all over Neel, and you've turned your husband into a yes-man, and all of them have to play along with your stupid —'

'Stop it right there. You're going to regret what you've said and all of it is nonsense, anyway.'

'I'm not going to regret it. You don't want to hear me out because you don't want to look at yourself —'

'Neel, can you bring me over that cup? I'm going to see if Anuj can glue it.'

Before the instructions even struck Neel's eardrum, Mae was up off her chair and standing over the incriminating porcelain. By the time Neel saw what she had planned, Mae was already stamping on the cup again and again until it was as irrecoverable as Humpty Dumpty after his fall, no matter how many kings and queens, memsahibs or servants tried to stick it back together again.

'Neel, can you call the airline to change my ticket? I'm going home,' she shouted as she headed straight to her room to pack. She didn't look back, even to notice the flicker of relief that spread over Tota's face at these words — the first and only words she had wanted to hear from Mae's lips from the moment she arrived at Indira Gandhi International Airport.

Thank God. Hai Ram Bhagwan.

At last Tota would have Neel back and there would be no sense in him ever seeing the girl again once he had dropped her off at the airport. The relief of it. Mae had already stuck her tongue out so far that she tripped over it. Now there was no other option but for her to disappear from their lives altogether and never come back. The wedding was surely off.

Finally, success.

THE WORRIES OF THE WORLD

SIDDHARTH WAS ON his way home when he was summoned by his wife to face the shit on the fan — the *punka* and the air conditioning combined.

'Come home quickly,' his wife ordered. 'That girl is creating such a big *tamasha* it's quite horrible here.'

That's when the first faint signs of his heart murmur started, on the Mehrauli—Gurgaon road. His wife's words then reached down to create an uncomfortable feeling in his stomach — and this was even before he ate the greasy channa bhatura that night.

He tried to dismiss these small symptoms as his car travelled down the MG Road, but his heart was insistent. It whispered from inside his ribs: *Take me away. Anywhere but here. Free me from this cage.* Siddharth instructed his driver to take him to Chattarpur Farms instead of home, so he could see his oldest and dearest friend, Hari. They had studied accountancy together in London when they were young and single, and whenever they were together they relived their experiences as young men who for four years had been free from rules. Free from responsibilities. Free from parental expectations and arguments with wives. In the days when Hari was called Harry and they shared a room in Hammersmith between a mosque and a girls' school, spending far too much time studying girls who were far too young for them and far too different, wearing skirts that were far too high.

Hari would understand the anguish Siddharth experienced occasionally on his way home, and he also knew about the family's resistance to the upcoming wedding, so it would be no surprise to him that Siddharth should be taking a left turn off the MG Road into Chattarpur Farms.

'What's wrong?' he asked as soon as he saw his friend, not expecting an immediate reply. He poured Siddharth a whisky and watched him as he stared at his poison, swirling it around the glass. Still no response. Hari watched Siddharth turn off his mobile phone to hush the harsh ringtone that seemed to accompany his wife's calls.

'Bloody Neel. I should have made him study in Delhi where we could all keep an eye on him.'

'And deprive him of the fun we had at his age?'

'Yes, yes, but we came home — that's the point. We came home and we got married.'

Neither of them went any further into the rightness of this simple path — the coming home, that is. It was as if there was nothing else up for contemplation. No option to do the 'wrong thing'. They were both being groomed for their family businesses, as Neel was.

'The problem with this generation,' said Hari, 'is that they have no values. Absolutely no reason to listen to any of us. Who knows what these values we've been nurturing for aeons will look like in the future? Who knows what they will take with them and what they will leave behind in their rush towards their robots.'

'Do one thing, Hari, and please get your servant to fetch me some anti-acid,' Neel replied. 'Too much eating out.'

'More like not enough eating in,' Hari laughed.

'Don't lecture me, yah? I've had it as it is.'

They didn't talk again about Mae and the difficulties ahead. The rest of the evening was a revisitation of their shared past, away from Siddharth's utterly unappealing future back at home. The ordeal ahead was only recognised when Siddharth stepped into his car a few hours later and Hari called out, 'May you live in extremely uninteresting times!'

Siddharth's murmur turned to a squeeze in his chest just as Hari's uniformed guard saluted him at the gate. He inhaled deeply to check that there was still room in there for some air, because if oxygen couldn't reach his lungs before he arrived home, then what chance would it have once he was listening to his wife?

Savitri was waiting for him at the gates of the farmhouse like a premonition: her eyes red, her face streaked with kajal and panic as she hopped into the car in tears.

'Neel's cut his wrists ...'

Siddharth tried to take another one of those deep breaths.

'You're lying to me?'

Siddharth started shouting at the driver to stop the car in the driveway.

'Tell me you're lying to me, baby.'

'No, Papa, we found him crying and there was blood, he had this razor blade.'

'*Hai Ram Bhagwan* ...'

Siddharth got out of the car and started running towards the farmhouse. Savitri ran after him, as if he was the centre of safety and good sense in the universe. And as she ran, she drew her arms around herself, breathing deeply, then gasping for air as if there were a limited supply. He could hear her thoughts, with a senseless rhythm that sang, *Why did he do it, Papa, why did he do it, why did he do it?* And then, *Papa, no, Papa, stop this, Papa, no, Papa, stop this. Make it go away, make it go away, make it go away so it never happened.*

If he could have made it go away he would have, but he had turned off his mobile phone to block out all of this. He had chosen his own peace of mind over his son, and now his heart was thumping against his ribcage. He should have been there. He deserved this pounding in his chest. He deserved to have the sorrows of the world as his punishment for turning his back on the sorrows of his own family. He should have seen Neel's outstretched hand seeking comfort, wisdom, or even just his fatherly presence. But instead he had gone to Hari's house, dammit, with his phone switched off.

Siddharth made his way to Neel's bedroom and stood outside the door, where he could hear Neel's thoughts as if they were being broadcast through a loudspeaker. *Mama, why didn't you finish me off? Why didn't you do it with a knife as well as with your words? How are you going to tell the Khoslas and the Bedis and the Jains about what you did? What are you going to say to them all when they ask how the wedding plans are going? You're full of lies, lies, lies — you'd rather I jumped into the fire than walked around it with Mae. Oh my God, Mae — why, why couldn't you just keep that mouth of yours shut?*

The thoughts were being amplified so loudly that surely the entire neighbourhood could hear them.

Siddharth quickly opened the door and began to blink uncontrollably as he saw the ghastly sight of Neel with a bandage around his wrist. He continued trying to blink away the apparition, but the bandages remained. Buddhi Ayah who had once wiped the dribbles of milk from the side of his mouth was now sitting down at Neel's feet, holding them as if they belonged to a saint as she sat on suicide watch.

Siddharth went straight to Neel lying on his bed, and not knowing what else to do he lay his head down in his son's lap without saying a word.

'Papa, please, why are you doing this?'

Siddharth didn't move his head; he just continued listening to Neel's thoughts.

I don't know how to show him that I love him ... my God ...

'If you love me, Neel, you'll do one thing.'

Neel felt his thoughts being intercepted, and the shock of it took him out of his own head enough to listen.

'You'll promise never to do this again.'

You can't stop me, even if it wasn't you who made me do this.

'Nobody has made you do this,' Siddharth said, seizing the thought in the net of his curse. 'You did this to yourself. You cannot, cannot, cannot say that anyone did this to you.'

'She wanted to stop our wedding.'

Siddharth moved up the bed so that he lay next to his son. As he spoke, the light above the bed seemed more fluorescent, the room more grey.

'How do you think she will feel about that now?'

Siddharth hadn't needed an answer to this question once he entered the house. He could hear the whizz of his wife's thoughts skimming the air in their upstairs bedroom like daggers instead of fan blades.

'I don't care how she feels. She has to take some of the responsibility.'

'What happened was an accident.' Siddharth had always felt that suicide was an accident — an accident of thought — and as much as he suspected his wife's motives, she had not cut the wrists of her son. She would not. Surely it was not within the heart of any mother to do such a thing.

❦

Ram Lal was calling out from downstairs, telling them that dinner had been served. He knew about what had happened to Neel because Buddhi Ayah had come running downstairs to the kitchen in tears, screaming and asking for the bandages because 'Baby' had cut himself. He knew immediately that this was a self-inflicted cut. It was something in the scream of the woman who had looked after him so fearlessly, replacing Neel's parents for long hours of a lonely childhood. It was a mother's scream: a mother fearful of losing her son. A scream to the gods for help — for anyone to help. Budhhi Ayah's eyes were half blind and wet as she rummaged in a drawer that produced only small plasters for lesser injuries, not the long white bandages needed to patch up the gashes of a family disaster.

'Send the driver,' Buddhi Ayah had insisted. 'Tell him to go to the Alchemist.' The Alchemist was the nearby village store, artfully named because it was a chemist that also happened to sell alcohol. If Buddhi Ayah had known what an alchemist was, it probably would have occurred to her that a metaphysical intervention was exactly what was required.

The driver had been sent and returned quick smart with the bandages, which were whisked upstairs where everything as happening. The cook continued with his work, feeling queasy in his stomach, which had been doing somersaults since he'd picked up the broken cup and saucer like someone cleaning up after a murder. He'd known that the day would turn disastrous from the moment he heard the white memsahib shouting in the living room — not just shouting at anyone, but shouting at his boss. And there wasn't a single employee in that house who hadn't felt like doing the same — it had given him some vicarious pleasure — yet it was satisfying and sickening at the same time, because the blonde woman had screamed in a future that was intensely unpredictable.

Ram Lal knew about the screeching of women. His wife, Rani, had this female affliction, but back home they recognised it immediately as the sound of possession, and in the village they had a simple solution for this type of ailment. His wife had all of her make-up and bindis and plastic bangles taken away from her and put into the forest to appease the spirits. The screaming had stopped instantly. (Although in a strange coincidence, he had also brought his wife to live at the farmhouse, far from his parents where she'd been left for years at a time.)

Later on there were more screams from the white memsahib — but this time it appeared that she was screaming at Neel. All the servants watched from the kitchen window as Neel ran through the grounds after Mae, who was trying to carry her bags to the gate. She refused help, continuing to scream at him like an *asura*. Later that day, when all of the yelling had stopped, the farmhouse was overcast with such a reactionary silence that you could almost hear Neel's wrists bleed into their bandages. It was so quiet that Ram Lal jumped when Buddhi Ayah came down after a few hours, looking older than old, and told him that memsahib had ordered him to make channa bhatura for dinner.

Channa bhatura. Of all the things she chooses to order ... tonight we must all eat channa bhatura!

The thought of it made him feel even sicker than he already did. All the servants knew that this was the dish Tota had pretended to cook after her wedding. The legend had been passed down through the lines of servants who had done her bidding since she first stepped over the threshold of this house with wedding bangles up to her elbows and henna lattice staining her hands and feet. Channa bhatura had come to represent her personal rebellion against her family by marriage. It was the dish of the conqueror. The dish that commanders eat. It was Tota sticking her finger up at the world with masala on top.

Only Tota and Siddharth sat down for dinner that night, because the children had taken to their rooms and Dadi was too sick. Tota seemed to relish the channa bhatura, but Siddharth was consigned to feeding his body in a ritual of endurance, lipservice to the need for survival, hardly digesting, simply swallowing each bolus of chickpea and batter, each mouthful going down with a dark thought that wasn't of his own making. He felt sick before he started on the food, but even sicker as his wife voiced her familiar concerns.

'How are we going to make sure that Neel stays in India? How do we know that he isn't going to whimper and wail and go running back to her over there?'

'He's not just whimpering and wailing,' Siddharth replied. 'He's feeling very hurt and very angry. Do you think, my darling, that on this one occasion you might have taken things a little too far?'

'Nonsense. You weren't there and neither was Savitri. We had a perfectly civilised conversation until she suddenly started throwing around the crockery. She's crazy — you don't understand.'

'And you're not?' He took another deep breath, checking that the air wasn't going to vacate its rightful place in his lungs, hoping it would stay on his side throughout this confrontation.

'*Arré*, whose side are you on? What do you want? Your son's life destroyed by a mad woman, or to live with that mad woman and have our crockery thrown around whenever it pleases her?'

'I would like my son to be happy. And if not happy, at least alive.'

What kind of new world was this, and was it worth fighting for? Neither of them knew the answers. Even Tota seemed to exist in a land beyond defeat, where victors lived among Pyrrhic regrets.

As for Siddharth, he was intensely aware of the channa bhatura shuffling along his gut, piercing his heart and squeezing out its poison as it went.

BLOODY DIAMONDS

THE DAY AFTER Mae left the farm, the entire household was confined to bed, as if she had cast a spell with the sound of smashing china. Siddharth had taken the extraordinary step of cancelling all his meetings to stay at home and meditate, just as Guruji had taught him, in the hope that he could silence the screeches in his ears and the pain in his chest. And by staying at home, he was also offering himself as a human shield between his wife and his son. He knew that he would have a role — even if it was the role of a cursed martyr, offering advice that would never be taken.

But no amount of meditation could stop the sound in his inner ears: the sound of a knife scraping a bell, deep in his head; a sound that intensified whenever Tota yelled out her constant instructions for Buddhi Ayah to bring some chai, press her feet or oil her hair — anything to calm her nerves and re-establish some sense of order in her mind. She was so preoccupied that she didn't ring to cancel the dance practice for the wedding, and some of the cousins turned up at the Taj Hotel, as did the dance master.

'Aunty, should we start the class without you?'

'Go ahead and practise without us,' Tota replied. 'Everybody is sick.'

She was right, of course. Siddharth interrupted his meditation and answered with his half-moon eyes. 'Tell them the dancing is over. Tell them the wedding is off.'

Tota hadn't acclimatised herself to this new atmosphere of shame. It was an admission of failure and she wasn't quite prepared to admit defeat. 'We will dance again one day,' she said. It sounded like a wise-ism rather than true wisdom or prophecy, but she continued: 'Neel will get married to someone decent and we'll all be dancing again, just wait and see.'

Siddharth continued his meditation, and as he did so his wife's thoughts floated in through his aching ears. *Maybe someone should just go and fetch the stupid girl. Neel will know where she is.*

He closed his eyes once more and the internal dialogue became his own festering thought process. *I was right all along about her. If Neel had listened to us and married Chandini, the wedding would have been done. Finished by now. But those people? Those people over there don't know how to behave.*

Siddharth opened his eyes to try and cut out the conversation, but when his eyes were open he started to hear Neel's thoughts, floating through the walls like ghosts. With his eyes open he could even see Neel, standing against the window, looking at his phone, stroking stoic glass as he scrolled down the list of old meaningless messages, seeking out the digital blip that might indicate that Mae gave a stuff. There was no such sign. So instead he rehearsed a conversation with her instead, summoning her presence. *I warned you about them. I told you it would be better to get married in Australia.*

If you hadn't wanted this stupid Indian wedding circus, then there'd be none of this.

There was a break in the thoughts. A sigh.

It's so easy for you to walk away from this, but you've left me stuck ...

Siddharth could see Neel now, even without looking. He caught a glimpse of him leaning out the window, looking at the ground below, measuring the distance. Then he watched as Neel slammed the window frame on his world so hard that the knuckles of all four fingers cracked.

'Shit!' Neel's real words, not the thought forms, were so loud by comparison that Siddharth jumped.

Where was Buddhi Ayah? Had she been locked out of the room? Siddharth found himself willing Mae to send Neel a sign, a text, an apparition, anything.

Oh, the discomfort of waiting — of wanting to help but having no ability to make people see differently! The treachery of a world seemingly out of control, ruled by desires that could never be fulfilled ... Oh my God. So this was what it meant to carry the worries of the world.

Mae was not oblivious to the passion. Even though she had walked out as a demonstration against Tota, she knew that Neel was having to pay the consequences. And her solution was to shop — to somehow take back some of the beauty and love and hope she had expected from India. The India she'd once dreamed about and longed to visit.

She checked into a hotel in Paharganj and instinctively found herself roaming towards the Tibetan trader in Janpath where she had bought the embroidered Kashmiri cushions — the now fatal gift she had felt so clearly articulated the sacred confluence of two rivers: East and West.

The man who had sold her the cushions was delighted by her return. Delighted, too, that madam had returned to his shop the day after a fresh batch had been delivered — a batch that now sat in a tall pile that stitched together swirls and dots of sacred art from a far continent.

'I make you special price because you have come back, madam,' he told Mae. 'I have many more designs in my shop. Please be coming inside. You are my first customer today; you'll bring me good luck.'

She didn't know why she was following the man into his shop, or why her feet had brought her to the familiar cursed cushions, but she couldn't stop herself from going into the darkness at the back of the store, where the shopkeeper pulled open a large plastic bag and started to lay the cushions out, one after the other, in a decadent spread of evil temptation. She found herself picking them up, examining the stitches for faults, thinking about what the Indigenous designs represented. The horseshoe shapes were women sitting at a corroboree. The broken lines were tracks to a waterhole. The most innocent symbols of art and storytelling.

'If you're having trouble making up your mind, perhaps you should start with your favourite colour.'

Ignoring what seemed to be a pre-recorded sales pitch, Mae's thoughts turned to Neel's mother. What had she done with the cushion covers? Were they exhibited now in the farmhouse living room as a sign of Tota's success in stealing back her son? Deciding that they had probably been chucked out, Mae began to choose *herself* some replacements. She stroked the bold designs, and as she did so, large tears dripped onto the Kashmiri embroidery.

'Please, you must have some tea, madam.' Clearly, the lucky customer shouldn't be weeping. He whistled and the chai wallah came running within a minute with two cups of emergency chai in tiny plastic cups, which the shopkeeper hated, being from the old school of chai in clay pots.

Mae didn't want to be held hostage to a sale on account of accepting a cup of tea, but her hands reached out in desperation and she drank the warm, sweet fluid in tiny sips, as if to preserve the very last pleasure she would ever have in life.

Now she would have to make a purchase. She took a deep breath.

'How much would you charge for a thousand cushions?'

The shopkeeper couldn't tell if she was serious, because her eyes were wet and her hands were shaking as she asked. Perhaps the *firangi* was a little unstable. Certainly, she wouldn't make a reliable business partner.

'That would be a very high quantity to be buying, madam.'

'How much?'

'Maybe four lakh rupees.'

Mae wasn't very good at maths, but she worked it out in her head to be around eight thousand Australian dollars. She looked at her ring. It would have to be worth that much money, with all the diamonds and the rock-sized ruby in the middle of it. What would be the use of this thing now? She'd no longer have any Indian relatives to impress, and her friends back home would never care whether she was wearing diamonds or diamantés. Besides, it had been given to her by Tota, not Neel — it would have been a symbol that she'd married a family, not just a man.

'I'll come back,' Mae said, finishing her hot tea in one gulp, driven by a plan she was convinced would see her using the lemons she'd been given to make lemonade — or *nimbu pani*, as they called it in Neel's house.

She strolled to the end of Janpath and pushed past the people squatting over cotton shirts and pants and hankies and locks and ties and mirrors and Rajasthani puppets, around to Bhole Nath, the boutique jewellery store where Neel had taken Mae to get her ring enlarged when she had just arrived in Delhi and the future was still in its construction phase, fashioned in sand — before it had turned to concrete.

Bhole Nath was a discreet size considering the caverns of wealth inside. Mae recognised the jeweller, and most importantly, he recognised her as the future daughter-in-law of one of his long-standing important customers, which warranted a cold Limca, ordered at the snap of his fingers, together with a moving display of all the jewels he could possibly showcase.

'I'd like to buy something special for the wedding,' she lied.

'No problem. We will find something perfect,' the jeweller purred, and ordered his assistant to bring out display after display of dazzling, perfectly rare jewels. First there appeared a peacock-coloured Akoya pearl necklace strung with exquisite diamond motifs. Mae tried it on.

'I personally chose these pearls, madam, and I can tell you I have never seen any of such perfect hue. They simply do not exist in these colours on this planet ... but sometimes in nature we have exceptions.'

Mae began wondering at what point she should bring up the news that she actually wanted to return her ring, not buy something new, but they had begun the royal treatment, so she sat like a reluctant queen and tried on a pair of peacock earrings designed from clusters of sugarloaf sapphires. Then a maharani's necklace with chain after decadent chain of pearls, emeralds and diamonds. Finally, a cocktail ring with a gobstopper-sized Burmese ruby as a showpiece. How remarkable, she thought, that the culture that promoted non-attachment had designed so many extraordinary objects of desire. And every one of them reminded her of the life she was leaving behind. None of it of any relevance now that there was a plane seat booked, ready to return her home.

'How much money would you give me for this ring?' she asked casually. 'I was told it was made from flawless diamonds and each stone came certified from your shop.'

The jeweller was clearly taken aback.

'It is not meeting your expectations?'

'No, it's just that it's not what I want.'

'And there is no other ring that we could exchange for this one, madam?

'No. I'd just like to have the money ... And then I'd like to go.'

The jeweller was taken aback, but he knew the woman wasn't in possession of stolen goods. He examined the ring through his eyepiece, thinking diamond strategies. She had every right to sell the ring, but he also had every right to buy the ring back at a most discounted price. She was probably never going to buy the Akoya necklace she clucked over, or the peacock earrings. She would probably never walk in through the door with Tota, Neel or any of his other clients in the future. The wedding was off, no doubt about it. Mae's status had suddenly swooped lower than she could have possibly imagined.

'Five lakh rupees. I believe we sold it for around this price.' He was lying. He had sold it for much more, but there was no way she would know that.

Mae was relieved to get out of the shop. She felt lighter without the burden of that ring on her finger. She was freed from Tota, and free now to turn diamonds into cushions. She could already see herself sitting on a rug at the Byron markets, where she used to paint henna patterns on the hands of locals and travellers, surrounded by cushions that people would gather around.

She went back to the Janpath shop to make her order, and told the salesman she wanted only Australian Indigenous designs. She could already imagine her future customers: a hippie couple with only two weeks left before they returned to Germany, travelling around Australia in their Wicked van, with not enough cash left to buy an Indigenous painting to remind them of their trip into the outback. The cushions would be affordable, and nobody would ever know about the diamonds that had gone into their making. She could return to her humble previous life and forget that she had ever dreamed of love.

BROTHERS

SIDDHARTH STAYED AT home for three days waiting for a phone call from Mae and listening to the desperate concerns of his family; he heard their deafening thought forms in spite of the irksome silence. Neel was moribund, Savitri was permanently mortified, and his wife just seemed to mock them all without even realising she was doing it. *So stupid he is. He was going to marry a madwoman and an idiot who would bankrupt him and destroy the family fortune. He would rather sit by the side of the street and beg than honour his parents' wishes, pick himself up and find another girl. What an idiot — a spineless idiot.*

Against Siddharth's advice, Tota had gone and told Neel that Mae had returned the ring. Bhole Nath Jewellers, in a fit of loyalty, had decided they'd better inform their long-term customer of the fate of those diamonds and the now bleeding ruby.

Siddharth had tried to stop Tota from spilling the news, and he could hear exactly the thoughts that preceded her delightful revelation. *I'm going to tell him exactly what she thinks of him. Just what that stupid female did with the ring, and how she accepted a pittance in return.* Through the screen of thoughts Siddharth could hear a more ghostlike notion occur: *Bhole Nath would never have done such a thing to us ... but she isn't us ... they would never have tried to pay so little for the ring if I were to sell it to them.*

'Don't tell Neel about the ring,' Siddharth requested.

Tota turned to look at her husband, but there was no suspicion that he could read her thoughts, her worries or her fears. She just took it as the normal convergence of minds that takes place when you live with someone, share a life, a bed and children together. These were shared worries, which naturally formed webs between parallel minds.

Surely?

'It is my duty to tell him so that he can stop moping around hoping for a phone call from a female who will let him down far more severely in the future.'

And so Tota dropped the news — as if it were a report she'd heard on the radio or read in the newspaper — while they were all having dinner together that night. It was a way of overcoming the silence that hung over them at every meal these days.

'Well, you better forget about your perfect Australian girl, because she's already sold the ring we gave her.' It was delivered with brute force, with Tota staring at her only son, waiting for a response.

'Why are you even telling me this?' Neel asked.

'So that you can start thinking about building a proper life.'

'Nobody has a proper life in India,' Neel replied. 'They just pretend for everyone else that they're having a great life. It's a shit place. Everyone pretending they're happy when they just spend all day doing as they're told. It's supposed to be a democracy, but nobody's free.'

'Yah, yah! It's going to be better in your beloved Australia, is it, where life is so perfect?' Tota was on a roll now and couldn't stop the next insult. 'And all the women are perfect, just like Mae.'

'She's more perfect than any Indian girl I've ever met. She'd be interested in me even if I was a beggar. How many Indian girls do you know who would want to marry me if we had a plot on the MG Road where we begged, instead of a farmhouse?'

Siddharth could hear his son's inner revolt: *Oh please, oh please, why did I ever bring Mae here? I should never have come home. We should have stayed in Australia and forgotten about this godforsaken country. We could have been so happy.* But then he thought about how pretty the ring had looked on Mae's finger, and how proud he'd been that his mother had indulged his future bride so generously, and he started to sob with hatred and love combined. The sobbing became so loud that even Tota had the good sense to stop provoking him.

Siddharth simply put his hands over his ears. He had begun to do that a lot lately, and Tota took it to be a sign of rudeness. In her mind, Siddharth had become a kind of holier-than-thou monkey that could hear no evil. *You think I'm the only evil one? You and I are steeped in this together,* he heard her say. *And perhaps,* he thought, *she is right.*

At which point Siddharth got up from the table and went to see his mother, as a way of returning in some way to the peace of the last century.

Dadi was in bed, looking at the ceiling as usual, not expecting anyone to visit her, sensing that under the circumstances she was perhaps the last of their concerns. When her son came into the bedroom and lay down next to her, something he hadn't done since he was a child, she put her arm around him, remembering the early morning visits he used to make in his pyjamas. She could remember the pyjamas, clearly, with their rocket ships, and how his body had fitted so completely into her curves.

Siddharth could see the pyjamas too, and wept as Dadi patted him on the head with the exact same regularity he remembered from childhood, when he'd broken a toy or been scolded by his father. *I'll always love you, darling, and I'll always be there for you, with God's grace even after this life. I will shower you with flowers from the life beyond and you will feel yourself being adored, even when there is no mother anymore here on earth.* He could sense these words, and pure and positive as they were, he could also feel the sorrow behind them. He could feel his mother's sadness that one day she wouldn't be able to pat down his grief. And then he felt his own tragedy: that his cosmic source would soon be removed. That there would be nobody in this room. That there would no longer be another soul in the world who prayed for him every day. Yes, soon there would be nobody in this bedroom. *Nobody* in the room.

Even when I'm not here, my love for you can never die. He continued to listen to her thoughts and was surprised by her unspoken concern. *If only you believed in God. If only you had faith. Then I would know that you'd always be in good care ...*

'You should go and see Arunji, *beta*,' Dadi offered as consolation. 'He will help you, I know he will. You don't have enough faith — that is your problem. You have to trust in God that your problems will be sorted out.'

'But Arun is not God,' Siddharth pointed out, trying not to sound too rude or obvious.

'*Chup, chup,*' she soothed. 'He knows God's will, of this much I'm sure. And he loves all of us and cares about us like we are his family. He is a true brother to you. A brother that I didn't bear, but a brother nonetheless.'

Of all the sentimental Indians, his mother was probably the most tender and nostalgic and misty-eyed of them all. It was true that his brother through happenstance had always been incredibly loyal, but at the end of the day he had always gone back to sleep on a charpoy shared with his parents in the servants' quarters while Siddharth went back to his comfortable bedroom where his ayah slept on the floor nearby, ready to wake up and wipe his brow should he startle in his sleep. What kind of brotherhood was it that could create such different dreams?

Nonetheless, after his grandmother's petition, Siddharth did book a time to see the family astrologer, to try to get to the bottom of the planetary pile-up that had resulted in the disaster at his house. What he didn't realise was that Savitri, having been given the exact same instructions by her grandmother, had left Arunji's premises just a few minutes earlier, allowing the cosmic detective only a few minutes to compose himself between visits.

Arunji took a deep breath as he answered the door.

'It's been so long since we met. You look so well,' Arunji lied. Siddharth's eyes seemed to sag a bit in the lower lids, giving him the appearance of greater wisdom, which worries can sometimes do. In the time since he'd received the 'gift' of the curse, he had begun to look much older than the two-hundred-year-old guru who had been responsible for dreaming it up.

Siddharth didn't bother to say that Arunji was being unduly flattering, because he could hear the astrologer beginning to worry. *Shit, he looks terrible. I'm going to have to try and keep the worst from him.*

'You know why I've come, don't you?' Siddharth began.

Arunji felt caught out in a way he couldn't disguise. *I wish that Mataji hadn't told him to come.*

'My mother wanted me to come to you because she trusts you with her life, Arun, and I'm about to trust you with mine.'

Please don't.

'She trusts you because she brought you up to be trustworthy.'

'I adore your mother like my own,' Arunji said. 'How is Mataji? I've been meaning to come by for so long.'

'She spends her life waiting, of course. You know why. You've told her about these problems. But I want to know exactly what we should do. And I don't want any messing about. I need an answer that's crystal clear — I don't want any metaphors or games or sloppy predictions. I want to know precisely what we should do about Neel. Should we try and find him another wife? And how long should we leave it before ... until he gets over this girl? How long is he going to be *matlab* ... so depressed?' Siddharth wanted to say 'suicidal' but the word didn't come out. It was absolutely unimaginable for him, even though he had heard the thoughts himself and had seen the blood-stained bandages.

Just as Siddharth asked his supremely stupid question about finding another wife, loud banging began, but not in his ears — it was coming from upstairs. Siddharth soon realised, from listening to Arunji's inner fury, that there was an illegal construction going on above the apartment. *Bloody hell, I preferred India when it was poor. Give us a few years of a free market economy and look what corruption we have! That man building upstairs will always win because he has money, money,*

money. *And nobody gives a shit anymore about where that corrupt bloody money comes from. I give my life to this country and this is what we get ...*

Siddharth was almost amused to hear these concerns. He'd picked them up everywhere since he'd been given his gift — this resentment of corruption and the way that the beloved motherland, rich in values and culture and history, was simply being thrown to the dogs now that there was money to be made by the crore. It didn't upset him. He just paid the bribes in voluminous amounts as need be: his dues to the new god of the new century.

'Oh my goodness, I haven't offered you any tea.'

'I didn't come here for tea.'

Siddharth followed Arun into the kitchen, somewhere he usually never visited. 'What are you going to do about the illegal construction upstairs?' he asked.

Arunji dropped the match he was holding to light the gas and looked deep into his brother's eyes. Nobody else knew about these troubles. Not even a lawyer, because there wasn't a lawyer in Delhi who would take on a nobody professor with no money to bribe anyone.

'It's a man called Bharat. Nobody you know. One of the new rich.'

'There's no point raging about the new India. If you can't beat them, join them.'

Arunji had known about the curse through his calculations, but he hadn't known exactly how powerful it was. *My bloody goodness. He really is hearing me think.*

'That's right.'

Siddharth had no qualms now about the two-way conversation he could have with Arunji. And Arunji was no longer deluded that he was sitting safely within the privacy of his own thoughts.

Arunji began his confession. 'I knew about your curse.'

'So why didn't you tell me before I went to see Guruji?'

'Because it had weight and power and ... inevitability.' *And you never asked. You were never interested in astrology. You never came to see me for a consultation.*

'You could have rung me up and told me. If it was important enough. If something serious was going to happen to a brother, you would want him to know. You'd want to at least warn him so he could go ahead in life more prepared.'

Arunji thought quickly about how he could respond to this accusation. *But you always laughed so much about the golf ball incident.*

'I'll admit it — I didn't believe in astrology, but I didn't believe in a lot of things before. You should have told me out of some sense of duty.'

Arunji, not knowing exactly what his mind would reveal next, immediately confessed the most detectable thought he could find at the surface of his consciousness before it was captured by stealth.

'Savitri and Mae were here some time back ...' He decided to be a bit more honest. 'Actually, they left just a few minutes before you arrived.' And then he was more honest still: 'Because I told them you were coming.'

Siddharth let out a long sigh. His mother was right. Mothers are always right. He was meant to come here all along. It had been predicted that it would unfold like this, as it had to.

'Why did they come?' Siddharth asked, with deadpan determination. 'And what was Savitri doing with Mae?'

Arunji tried to speak quicker than his thoughts so that Siddharth couldn't catch up with them, until there was little space between the words.

'It was based on a promise. Savitri had promised to bring Mae along to meet me. Mae is staying in Paharganj and is about to go back to Australia. She has a business plan and apparently Savitri is going to be her new business partner.'

Siddharth looked across the table at Arunji, with his perfectly placed comb-over, and knew he was telling the truth. He felt for the first time since the curse was bestowed that he was in a tantalisingly powerful position. Business. Well, he knew an awful lot about that, at least, and perhaps he could even help.

'Did you cast a chart for their business?'

'Yes, and Savitri is going to be the one who really benefits from this ... this enterprise.'

'Is she going to go and try and visit Mae?' Siddharth had stopped saying the word 'Australia' because its meaning had become tainted.

'This is what I advised.'

'Ahh, *bhaiya*, there are more important things we have to arrange for that girl ...'

But she'll never find a husband over here.

Siddharth answered Arunji's thought almost before he'd finished it.

'We've tried so hard for her, but you know the problem.'

Yes, she was born a Manglik, and you think that doesn't matter over here?

'Arun, you believe in fate or *kismat* or whatnot. Tell me one thing: do you think it's really worth knowing what you know about the future?'

Arunji began his defence. 'Let me answer your question by asking you this question. Do you think it's good knowing about other people's thoughts? Do you think it's important to know about each and every person's worries? Wouldn't you rather not have to carry around the worries of the world — aren't yours enough, *bhaiya*?'

'Is there a way to get rid of it?'

'You must live with it for a while yet, and you will learn to be grateful, believe me. You have powers that some people would murder for. You might not yet know it, but these were given to you as a blessing. And the concern that grows from these powers will be a boon for all those who know you.'

Hearing such a positive prediction, Siddharth immediately decided to try and do something about the *goonda* illegally building an apartment on top of Arun's flat. He knew exactly who he'd send to sort it out — his office manager, Kapil. He'd been working for Siddharth for years with an open brief (and a briefcase filled with cash) and a remit to 'smooth the way'. When he had first started working for Siddharth he'd requested a business card that folded over to leave behind one-hundred-rupee-note bribes in government offices. Nowadays, he was carrying briefcases for the lakhs of rupees he paid on account of inflation. Last year alone he'd bought twenty-five new briefcases for the purpose.

Siddharth left without the clear-cut advice he'd hoped to get about Neel. Bloody astrology, it never got to the point directly, always spoke in riddles. Unlike a Mercedes that could take you from A to B, astrology took you dancing around trees like a bad Hindi movie.

At least he'd been given the good news that Mae hadn't fallen off the edge of the world and entirely out of their lives. Somehow the stars, along with Savitri, had caught her, and there was hope yet in the world for Neel.

DARK POINT

THE WATER WAS rough the day Mae returned. Good. She walked purposefully along the sand at Tallow Beach, watching her blue toenails and witnessing each step that took her closer to the sea. In her hand she held some frangipani flowers she'd collected earlier as an offering, a symbol of gratitude, an apology even, for having left 'her' beach to go to India. The flowers were also an offering for her grandmother's good health. As she placed them in the enthusiastic waves, Mae witnessed her feet touching the cold water and then observed them as they sank into the sand, immersing her crystal-laden anklet until the gemstones glistened. She inhaled deeply, bracing herself as the cleansing foam and swell of Australia's most easterly waters took possession of her legs, then her bejewelled pierced navel, then over her head. She was back home, in the surf — the amniotic fluid of her childhood which was as constant as the tides. Thank God Australia couldn't evaporate like a relationship. The waves could slap at the shores all they liked, but the land was too vast and too old to destroy — instead, the torture of the waves resulted in stretches of magnificent sand.

She'd often thought about dipping herself in the water at Tallow Beach when things became really bad in India. In the long Northern Rivers region with its cornucopia of beaches, from Brunswick Heads to Golden Shores to Byron Bay and beyond, there was no other beach that belonged exclusively to her, and when it became clear that India would never be hers, she took to returning to Tallow whenever she became too hot at night in Delhi, mistaking the salty dampness on her skin for sea spray in her dreams.

Coming to Tallow Beach made Mae think of her grandmother. She'd always called her grandmother Dolly rather than Granny, and having a grandmother named after a toy made for a playful, enchanting relationship. Dolly had brought her to this beach after school on Mondays when she was a kid, and they used to call it Monday Beach. Later it became Moon Day beach, or simply Moon Beach, and Mae used to go there on full moon and new moon nights through her teenage years. She'd made love to at least three different local boys on Moon Beach, and she'd even seen someone drown while swimming with the happy pods of dolphins that would appear like sirens. For her, Tallow was eternally tangled up with the moon, the dolphins, sex, death, redemption and love — and Monday afternoons, of course, which in the summer seemed to last until midnight.

Every time a wave came at her, Mae thought about Neel and willed the wave to wipe away her memories. That memory of the patch on his stomach she loved. The image of the stretch of skin from his shoulder to his chest. Wave upon wave smashed onto each memory. Onto her knees she went and let the surf crush every thought out of her brain; like a liquid hammer, down it went on her skull. And then again. That one was to wipe away the first unblinking gaze of his, way back at Anjuna Beach in Goa. A tear pooled but was instantly rendered meaningless in the salty ocean, where it could never take form again. The swell bashed at her, again and again. All she had to do was think of him: here the sea would punish her for every thought, and every image of him could sink to the bottom of the ocean.

Yet for every new wave there was a new thought, gaining oxygen in those deep and violent waters and emerging on the surface again and again, until she felt there would be no end to the remembrances she offered to the ocean. As if love really was the seventh wave, returning relentlessly to knock her out, voluminous and overpowering. Enough to kill. She thought of the man she had seen drowning out here at Tallow. They say that when the waves take you out here, they spin you until you don't know which way is up. All she would have to do was immerse herself that little bit more.

She wished she'd never met Neel. That she'd never gone to India. If only she could be here again on a Monday afternoon with her grandmother, with nothing to worry about but a bit of homework. But Dolly wasn't up to going to the beach anymore. She was as frail as Neel's grandmother, sitting in God's queue of forgotten refugees, lost between worlds. Thinking of Dolly made her cry again, and she let the sea knock all that out of her, too. *I was born tough and I'm staying that way*, she told herself. *Save the salt for the ocean. It's wasted in my tears.*

Mae kicked the sand as she walked out of the surf, ran from one side of the beach to the other to dry off, then wiped the last remaining drops from her skin before sprinting up the stairs to her car. There was work to be done. A business to start. She had to look after herself. After all, the Indian astrologer had told her that she'd have to be strong.

❧

Mae was beginning to wonder what the Indian astrologer had planned for her when he said that Savitri and she should go into business together. She'd been too upset to even contemplate any kind of future success. Yet on the penultimate day before she left, Mae had been swinging her pendulum over the phone. Should she call Neel? No. Should she pick up any of the calls coming from him? No. But then the phone had rung and she'd seen Savitri's name and before asking her pendulum whether or not she should pick it up she'd pounced on it, hoping for some news.

'Remember I promised you that I'd take you to meet our family astrologer?'

It was just the right kind of divine intervention she'd needed, and within two hours they were sitting in Arunji's living room.

Mae had remembered talk of Indian *jyotish* masters from when she was a kid in Bryon Bay, back in the days when carpets could fly, magic puddings could talk and possums could transform by eating a lamington. Back then, sand was still sand, and it shifted and shaped into castles and kingdoms and was never used to form immovable, unquestionable concrete. Back then she'd heard about *jyotish* masters who could tell you who was going to visit them years in advance And yet when she'd finally had the opportunity to meet with one, she'd stopped believing in love, which may as well have meant giving up believing in anything miraculous at all.

'Why are we here?' she'd asked Arunji when she'd met him, chin up, blue eyes piercing.

'You're here because you've booked a flight tomorrow, you've been promised a visit to the family astrologer and you've just had a terrible parting with Neel.'

Savitri told you all that, she thought. *Useless.*

She watched as he examined her date of birth and scribbled some numbers around it, as if he were mapping out galaxies.

'Is my grandmother alive?' She thought she'd start with a simple question. He had a fifty per cent chance of being right.

'Yes, but partly because she's awaiting your return.'

'Will I ever return to India?'

'Yes.' Arunji was not giving anything away.

Savitri, started the conversation afresh as if the previous exchange had never taken place. Mae noticed that she was far more polite, clearly believing that propitiation was the best way to revelation.

'Uncle, please do one thing — tell Mae what she should do next now that she is leaving us, leaving India, leaving Neel ... that is ... like this ...'

Arunji addressed Mae now in the third person, as if Savitri were her interpreter, which made her feel like a child. 'She should start up a business in her hometown and forget about India for now ... but it will only work if you go with her ... everything will change for you once you go. And Mae will look after you very nicely.'

Australia had always belonged to Neel in Savitri's eyes, so she had never trespassed there with so much as a thought. While Neel had been studying at Sydney University, her parents had gone twice: first to settle him in, and again when he had started saying that he wanted to live in Australia. Savitri had stayed behind on both occasions to look after Dadi and the house and the servants, as was her wont.

Australia? No, it would never suit her ...

Yet here she was, on this continent so far away from the centre of her world that she could almost drop off the end of the earth.

Mae picked her up at the airport early in the morning and they didn't stop for Sydney — instead they began the day-long drive up to Byron Shire.

As they drove up the highway Savitri looked over at Mae's legs. The foreign ankle was circled with small gemstones. Her Australian shorts were extra short and the brightest imaginable yellow, and her toenails were purple, her left foot tapping to the beat of some roaring singers whose voices streamed effortlessly through the wide-open windows into the breeze. *These must have been the reasons Neel loved Mae,* Savitri thought. The short shorts, the proud bare legs and the freedom and bravery of it all.

Savitri took off her shoes and felt the freedom of putting her legs up on the dashboard as they cruised past gum trees and tangled vines with the velocity of rushing air. Nobody was watching. She pulled her block-printed skirt a little higher to capture the feeling of the sun, and it soon began to sting her legs. How strange it was to be able to feel the sun like this, so intimately. She pulled her skirt up even higher, so that she was exposing even more of her brown legs to nobody but the sun, generously, which the sun blessed in return. Mae didn't even turn her head to notice this transgression of a few centimetres of cloth up a leg. For her, bare legs were a basic human right.

'I can see why Neel loved your country.' She took in a deep breath to smell the riches of the earth in the eucalypt forest: scented, ancient-looking sentries at the side of the road. 'The smell ... I don't know what it is — Ayurvedic herbs.'

'Casuarinas and silky oaks,' Mae said, clearly changing the subject from Neel, swerving into a small lane that went off to the right. 'You're going to love this place we're going to. I took your brother here when we first drove up to see my parents. It's called Dark Point.'

When they arrived, Dark Point seemed oddly misnamed, because Savitri's eyes were blinded by the sunlight reflecting off large dunes. They walked through the camp site, where some spindly, tall, blond grass held together the soil at the edges of what looked to Savitri like a small Sahara Desert.

She tucked her long skirt into her underpants so she could continue the short-skirted feeling and took off her *chappals* so that she could walk barefoot along the path through the gum trees. The sand was covered in grassy stars that looked as if they'd been artfully placed by some goddess of the dunes.

'It's so lonely here,' Savitri said, and as she did she noticed Mae wiping away a tear.

'Neel and I camped here the night once, and I remember being so amazed that he'd never camped before.' She seemed to be holding back her tears now, and instead started to laugh. 'He told me that his father wasn't a colonel, so of course he'd never had the chance to camp — would you believe it? As if you'd need a colonel father to go camping!'

'Do you miss him?'

'He changed when he was around his parents.'

Savitri hadn't intended to try and patch things up or facilitate any sort of reconciliation; Arunji had warned her that the trip would go awry if she tried to get the two of them back together again. No, she was just curious.

'Do I remind you of him?'

Mae laughed. 'Have you ever gone camping?'

'No.'

'I guess you're like each other, then. You're both from another planet!'

But in that moment Savitri didn't want to be from another planet. She wanted to be from the same one. She wanted to try all of the experiences that Australia offered, over here in this land of sun-blest dunes and bare legs; this land filled with illicit pleasures of the type she'd never been allowed to enjoy in her own country — the trees smelling as tempting as the paan sold by the roadside, which was never safe enough for her to try back at home. Walking barefoot along the dunes, she felt as if she had permission to savour it all.

They strolled over several more dunes until they reached the lake, and there, like an omen from another planet, was a swan that was not a swan. Even in Delhi, where they glided on the Old Fort's moat alongside the paddleboats, they were white. Here in this place they were as black as South Indians. She felt like telling Mae about how the swan was considered the *vahana*, or mythical animal, of Saraswati, goddess of music, art and literature. It was Savitri's secret symbol — and here in Australia it was even closer to her skin colour! But she didn't want to reveal her closet affiliation with swans. Instead she said, 'I can see why Neel loved it over here.'

'Savitri, do you mind if we don't talk about your brother? I know it's hard ...'

Arunji's warning returned. Savitri should not even be seen to be attempting a reconciliation. She knew the plan she'd been advised to follow, but even in the telling of the plan Arunji probably hadn't revealed all the truth, as was his way. And anyway, the truth was as vast as continents, as richly coloured as the green and red parrots she caught in the squint of an eye, framed in blinding coloured light. How could Arunji really know the sum of it?

Truth. It was like the tumbleweed that rolled across the sand now, alluring to behold from afar. In a few minutes it would roll over the tip of a dune and disappear from sight altogether.

DEFENCES DOWN

EVER SINCE HIS marriage, Siddharth had been niggled by a sense that his life was no longer his to command. Now, with his daughter away in Australia and his son off on a distant inner continent, he felt as if any steering wheel he'd ever owned had probably been a toy, and not even a battery-operated toy at that. Like a child, he had driven at the wheel of life relentlessly — unplugged — quite the deluded controller of the universe, while the sun rose, galaxies swirled and constellations reconfigured around him with mechanical precision, like true commanders. And now? Why, he could take his hands off that wheel and feel as if not an iota of push and shove, intent or will, bribe or punishment could change a thing. It was as if the driverless car he'd discussed that day in Goa with Delhi's champions of industry had finally arrived at his front gate — and it was powered by cosmic forces quite beyond the algorithms of its inventors. It had arrived with full force and whisked his family off for a cruise into whatever future it decided they should take.

Furthermore, the curse had made him realise that this future was populated by the more complex competing algorithms of needs and desires, worries and preoccupations, of more than a billion others. In his prior life the world had contained only a hundred people, no more (of course, the three thousand people in his company counted as a single unit). Now it was as if the bursting billion-odd people of India were invading his consciousness at any given moment, each one presenting a new challenge in computation.

This fact was confirmed that very day when he walked past a chai wallah who had set up on the street corner outside his office in Gurgaon so he could glean some business from the guards who sat in the heat of their gnome-like cubby houses all day. This boy hadn't even entered his peripheral vision before, though he had worked there for the past year, but that was before Siddharth had been given the curse. He had walked past this boy on countless occasions on emotional autopilot, rehearsing conversations and constructing to-do-lists in his head on his way to the office. He had never seen the boy ... until that day.

That day the autopilot wasn't working and he heard the boy's unmistakable whispers of desire — something you might describe as wireless wishes. Distinctly among those thought waves, Siddharth overheard the urge to become one of those guards making temporary identities for visitors — identities that would give them legitimate access to the kingdoms of commerce inside. Yes, it seemed that the little chai wallah boiling leaf tea, milk, sugar, ginger and cardamom would prefer the grand job of issuing slips and lanyards, and recording the presence of laptop computers in bags that entered that building. He wanted true purpose, and the uniform that came with it.

Fascinated, Siddharth stopped and ordered a cup of chai from this unsuspecting child, who would have been all of about fourteen years old but looked around ten, dwarfed from the usual conditions of undernourishment.

'Why aren't you at school?' he barked. It was the sort of question that Siddharth's mother might have asked. The boy shrugged, reluctant to invent an excuse, but Siddharth heard his thoughts. *Maybe the big sahib will give me a job?* (He hated being referred to as 'the big sahib' but he forgave the child — poor boy, he didn't realise that the big sahib could hear it all.)

'Can you read me this sign?' It was the same sign that was outside every office block along Siddharth's road: CHILD WORKERS PROHIBITED ON THESE PREMISES. Siddharth was particularly careful of this prohibition because corporations around the city had recently been targeted by government officials — hungry for bribes, as always.

'I can't read.'

'Why do you want a job as a *chowkidar*? Why just stop at the gate? Go to school and get yourself an education so that you can take my job one day!' It was a rude provocation, coming from nowhere as it did, without a scant thought for the inequalities at stake.

This is my opportunity! I will ask him for a job. But the boy was silent, unable to articulate the request that hung immobilised above his head and above his station.

'You want a job with me? Okay — I'll employ you the minute you've finished school,' Siddharth continued, trained as he was to trumpet these words with the triumphalism of elite male private-school privilege. The words came to mind without a second thought — he was, after all, from a family that had helped transform a washerman's son into a professor of mathematics.

The boy remained silent. He had been given the ultimate offer, like a taunt that would be pulled away the minute he reached out for it.

Is he going to tell the police officer I'm working?

'I cannot go to school, sahib.'

Then somewhere, behind these words, Siddharth picked up on a subtle worry about money, not even articulated as thought — just a concern for a mother, yet again. The boy was the main provider in the family, that much was clear. Siddharth had always heard about this big social issue but until now he had never truly listened, because India had so many competing social issues that even if you counted them on your fingers and toes and all the hairs on your head, you wouldn't be able to add them up or take them all in. Or so he thought. But he'd never before been so entirely captured in the empirical presence of one of them — a chapped-skin child with no shoes and the wiry, lustreless hair that comes from sleeping on the ground and living on the street.

He already knew all the arguments about child labour. Do you refuse to employ the kids and destine their families to financial ruin, or do you employ them, reap the benefits and face massive fines from the government? There were balances and checks involved — it was a transaction and a trade-off. Until now. This time it wasn't just an issue of child labour: this was an issue regarding a boy who had large brown eyes and a beautiful frown. Siddharth couldn't help but think of the child's mother. She probably had the same enormous pleading eyes. What had happened to her? Why did she need her son to go out onto the streets and work for her?

He could almost see that mother through two soft, watery eyes. She was pleading on behalf of her son.

Siddharth hadn't meant to become so emotionally involved in a single story on a street corner, but somehow the curse had hijacked his heart and his tear ducts. Why could he no longer walk past this boy? Why was he suddenly so bruised by the fact that the midget was a breadwinner — mimicking another million such stories on other street corners? The boy wasn't known to anyone, for goodness sake. He was an unknown person from an unknown family.

The unknown unknown. Life had been so much simpler when this category remained hermetically sealed, not prompting him to learn more, to know more, to feel more. Now Siddharth's heart was squeezing irrationally, almost mimicking the boy's heartbeat in the terror of interrogation, the boy's dilemma quite palpable, echoed in Siddharth's palpitations.

'Of course — you need money. I will send someone to come and see to it.'

Siddharth wanted to get back inside the office and out of the heat — the emotional heat as well as the physical heart-seizing sunshine. His pulse was skipping as he made his way past the guards in their much-coveted uniforms.

When Siddharth had said that he would send someone to 'see to the money', the boy thought that Siddharth was referring to the five rupees to pay for the chai, because the 'big man' had walked off distractedly, obviously not having the small change required to deal with the likes of him. (He charged the guards three rupees for a small plastic cup of chai, but he knew he could charge the big boss five rupees because he wouldn't be bothered with change.) But just as the boy was thinking that a peon would be sent out later with some change to pay for the chai, Siddharth turned round and gave him a five-hundred-rupee note, and the chai wallah found himself speechless, dazzled by the two zeros that had been added to his already inflated price — a price he hadn't felt comfortable to state in the first place.

And that was the end of it, or so the chai wallah thought. But then the person who was sent to 'see to it' — Siddharth's secretary — came with the promise of more money, to be paid to his mother, if he began at St Columba's School, where a place had already been secured after the payment of a handsome 'gift' to the school building fund. (Otherwise, who would have accepted a chai wallah to study among the children from 'good' families?)

It could have been left there. A chance encounter on a street corner outside a star-aligned office in Gurgaon. It could have been just a one-off seizure of the heart, a sudden bout of empathy triggered by a story that hit a sweet spot at precisely the right time. But Siddharth started 'seeing to' many such cases as the days went on, because stories poured out of people across the ever-complex network of thought: so many bewildering, broken, unspoken stories that no frail human could ever intervene to give a happier ending to their totality. And yet the more interventions he made, the more he felt their necessity, as if it were not he but his gift or curse that made the constellations align — as if another controller of the universe was acting through him (which became, over time, a convenient way of thinking through the extraordinary happenings that now occurred in his life on a daily basis).

The need for money was a familiar story, and he heard it again and again on the 'waves'. But the worries of the world will never limit themselves to such banalities, because worries tend to breed and they do so beyond their species. Just by listening in at a board meeting that same day, Siddharth was able to hear that his chief financial officer, Manish, was worried about having lost five crore of company money on the acquisition of another start-up, a company called Janmashtami Enterprises, run by a next-generation entrepreneur called Isha Patel.

'No profits to report this year yet for Janmashtami,' Manish said to the meeting in a cursory fashion. This wasn't news to Siddharth — start-ups rarely made money immediately. Fail forward, fail fast, it was always about failure, and though failure hadn't been Siddharth's mantra, he understood it as something trendy the young ones liked to entertain. But then he began hearing Manish's true thoughts on the matter. *The losses can be hidden against the gains Neelkanth Enterprises has made in the US.*

Again, Siddharth took little notice of this news. It was not unusual for chartered accountants to manage their books in such a creative fashion, and who was he to intervene in such an imagina-tive balancing act? But Manish's thoughts continued unabated, for the CFO clearly had no idea that they were being broadcast on a virtual free-to-air station. *And once Sangheeta has transferred the profits into her name, then we can announce that the losses cannot be recovered.*

One of the other managers was now speaking about hiring a new manager for client engagement, but Siddharth's ears could tune in to one station and one station alone.

Of course, Siddharth knew that the responsibilities of manage-ment came with the right to illicit tithes from the profits — that was the way in India, unfortunately, but now the deceit had been unveiled and was begging for his intervention.

What if the visas don't come through for us all to leave once this is done?

Siddharth was now so intrigued he actually found himself physically leaning in towards Manish — not that this made any difference, because these worries might as well have been on loudspeaker.

Should the US visas fail, Isha can take Sangheeta and go on a student visa to the UK ... but then we would all have to live without her nearby.

His ears were almost growing now in the direction of Manish. Siddharth reached for his water as if it were whisky, his heartbeat skipping and speeding with familiar arrhythmic beats.

Or maybe the losses will never be tracked and Isha can get a management job at Neelkanth Holdings and work here, without anybody suspecting ...

Siddharth got up from the meeting at this point and left the room. Feeling a little dizzy, he held on to the corridor wall as he made his way to the nearest staff bathroom, not his own private bathroom, uncertain what to do next. He was one of them. He could hear their thoughts. This was truly a blessing and a curse — an opportunity to understand how to make the lives of his employees better, as well as making him vulnerable to every criticism about management. He went to his desktop, confirmed the losses, and then walked straight back into the boardroom.

'Is Isha Patel from Janmashtami Enterprises your son-in-law?' he asked Manish outright in front of all the other board members.

The look of shock was replaced in a reflexive switch to accustomed obfuscation. 'Sir, we never felt it would be appropriate to state the family relationship as you were the one who wished for the acquisition to take place.'

This was not the way Siddharth remembered it at all, nor anyone else in the boardroom who had heard Manish sell the potential of Janmashtami Enterprises with such passion and conviction just a few months earlier, sharing his credo of 'bought innovation versus sought innovation' — something that didn't really make sense but rhymed, so it was taken as well-considered.

'We must speak about this later,' Siddharth replied, and the board meeting continued.

Later.

Siddharth was exhausted by the burden of this clairaudience, and simply wanted to sit at his desk and stare at his computer. He did not know what to do about Manish, who had worked with him for over six years as his most trusted financial officer. And here he was, slicing away a dangerously large tithe for himself, in his daughter Sangheeta's name, and planning on skipping out of the country once he had fudged the books. When Guruji had said that he was giving him all the worries of the world, Siddharth hadn't believed him, and now they were taunting him with their abundance. Worse still, these worries included those bred by illegitimate gains — the worries of the new India, hungry to tithe and tax and steal outright, and make bastards of ancient values such as loyalty, duty and honour. If he had to add these worries to his ledger, would his books be expansive enough to hold them?

Kamna, Siddharth's head of staff, entered his room at that point, and seeing him so wiped out she asked if she could bring him a cup of tea.

'If you think it will help,' he answered lamely.

Kamna came back with his tea and once more the airwaves started heating and vibrating, but this time with feelings rather than words — her worries seemed to be embodied in flesh, rather than thought; yearning, as if the nucleus of every cell in her body was missing. Loneliness. Something he couldn't really help her solve because he was surely the loneliest person in the world.

'Drink this. You need it, sir. You are looking quite flushed and I don't think I've ever seen you looking so unwell like this.'

'Thank you, Kamna. Please — sit.' He was touched by her caring. How could someone know how to care in such an authentic way and still be so lonely?

'What are we going to do, sir?'

It had been a long, excruciating meeting, and he didn't wish to speak about Manish, because every time he thought about the man he felt pickled in hideous anxieties that were not of his own making. He felt ugly and greedy and deceitful ... in front of Kamna, who was not responsible for any of it. It was like bringing an ogre in front of Mother Teresa.

'I have no idea what we are going to do, and I don't want to think about it. And it's not about the money. I just feel so desperately betrayed. Do you know that feeling?'

She knew. He could feel it.

Why is she alone? He closed his eyes but he could still see her, staring back at him, her eyes curious, her face strong, framed with waves of sculpted black hair. *Why is there not a man in this world who can look after you, Kamna?*

When his driver took him home to the farm later that day, he had both Kamna and Manish and the bewildered chai wallah on his mind, competing as the car pulled up the red gravel driveway leading to the wedding cake that was his house. He could feel their thoughts from afar: Kamna reflecting, thoughtful, saintly, and Manish, distracted, shaken, conspiring. He brought them both into his house with him, together with the midget, because the worries of the world don't stop at the front verandah and wait outside the house politely on the rattan chaise longue, lounging carefree.

And then the worries were waiting inside for him, in the form of Tota, who began crying as soon as Siddharth walked through the thick, carved teak doors and arrived in the marble atrium at the entrance to the house.

'What happened? Why are you crying?' He didn't feel ready to take on any more, but he had no choice.

'I called Arunji to the house today but he couldn't come.'

Tota was always so rude about the family astrologer — why did she even consider consulting him?

'Today's the day we set aside for the wedding, remember, and he told us not to ...'

My God. The wedding. Today. Yes. My God. Neel.

How could he have forgotten this day of all days? After all the dance classes at the Taj? After all those meetings with the wedding planning company? The cancelled orders, the peons who had been sent to inform all their family and friends that the wedding had been 'postponed' due to family problems. After everything. This day had caught up with them, finally.

Even worse. Siddharth could sense now why there had been tension in the house from the moment he arrived. It was ordained. This was the day when there should have been bliss and union, dancing and feasting. This was the day when Neel and Mae were meant to take each other's hands, tie the cloth and walk around the fire seven times. This was the day they were meant to recite *shlokas*, committing to a marriage that would last ten thousand years through life and death and life again.

'Arunji said on the phone he knew that the *shaadi* wasn't going to go ahead! And I had the phone on loudspeaker, so this was in front of Neel, I'm telling you. In front of Neel! *Arré Ram Bhagwan!* And if he knew that the bloody date was going to end like this, then why didn't this wise bloody astrologer of yours tell us so?' She was yelling now, as if she was blaming not only the family astrologer but Siddharth too, and all his ancestors and the fates that had conspired to make her step over the threshold into this house as a new bride all those years ago, only to give up her life for this hopeless family. 'Why did he make us shame ourselves in front of everyone? Why did he even let us put our good names out on those invitations?'

Siddharth didn't know the answer to even one of her questions, and neither did he believe it was the fault of the astrologer, although his wife did raise some curious questions.

'Don't worry about what Arunji says. None of it is to be believed, anyway.'

'Then why did you let him send our daughter away if you don't believe his shit?'

'Savitri wanted to go. It had nothing to do with Arunji.'

'What if he knows that something terrible is going to happen to her over there and he doesn't care to tell us?'

'Nothing bad is going to happen to her. And when did you start believing Arunji's predictions, anyway?'

Siddharth didn't need the answer. It was desperation and fear, of course. He could feel her body emanating waves of heat. He tried to hold her hand but she tossed it away.

'It was like he was suggesting it was *my* fault!'

'He wouldn't have said that. That's not how Arunji speaks.'

'He said I should kindly not worry and step out of the way. That's the same thing.'

'And maybe it was good advice ...' All Siddharth wanted was a little bit of recognition that his wife might have played some part in the way the stage had been set for Neel and Mae.

'Get out of the house. Get out. How dare you say that to me? Get out.'

She was pushing him out of the house now, and he was letting her, putting up no resistance whatsoever. The driver still hadn't gone to his quarters, so Siddharth simply stepped back into his Mercedes and instructed his chauffeur to go to the first hotel on the MG Road, then return to pick up Neel and get some clothes.

Siddharth gazed out at his perfect lawn as the Mercedes circled it. Every day his gardeners picked up every leaf that dared to land on the carpet of grass, in an attempt to hold back the chaos beyond the walls. *If only the worries of the world could be removed with such perfect precision.* The Mercedes hugged the red-earth road with its perfectly punctuated flowerbeds, went around the sculpted waterfall and out to the front of the farm, where the *chowkidar* couldn't open the gates quick enough for his escape. If it weren't for his mother and son inside the house, he felt as if he could leave now and never return — give up his business even, drive up to the hills in a driverless car.

The Mercedes pulled up in front of a flat, nondescript, single-storey hotel. The foyer showed signs of a modernist influence: a fake Brancusi on a central table and a fake Husain on the wall; it was an otherwise elegant enough venue in which to spend the evening, and possibly even the night.

If it hadn't been for his wife, they would be spending the evening at the Taj Hotel, no doubt about it. The entire family would have been present for the wedding in their full regalia: pearls, rubies, emeralds and diamonds competing with brocades, bejewelled chiffon silks and embroidered fabrics from every corner of India, elegantly draped on shoulders and around navels. Silver bowls filled with almost one hundred dishes would have lined the room, and chefs in starched white uniforms and polished shoes would have served the guests as they feasted. After the family had stepped off the stage having completed their choreographed dance, Bollywood dancers from the Kingdom of Dreams were booked to perform for the next two hours. And then, in their midst, Neel would have arrived in a *doli* on top of a decorated elephant, illuminated by the planetary blaze of fifty lanterns raised high by turbaned light bearers. (Not the ones in the dirty uniforms who sleep beside the white wedding horses on the roadsides of Delhi.). He would have arrived to the sound of trumpets, French horns and the *shehnai* announcing the arrival of good tidings and brilliant fortunes.

There was a knock at the door. It was Neel, arriving surreptitiously in the night, still dressed in the kurta pyjamas he'd been wearing for the past five days through day and night, stained a little around the Nehru collar with some dish he'd eaten containing *haldi*.

'Papa, you been kicked out, yah?'

'Yah.' He liked being with Neel and he liked talking like him — it made him feel like a youthful man again. They were two young men, refugees together, hiding out from the home fires of fury.

'I wanted to spend tonight with you. I know I'm not nearly as fun as Mae, but I just wanted to be with you, no matter what.'

Neel sat on the bed next to his father and gave him a hug.

'Yah, twenty guests still turned up at the Taj who didn't know that the wedding was cancelled. We could have invited them round here for a beer.'

Siddharth didn't want to have any guests. He was glad to have this time with his son, far away from the wild action of their home — happy to talk, order club sandwiches, raid the bar fridge and watch TV. He picked up the remote, something he hadn't done for months, and then the oddest thing happened. He heard an attractive anchorwoman presenting the news on Zee TV, and while they were talking about Kejriwal and his drive to conquer corruption, he could hear the anchorwoman's thoughts, even though she wasn't near him in person.

My God, she's wondering if her lover is watching ...

It was extraordinary — this thing of his even worked over mass media. The anchorwoman's musings made him think of Mae.

'Do you want to go to Australia and meet Mae and Savitri? I'll pay for it. It'll be my wedding present.'

'For a wedding that didn't happen — and go to see a bride who never wants to see me again?'

'That's not true.'

But she hasn't rung and she refuses to pick up her phone when I ring. Savitri says she doesn't even mention my name.

'Maybe she just doesn't want to see your mother again?'

'How can I marry someone who will refuse to talk to my mother?'

'How often do you think your mother talks to Dadi? I don't think she'll even tell her that she's kicked me out of the house.'

The two of them laughed. Neel remembered something Arunji had said earlier that day, about this wedding being a piece of history that was being replayed with a difference — cryptic references that probably meant something to the astrologer but didn't translate without a belief in hocus-pocus.

'You know, there's one reason to be happy about tonight,' Siddharth said.

'What?'

'Nobody has to see me dance.'

Neel laughed, even though he didn't feel like laughing.

I'm stuck in time. I'll never move from here. Nobody will understand. I'm a burden on all of them ...

Thoughts from the groom-who-wasn't-to-be kept populating the room like the wedding guests who hadn't been told that the *shaadi* was cancelled. And between them were the thoughts of the anchorwoman. *I shouldn't have slept with him. He'd have texted me by now if I hadn't gone to bed with him.*

Neel never went to the room that Siddharth had booked for him. They both slept with their clothes on, without even covering themselves up. There were crumbs on the bed and half-empty glasses of whisky under the bedside lamps, and the lamps were left on, like the TV, which continued to broadcast conversations, both external and internal, that permeated Siddharth's dreams.

And Siddharth dreamed that he was listening to the radio at the wheel of that driverless car, driving without driving. He took his hands off the wheel and it continued without him and he felt strangely relieved to be so out of control. Should he worry about this? No. He unbuckled his seat belt to maximise the trust factor, and stretched back so that he was almost lying flat in the driver's seat, still touching the wheel, just for reassurance, just to be sure — surely, surely sure — that he was safe. He wasn't even looking at the trucks ahead, but they were driving up the twisted roads that led up to Badrinath, up to Uttarkashi, the holy hills above Rishikesh. These roads were dangerous, prone to avalanches — what would happen if he let go of the wheel entirely? Should he be worried? Should he sit up again?

No, he shouldn't worry, because if he did so he'd be adding to the worries of the world, over which he had no control.

Adding to the worries of the world.

No more adding to the worries of the world ...

No more ...

Worries ...

No ...

He let his hand slip entirely from the wheel, put his seat into full recline and simply gazed in awe at the peaks around him reaching for the sky, high above the plains, as the dreamy driverless car ascended, up, up, into the Valley of Saints.

WEARING SHIVA

'I NEVER WANTED TO return here to live,' Mae told Savitri as she turned the key to the side door of her family house in Brunswick Heads. 'Especially after I met Neel.'

The house didn't look like something anyone would want to run away from — a welcoming tropical weatherboard on short stilts, on a broad road dotted with barefoot holiday-makers and lotus-eating locals. It looked like it could be blown away in a gust of wind, like a fairytale, with none of the sturdy brickwork of their Delhi home. There was a pretty reception area as you walked in, with a stone Buddha to welcome you, and shelves displaying an assortment of candles and Tantric objects and shells that had been made into toys in places like Mahabalipuram. It was nothing like the austere cream-coloured marble foyer of their farmhouse; there were none of the echoing spaces or balconies that allowed the inhabitants to observe the activities of the servants from lofty heights. This wasn't even a foyer, but more of a charming, intimate, sacred space, with wooden floorboards and an old kilim laid out like a prayer mat in front of the Buddha. She felt instantly happy. Until then she had wished she could spend some more time alone with Mae, but seeing the house she was intrigued to find out what kind of parents might have created such a hideaway.

'My father's surgery is on the left. We don't go in there too much, and you'll need to knock because he often has patients. I'll show you your room.'

They walked through a living room covered with Indonesian ikats, through two white Indo-Saracenic arches and out onto a broad wooden balcony, where a cornucopia of tropical plants hung like a still life all around them: crested bird of paradise flowers next to pandanus grasses, banana palms, wayfarer palms, and small red purses hanging like rich promises off the long tail of a plant she'd never seen before. And there in the middle of it, a ship's lantern on a low table, surrounded by low cane sofas where you could sit back and sip herbal tea while inhaling the warm earthy smells of this tropical sanctuary.

Mae's spare bedroom was in the middle of this Garden of Eden, complete with a Balinese bed draped with a white cotton mosquito net hanging off thick bamboo runners. The only sign of a makeshift finish in this romantic retreat was a rattan mat that had been hastily pulled over the concrete floor.

'This is so-o-o pretty — I can't believe it. Where are all these plants from?'

'Well, that's a hibiscus with *flowers as big as dinner plates* ...' Mae was reciting words from one of her favourite childhood picture books in a singsong voice. 'And there's the Big Bad Banksia man. And that over there is George. Say hello to George.'

Savitri looked in the direction of Mae's pointing finger and screamed a primal, guttural, nerve-pinching scream that was utterly uncontrollable.

She hadn't meant to scream, but George was a python who had wrapped his long, sickeningly scaly body several times around a branch that was surely too thin to hold him, just a few centimetres higher off the ground than she was, and close enough to lick her scalp if his forked tongue was as long and scary as the rest of him. He was attached to the tree, it seemed, as if the branch were his second spinal cord, but he could leave it at any moment — shed it like a skin and begin to slither his way towards her ...

Mae laughed. 'Don't be scared of George. He's not here for you, but for the wood pigeons.' There were feathers on the pavers below the branch, as evidence of his culinary preferences. 'We've been meaning to call Den to remove him. He's magic with snakes.'

'My God! My God.'

Savitri looked at George's cold-blooded eyes — eyes that made alien, reptilian observations of the world — and winced. She had been trained by her ayah not to look at snakes in the street whenever she was out in Delhi. She had been told that the snake charmers would curse you if you glanced at them without paying, and that you would come back as a snake if you didn't pay them, so she always looked the other way. And in spite of averting her gaze whenever a snake charmer gathered a crowd, she had spent her entire childhood seeing snakes in folded-up bedcovers and dreaming that one had wrapped itself around her while she was sleeping. And here she was, with a snake on sentry duty outside her bedroom! She shuddered as those coiled-up memories unfurled. The snake, if you please, was virtually her bed companion!

'I can't believe you're not terrified having this in your garden.'

It seemed as if Mae was scared of nothing.

'Oh, they bite, but they don't kill ya. You've got to be careful if there are babies around, though, because they like the smell of mother's milk.'

Savitri screamed again.

'Yeah — in Australia sometimes they find a cow dead in a paddock with two fang marks in its udder, because a snake's stopped to have a suckle and the cow's tried to kick it off.'

Savitri was holding herself for protection now. 'Eeeee!'

'And bears drop out of trees here, too ...'

'You mean koala bears?' Now she was confused.

'Nah, only kidding — and they're not bears. Enough. Let's go and meet my grandmother, she's keen to say hi.'

Savitri knew that Mae's grandmother lived with them, Indian-style, like Dadi back at home, but she was always confused by the way that she referred to her nani by her first name, Dolly. She couldn't imagine calling Dadi 'Kamla'. The words simply wouldn't come out of her mouth, in case they tainted the relationship and reversed the true order of things forever. Nothing could seem more odd except the sight of her grandmother in pants, not a sari — immortalised in a photograph from the 1960s, taken on the Czechoslovakian border when she was a young woman. But that photograph was always kept at the bottom of their photo pile.

'I'd love to meet her.'

Savitri was led into another room off the Buddha corridor. Dolly was lying down in a purple room, complete with a purple mosquito net — so unlike her grandmother's sick bay. Dolly's grey hair was cut in a pudding-bowl style, clumsily, and her face was as creased as that of a Pahari woman who'd been carrying wood up Himalayan mountains all her life. Her eyes at their bluest core hadn't aged, even though the lids had sunk, leaving slim gaps of anaemic flesh showing.

'Dolly, Savitri wants to say hello.'

Dolly got up and down a few times, as if she was a little confused about how she would like to receive this guest: lying down or sitting up or in a chair. Savitri surrendered her hand.

'Savitri arrived from India a week ago.'

'Oh dear.'

'You live in a very beautiful country,' Savitri said, 'and I am so honoured to be here.'

Dolly nodded and stroked Savitri's hand. She didn't seem to want to have a conversation now that she was 'connected'.

'Oh, I don't see much of it nowadays, but Australia is really lovely.' She smiled, as if at a distant memory.

'Savitri had a shock when she met George,' Mae said.

'George?'

'The snake.'

'I thought it was called a python.'

'Yes, the python's name is George.' She was shaping the words in her mouth more clearly, and loudly, for her grandmother, who was so removed from the century and yet so fully in the moment of connection.

Dolly felt Savitri's hand and announced something that took the two girls by surprise.

'She's got the same gift in her family as we have in ours.' Her blue eyes sought out Savitri's. 'It's there.' Dolly seemed excited, as if she were at a reunion. It was as though she was alert to a possibility that could change everything. 'Mae has a touch of it, too, but she always says she can't feel it.'

'Dolly thinks I'm a bit psychic but I haven't developed it,' Mae said, lying down on the bed next to her grandmother and taking her other hand. 'Mum has it, but not me.'

'But in this girl's family it's running down the male line. Is it your father, dear?'

Savitri laughed. 'No. It's probably his brother. Well, sort of brother. The family astrologer. My father would laugh if you told him he was psychic.'

'You're going to have a lovely time here with us,' Dolly continued, smiling coyly as if she'd just discovered a secret too embarrassing to share.

'I'm hoping to enjoy my stay.'

'Yes, you might like to stay.' She giggled, as if she'd heard a joke that nobody else could understand. 'And you mustn't worry about your family while you're here. That'll only get in the way of your fun.'

Mae spoke, a little louder. 'Savitri's going to help me set up my business once the cushions have arrived. They'll be arriving in a few days.'

'Your mother won't be pleased,' replied Dolly.

'Whose mother? What about?' Mae seemed a little thrown by this reference to Tota, but it wasn't lost on Savitri, who understood that Dolly talked in tangents the way people do when they have Parkinson's with a touch of clairvoyance.

'Take her to the beach, darling. She needs to see the water that connects us with her country. You know India and Australia used to be the same continent' she said to the girl.

They didn't go to Dolly's Beach, as Mae's family knew it, but to the beach at Brunswick Heads, out to a small pier with a river to one side. The beach was covered with flat, finely ground sand; on the other side of the spit, long sandy stretches hugged the ocean all the way out to a white lighthouse in the distance. There were lots of young people on the beach at the mouth of the river. Mae decided they should swim in the calmer waters there until Savitri got used to the surf.

'We'll swim in the flat water at Torakina,' she said. 'Too many tourists get killed in the waves.'

She remembered how reckless Neel had been, swimming out too far in the choppy waters, where he'd been dragged further and further into the ocean by a rip. Mae had forgotten to tell him to swim sideways out of the rips so prevalent in Australia, so he had struggled, trying to get back in the same way the ocean had sucked him out, until Mae managed to get someone on a surfboard to go and pull the poor stupid foreigner out.

Savitri didn't care which beach she sat on; the sand was warm beneath her and she was enjoying this more than she'd ever thought possible, watching these happy people who knew how to love the sun — a love she'd never been taught. (In spite of the fact that she was named after the daughter of the sun god!)

There were mothers with small children, bare-breasted, wearing strings for bikinis— all this in front of the men, who hardly noticed. Were they just being respectful? In India they would have been setting up their mats in rows to watch! It made her think: why had Mae ever wanted to leave this perfect place where she'd happily arrived through the accident of birth?

Mae dropped her beach bag and simply took off her clothes, taking off her top and stripping down to her bikini. Savitri struggled inside her towel, and several minutes later emerged in her one-piece, feeling as if she'd arrived at the beach in her winter school uniform. Nobody seemed to notice her discomfort any more than they noticed the women with bare breasts.

As Mae began putting suncream on Savitri, a young man came over and sat down next to them. Savitri watched in awe as Mae stood up, half-naked, and they hugged — yes, they hugged. She watched as his chest touched hers, with no fabric to separate them, just like that, as if they were in bed together, with casual, familiar intimacy.

'Savitri, this is Nitin.'

'That's an Indian name.' Savitri was still reeling from seeing Mae pressed up against the chest of a rather handsome boy.

'Half the town has Indian names,' Mae replied.

'Yeah,' said Nitin, 'there's Casadevi, and Maya, and Aman over at Ocean Shores.'

'Then there's Kazza — Karen Moxham — who sounds Muslim even though she's not.'

Savitri tried not to look at Nitin's body; she tried extremely hard to adopt the same casual lack of interest the Australian men seemed to have towards topless Australian women, but she knew that her eyes were fixating on the glory of that bare chest, which didn't have so much as a vest for modesty. And then there were the muscles, along with sleek skin, not too much hair and the sort of tan that didn't make the skin go brown like her own, but golden.

'Do you girls want to join me for a swim in the surf?' The beautiful young man was now tying his hair into a bun, making Savitri think of the sadhus who competed to dip in the holy waters at the Kumbh Mela.

'Too rough today,' Mae answered. 'Savitri's not a strong swimmer.'

'I'll swim with her.'

'No — she shouldn't.'

'But I'd like to give it a try.' Savitri didn't want to lose this opportunity to ... to ... well, risk her life. Why, she would have a lifeguard who was even more attractive than the one at her mother's pool!

Mae recognised this bloody-minded female intent and responded with a knowing smile. 'Righty-ho, I'll stay here.'

Nitin, oblivious to the unspoken collusion, took Savitri's towel and they walked over the spit together. The choppy ocean stretched away into the distance, the coast's bell-shaped curves like a female form — perfect sanctuaries for delicious summer days.

'You must be Neel's sister, no?' He was waiting to interrogate her once he had her on her own.

'Yes.'

'I really liked your brother. He gave me this.' Savitri looked at the necklace Nitin was holding. It was the wooden Shiva that Dadi had given Neel when he first went to study in Australia, for protection.

'I remember that.'

'Yeah? I told him what an amazing necklace he was wearing and he took it off in a flash and gave it to me, just like that. So cool. I've worn it ever since. It's got special meaning for me.'

Maybe that was why she was drawn to his chest! Knowing that her brother had liked this boy and that he had a talisman from her grandmother made Savitri walk confidently to the water's edge and let the ocean spill foam over her feet. She was happy here.

This was her lucky day. She didn't really know why she liked the Australian boy with an Indian name and an Indian god around his neck, but she suspected it was because he hadn't been presented to her as a suitor — a yes/no choice. He was the incarnation of uncertainty.

'It's cold.' She didn't say this in complaint. The temperature was a challenge.

Nitin was splashing to keep up as she pushed forward into the surf, up to her waist, then past her chest, running against the waves and against the current, confronting the shock of the new and the cold and the deep all at once. The waves began their assault as soon as they had her in their thrall, and one of the blooming, curling kind took her: knocked her down, spun her round and spat her out for lack of respect, grazing her legs in the sand before coming to a standstill. She had salty water up her nose, a numbing unease, just like when she was doing the Ayurvedic *nasya* treatments back in Delhi. Her hair was filled with sand and her legs were raw.

'Wanna hold my hand?'

'Let's try that again.'

She held his hand and they stepped out into the waves once more, and she copied him as he hopped over them more cautiously. But she felt that he was holding back. Savitri wanted to go further towards the cresting horizon, towards the confluence between the sea and the sky swaying rhythmically together now in front of her.

'Duck.'

A wave was towering above them and Savitri didn't duck, so she was hit once more and taken — this time holding a hand as she was hurled by tidal forces, deprived of oxygen, pushed and pummelled. Nitin's bare-chested body pulled up against hers, holding her confidently around the waist as soon as the water had given its permission and he could get close enough. She didn't know where the surface was but he brought her up to it, carrying her back to the waist-high water where her feet could touch soft sand and her head could face the sky, before he let go of her.

'You're crazy. That was dangerous.'

'But it was so-o-o much fun.'

She reached for his hand and he took it, and Savitri pushed towards that alluring horizon again, wanting to repeat the wet rhythms of the last encounter. Nitin pulled her back by the waist as a wave came at them. He held her close to his body so they presented to the ocean as a single, stronger entity, but that seventh wave knocked them both down, back to the sandpaper that scratched their skin at the water's edge.

At a waterlogged standstill now, he lay next to her and reached out to take her sandy hair out of her eyes.

'You're mad. We're not doing that again. I'm taking you back to Torakina.'

Nitin picked up both their towels and walked them back towards the spit, clearly pleased with himself for being so heroic.

'I can see why my brother liked you.'

He smiled.

When they arrived back at the flat waters where the Brunswick River meets the sea, they saw that Mae was surrounded by a group of friends. Nitin slapped hands with all of them and they sat down to catch up. She heard one of them asking about Neel.

'We've split up,' Mae said.

'Nick and Caroline told me they cancelled their tickets to India.'

'Yeah, I was going to go to the wedding too,' Nitin said. 'But I managed to cancel the booking before I paid for it.'

'I heard that his mother was a real bitch.'

'Err, this is Neel's sister, by the way. Savitri, this is Kerry, Brian and Jayden.'

'Nit, can you put some cream on my back?' The girl, Kerry, was clearly flirting with Nitin, and Savitri reacted in a way she couldn't have predicted, picking up her clothes and towel, and looking the other way. 'Mae, I'm going to walk back to the house, if that's okay.'

Mae caught up with Savitri on the thick wooden footbridge over the Brunswick River, past the young boys throwing breadcrumbed burley out across the water to tempt fish.

'I'm so sorry that Jayden was rude about your mum,' Mae said.

But Savitri wasn't upset that her mother's reputation had reached this far-flung corner of the world. She had far more important concerns.

'I think I need a bikini, like yours.'

'We'll get you one.' Now Mae understood everything. 'We'll get you one that would make the girls at your mum's pool blush!'

Savitri laughed. She felt as if she'd graduated from that pool. Now that she was in Australia, she felt as if she was ready to take on the ocean, one wave at a time.

IT WASN'T MEANT TO BE THIS WAY

SIDDHARTH WOKE THE morning after the wedding night to the sight of his son sprawled next to him, hugging a pillow, his mouth slightly ajar as if in mid-sentence. He brought one of the spare pillows closer and hugged it to himself as he waited for Neel to wake up to this post-apocalyptic world.

Shit, I left my phone at home. I could go and get it, but Papa is here ... If only we could stay here. We could book a room for Dadi, too.

Siddharth responded in his head. *How are you going to take Dadi, Neel? You'd have to take Ayah too, and the wheelchair ... and her puja table.* Neel's eyes were still shut, so he didn't feel like articulating his response in words.

Why on earth isn't Savitri calling to tell me what's going on and how things are? I told her to tell me everything. Something's gone wrong — she doesn't want to tell me ...

Siddharth responded: *Let Savitri be. She's just arrived. She's not going to be able to fix the mess. You're going to have to do it.*

Neel got out of bed and began looking for his father's phone.

I'll call Savitri from Papa's phone. She's more likely to pick up.

Leave her.

Neel picked up the phone, and Siddharth, frustrated that his son wasn't hearing his side of their wordless conversation, sat up to get the words out.

'Don't call Savitri. That's not the way to get to speak to Mae. It's unfair.'

'How did you know I was going to phone Savitri?'

Siddharth stared at Neel for a full minute, assessing him, wondering whether it might be helpful, at this moment, to tell him about the strange occurrences in his life. Apart from Guruji, the only person who knew about the curse was Arunji, and it was most unlikely that he would have told anyone — his revelations were reserved for precisely the most appropriate moment, or so it seemed.

'Neel, I can hear every word that you're thinking, and I know what you're feeling from the bottom of my very heart, as if your words and thoughts were my own.'

Neel laughed.

'No, really.'

Neel listened, and his father told him the story of the curse — about how he had been so abrasive and dismissive and impatient at the *darshan* he'd been forced to attend with Guruji. He told him about the deal he had hatched with Savitri — how he would learn to meditate only on the promise that she would settle down and start dating Mohan. He didn't stop at anything. He told him about Manish at the office, and about the way he had overheard the thoughts of the driver, the cook, his employees and his family.

Then he told Neel about the first time it happened: how non-existent cymbals had started a cacophony in his ears. He told him how the words that populated other people's minds, translated sometimes as feelings but at other times forming entire sentences, entered his consciousness fully punctuated. He even told his son about the thoughts that had emanated from the news anchorwoman the night before.

'What was she saying?'

'Oh, something about her boyfriend.'

'Do you know how Mama feels?' *He's just guessing that I would try and call Savitri.*

'She feels as if the world has given up on her. She feels as if she's not just ruined your life but hers too, and she wishes she could take back the words that broke your heart and ruined your marriage to Mae.'

What Siddharth didn't say was that Tota also thought Neel was a gutless idiot — or that she wished for a son who was strong and fearless, not a henpecked boy who had given up on his own family. He didn't say that Tota wished she could hold insect spray up to the very idea of Mae and have her disappear, like a cockroach. He didn't say, either, how she was contemplating bringing some suitable girls to meet her son in the near future.

'Your mother would love to see you happy.'

'Yah, yah.'

There was such a deep-seated unhappiness within his son. It obliterated any chance for him to see the conditions of happiness in any other person, let alone himself. Joyfulness, after all, comes from godlike ontological excess, and if he couldn't locate that well of abundance, it was hardly surprising that he felt bereft of the power to make his mother happy.

I will take you to meet Savitri's guru. Siddharth didn't quite know whether this was a good idea. He knew that people in need of spiritual revival were the most likely future fundamentalists. Could he bear to see his son don orange robes and set off for the hills at the behest of a supposedly two-hundred-year-old sadhu? Could the meditation he had learned, without the concomitant curse, cure his son of the melancholy that had smothered his reason, his power, his ability to love even himself?

Papa wouldn't make something up. So weird. I'll ask him if he can read my thoughts ...

'Yes, I can read them, Neel. I've heard you.'

Neel laughed, embarrassed. This was very awkward. *Now I've got the thought police listening to me.*

'I'm used to it,' Siddharth replied. 'It feels normal now. Nobody's thoughts are strange.'

'That's totally awesome.' *You wouldn't make it up?*

'Why would I want to make any of this up?'

'That's wild ... You know, this is something Mae's grandmother can do.'

'I can hear much more than you think, even. Things that you haven't quite thought but that influence your thoughts.'

'And you call that a curse?'

It was one of the first times Siddharth had ever really stopped to question whether it could be anything else. He remembered the day it started happening, and how Guruji had called it a blessing: a 'gift', because Siddharth already had everything material he could possibly wish for and more. Where, then, had this idea of a curse come from? Was it simply his resistance — his unwillingness to take on the worries of the world? What if he embraced them? What if he loved the ability to know and to help and to heal? Yes, with this ability he even had the power to heal. If he could turn around the life of a chai wallah, then surely he could use this gift to turn around the life of his son? And even his own life. He could turn the curse into a blessing.

The thought itself made him feel happy.

'Neel, I think we should find this guru and get him to teach you to meditate.'

'No, no — that's exactly what Arunji was telling me I should do.'

Arunji said the same thing? Interesting. Siddharth could see his son's issue. Meditation seemed too simple a solution for an overwhelmingly complex problem. He had experienced exactly the same reticence himself. This type of guru-worship was for grandmothers and sisters and sycophantic, obsequious, holier-than-thou types who liked to grovel at the feet of those supposedly wiser than they were. It was bad enough that he wanted his son to visit a guru, let alone one who was two hundred years old, if his disciples were to be believed.

'Forget the guru-worship, yah — let him just teach you about *thisthing* — *thisthing* that's there whether you want it or not, all the time, whether you see it or hear it or not.' He was talking about the milky ocean at the beginning of time, where the worries of the world exist like poison, alongside the diamonds and pearls fished out by the goddesses.

He could hear this idea fall on parched soil.

'What if you could change one thing — what would it be?'

'I'd still be with Mae.'

'Then you need to change yourself. The one thing you need to do is change yourself.'

Siddharth didn't enjoy sounding like the guru but he had no choice. His son was so irritating in his refusal to see this fact that should be glaringly clear to everyone.

'Do you think that Mae is the first girl in the world to despise her mother-in-law? Do you think that you're the first person ever to be stuck with this problem? This is a problem from the beginning of time, yah, when bloodlines were written and obligations were made between people and clans. This is a structural problem.'

'So what? Is Guruji going to take away this problem that's always existed?'

'No, that's my point. You're the only one who can take it away, yah.' Siddharth decided to use the metaphor that had arrived in his dreams. 'You're going to be able to take your hands off the wheel. Everything you've been trying to control that you cannot control will become irrelevant. You'll just let go of all of it. None of it will matter. It's hard work being the controller of the universe.'

Guruji had taken up residence at farm number thirty-three. This ashram in the metropolis could have been installed in Siddharth's farmhouse without looking too dissimilar. The environment in which Ram Avtar had set up the guru behind his high farm walls aspired to the same standards of fantasy. The two farmhouses had been styled by interior designers who studied at the same college. The gardens were equally ornate, their flowers blossomed in perfect synchrony and the same bees gathered identical pollen across the boundary walls.

On arrival at number thirty-three they were taken by a servant to the room where Siddharth had been whisked away to learn how to meditate, a moment that seemed to belong to a different lifetime. The two of them, father and son, were now seated alongside the same statue of Lord Krishna that was multiplied into an infinity of Krishnas by some strange seventies mirror effect.

Last time Siddharth was here he had been impatient to get away from the guru and back to work. This time he was impatient to see him get to work. Last time he'd sat in the same low seat on his own, looking at the expansive marbled hall outside the guru's suite. He'd behaved as if he were a banker or insurance agent, assessing how much Ram Avtar had spent on the construction and interior of his farmhouse, matching the space with the financial coefficient he believed accompanied every manifestation of life. This time he couldn't think about what the farm was worth or how much they were paying their guru. Instead, his gaze was absorbed by the swirling paisley patterns on the white marble floor. He was standing outside himself, seeing his past, observing himself and his son's knotted brow — his own thoughts, on this occasion, larger than Neel's.

There is no guarantee ... no guarantee ... what to do ... how to make sure this works? He was hearing his own rumination just as he heard the thoughts of others, but this time trapped in that marble hall, echoing and amplified. *If only there wasn't this ridiculous rumour that Guruji is two hundred years old — it would be so much easier for Neel.*

The servant knocked on an adjoining door and Guruji emerged from his suite. Siddharth looked at his son, who was suitably reverent and polite, bringing his hands together. *Good*, he thought. *He isn't making my mistake. He's smarter than I am. He knows what he needs.*

'Namaskar.' The guru reached out and held Siddharth's arms as if he were greeting a long-lost brother, and Siddharth's icy suspicion of the man thawed. Had he been so self-absorbed the last time they'd met that he hadn't noticed the welcoming, loving smile? Had he not noticed the fallibility of the man who had taken to white robes? The cocked, questioning head and arched eyebrows that sought the wellbeing of others?

'Guruji. This is my son, Neel.'

Neel and Tota were the only two in the family who had not been to see the guru. The man was curious, that was natural, but more than this, it was clear that he felt a paternal sense of responsibility for a son who wasn't his own. It was disarming, because Siddharth had always thought of the guru as disingenuous — only interested in receiving garlands and donations, neglecting any duties to contribute to the real world of commerce and karma.

'I've been longing to meet you. I've heard so many things about you from your grandmother and sister. And I heard that you're getting married to a lovely Australian girl.'

Surely he knows what-all happened to the lovely Australian girl?

The thoughts of the guru were harder to read — somehow more contained. They didn't spill over; they were hardly audible. Had Savitri not come round to tell him before she took off to Australia?

'Actually, it's off.'

'Maybe it's better not to be focusing on finding a wife for now,' Guruji said.

'It's hard not to think about her.'

'So today we can teach you to meditate. But you have to want to learn.'

'That's why we've come,' Neel replied.

This is going well ... better than I could have hoped.

'We can all meditate together after the small ceremony,' Guruji announced. 'That will help.'

Guruji lit his incense and began singing a Sanskrit song, offering blessings to the saints who had come before, represented in a painting on the altar where white-robed sages lined a river winding back to its source.

Siddharth could feel Neel's mind slow down to a silence that had no expectations, buoyant and light.

So peaceful.

He opened his eyes and saw a tear in the corner of his son's eye. And sensed that at that moment Neel didn't have a single thought about his own inadequacy. No oppressive memories about irretrievable losses, failed desires or cancelled weddings. The chaos and confusion were surrendered to the soft Sanskrit song. When Guruji had sung this song for Siddharth he had failed to hear the tenderness in the words.

Guruji then gave Neel a mantra and instructed him to sit down with closed eyes, and not to keep the time: to let the mind take its course — which it did in the most elegant way, sidestepping every obstacle in its path. There was nothing missing in his sunshine. Everything that the world had to offer was his, yet there was no need to shout about it or claim it as his own. It was simply there, just as Siddharth had said. The tear gathering in the corner of his eye fell, but there was no sadness in its salt, simply relief. That tear could have fallen into the saint-lined river that stretched into the distance ahead of them, behind the fruit and spirals of incense on the altar.

A bucolic silence held the three of them in its space. A buffalo called out to be milked. They all heard this call as a question mark that didn't need a response. For those few moments, there wasn't a worry in the world that could disturb them.

THE MAKING OF A NEW WORLD

MAE HADN'T WANTED to celebrate her twenty-second birthday, feeling she'd done nothing to deserve the attention, but she had no say in the matter. After all, her father, Terry, had pioneered the homebirth movement in the shire, and if birth couldn't be celebrated in that house, then where could the party be held?

Patti didn't expect her daughter to change for dinner — Savitri was the only one surprised that Mae didn't dress up for her birthday, but simply changed into a fresh bikini and draped an Indonesian sarong around her waist before helping Dolly get to the table.

Terry lit the candles on the table. 'Can someone go out to the van and invite Winsome and Sage, please?'

Savitri had met the young couple who lived in a van outside the house and had heard all about their adventures travelling around Australia looking for a place where they could have a homebirth and start their lineage. Finding Mae's father helped them decide on the shire, and as they didn't yet have anywhere to live, Terry had agreed they could give birth in the house. Winsome and Sage had often come in for meals since their arrival and Savitri always noticed Winsome's long black Chinese hair, immaculately straight and shiny, and her large pregnant tummy, which unashamedly peeped out between the top of her baggy pants and the T-shirt that no longer quite reached her waist. She loved the sadhu looks of Sage, too, with his neatly dreadlocked hair that grew past his shoulders in a ponytail, a long bearded face and green eyes.

'The moon's close tonight,' Patti said. 'Close enough to touch.'

Savitri had seen it earlier and felt its luminescent potency: large and close to the treetops above the trailer park that lined the road to the two beaches. There was a sense of mystery in the air. It was a night rich with possibilities.

'Terry will be called out halfway through dinner for a delivery, that's my bet — the women will be popping. Give those babies a full moon or a thunderstorm and the mums charge into labour.'

Savitri felt a tingle at the idea of such lunar power. Of course, it must be the same moon that hung above them in Delhi, but surely the smog over her city would obscure and discolour any force such a magic moon could conjure.

Mae came back first with the van-dwellers. 'Hey, everyone — Winsome has promised not to pop the baby tonight.'

Sage brought his hands together in a traditional namaskar, complete with a Ming dynasty bow, signalling the moon's daily passage over India, the Orient and every stop in between, with total irreverence for any cultural difference it might encounter on the journey.

Terry brought out a bottle of wine to go with the shepherdess pie, fried zucchini flowers and rocket salad, Mae's favourite. 'Sky juice for you, Savitri?'

Savitri sipped the sweet water they collected off their tin roof, filtered through a clay purifying system. *So much nicer than the Aquaguard water back at home.*

Mae returned again, this time with Dolly, who looked into every-one's eyes, one at a time, with lunar lucidity. The table was complete now, in full circle, and Dolly decided to do the birthday honours.

'I know you want to pretend that this isn't a special day, darling, but you can't ignore your birthday any more than you can ignore a husband on your wedding night.' She held up a glass. 'Here's to our Mae!'

Savitri winced. Damn. She knew Mae had warned all of them not to talk about Neel or weddings or even India as long as she was staying with them. She'd felt uncomfortable the other night when Terry had begun telling her tales of his Himalayan treks and the first homebirth he'd attended in Kathmandu, but she hadn't had the heart to stop him.

Mae picked up her wineglass and swigged hard, the red anaesthetic, sinking fast to the bottom of the glass.

'It was so lovely when your brother came to stay,' Patti started, ignoring her daughter's cues to switch topic. 'He was such a charming, well-brought-up, respectful young man. I can't tell you how upset we were to hear about the break-up.'

'What's broken up?' Dolly chimed in.

'Neel and Mae.' Patti was speaking louder now, directly into her mother's ear.

'No, they haven't. He was here just a few minutes ago.'

Savitri wondered whether Mae's grandmother could see Neel's astral body kneeling in front of the Buddha or sighing next to the koi pond. Dolly's mind seemed to have the porosity of a cloud, with the boundaries between the concrete and unseen worlds indistinguishable at their palest edges.

'Does anyone want to go for a walk in the moonlight?' Mae was looking at Savitri, Sage and Winsome with a desperate expression.

'Sure, but let's stop off at the van — I have a present for you,' Sage replied.

❧

Even with her large belly, Winsome reached up a leg and lifted herself elegantly into her van with the grace of a pregnant ballerina, without so much as a hand from her boyfriend, who stayed back to help Mae and Savitri clamber up with less panache.

'Welcome to our humble passion wagon.'

Savitri pretended she hadn't heard, but really it was a fairly accurate description of their bedroom: there wasn't much room for anything but passion. The mattress took up all the space in the back, and some uncomfortable cushions lined the sides of the truck. A couple of boxes at their feet must have held their worldly possessions, and goodness knows how they would fit a new baby in their van, even if it arrived the size of a doll.

They sat down and Sage began rolling a joint. 'An extra big one for the birthday girl.'

'Nah. I'm not smoking anymore,' Mae replied, turning down her present, but when the joint was passed to her she inhaled to full lung capacity regardless, and as she did so her phone rang. She took it from her pocket, sighed and pressed the red button. *It must be from Neel*, Savitri thought as she saw Mae take another deep puff of the joint she didn't want.

Savitri could feel her brother's anxiety and determination, as if they had been teleported over the moon's wireless water network. Mae passed her the joint and Savitri, not wanting it either, took it to her lips, like a shared conspiracy.

'You're full of surprises, Savitri.'

Savitri was determined not to cough, and instead took the deep breath that Mae had taken, filling her lungs with Mullumbimby Madness, grown by locals and harvested from various Aboriginal sacred sites dotted around the shire.

'She's never had this stuff before,' Mae said.

'Like Winsome until she met me.'

Savitri looked over at Winsome's round, pretty face and enormous belly. She took another drag on the joint and saw her again, as if for the first time. Why, this Chinese girl had the smile of a moon goddess, and she was stroking her belly, as if bestowing fertility on them all. As she watched, Savitri was acutely aware of her own body, feeling more powerful than ever before. She felt a yearning to be touched, somewhere, anywhere.

'Winsome hadn't even celebrated anyone's birthday before she met me,' Sage continued. 'This is all new for her.'

Savitri took another puff on the joint as she heard the goddess speak. 'Jehovah's Witnesses don't celebrate birthdays.'

'How did you two meet?' Mae asked.

'She tried to convert me. You tell the story.'

Winsome's voice seemed to come from a land without borders, with its Hong Kong lilt, Aussie easiness and stretched American vowels. 'My parents were unusual Jehovah's Witnesses because they wanted me to go to university before I became a missionary,' she began. 'So I hadn't been working for long when I met Sage.

I'd tried knocking on doors but people were so rude to me. Not that this mattered. We were told that the more people put us down, the more convincing preachers we'd become — and anyway, the people who refused to hear us were going to die in Armageddon.'

'That's all of us, right?' Sage was speaking to everyone in the van. 'We're all going to die — even the ones who have never heard of Jehovah's Witnesses.'

Savitri was only just beginning to feel like she could live, for the first time in her life. She laughed a little, wondering if anyone else noticed how different she was feeling.

'So I started trying to preach in the railway tunnels below Central Station in Sydney.'

'She used to hand out *Watchtower* magazines.'

'But only a few people stopped to talk to me, so I started testing out different spots where the worldly people would want to stop and talk, and I came across this yoga school, and the teacher, Zara, was really nice. She used to let me join the classes for free — and I agreed, only because I thought it would help me to teach more people and save more lives.'

'What she didn't realise was that she was a natural born yogi.'

'Yeah, I loved the yoga, and I loved Sage, because he let me practise preaching on him so that I'd get better at it!'

'Yay — great pick-up technique.' Mae nudged Sage. 'I'll listen to you preach, darlin', if you come back to my van afterwards ...'

'He was so much nicer than all the other worldly people.'

'So funny how you call us worldly people!' Mae remarked.

It didn't seem funny to Savitri. She felt as if the others were far more worldly than her; as if she were joining their world for the very first time. The joint came round again and she inhaled it like a remedy for innocence, there in the semi-darkness, hoping that the world could reach her. Yet the world was far, far away, perhaps far below them — they could have been on a flying mattress in a flying van, flying, flying, closer and closer to the dangerously close moon. She leaned her head on Mae's shoulder and Mae stroked her head like her ayah used to do when she was a child.

'But I soon realised that I was attracted to him, even though he wasn't a JW. And he was so sweet about it when I told him, and so careful to tell me that I was probably doing the wrong thing, and that he was just helping me practise my preaching and my yoga.'

'But I did admit that I was into you, didn't I? I was honest.'

'That's right. He was honest, and even though he told me he would never be able to convert, somehow I couldn't stop liking him.'

'*Losing my religion ...*' Mae sang.

'The elders tried to stop it, though.'

'Yeah, they held a meeting — and these were the guys who'd been asked to look out for me after my parents went back to Hong Kong. They asked me how many times I'd had sex, whose idea it was to have intercourse. Whether I'd enjoyed it or not.'

'Bloody perverts.'

'No, no, they are who they are,' Sage replied.

'And that's why I loved Sage. Because he wasn't rude about them and he wasn't rude about me, and he understood where I was coming from and he still wanted to be with me.'

The joint, which seemed to be the smoking source of all stories, came back to Savitri and the van rocked a little as Sage shifted to pass it to her. Who knows, it could have been rocking because it was flying over mammatus clouds, the bumps dislodging her remaining bearings with reality. She was listening to the story as if she'd never heard one before, savouring the illicit tale. She laughed. What would her mother say if she were to see her now?

'What did your parents say about you ... wanting a love marriage?' Savitri knew that these weren't the right words and that the moon goddess wasn't married, but like anyone being told a good story, she wanted to know how it intersected with her own. What would an Indian parent have said about such a scandal?

'Her parents refused to speak to her. They told her that she wasn't allowed to stay with them when she went to Hong Kong if she wasn't a Jehovah's Witness anymore.'

'Couldn't you just lie and say that you were?' Savitri said. 'Does it matter what label you put on yourself? All religions are the same.'

'No, they're not. We're different — JWs would be happy to sacrifice their family for their religion.'

'I'm Winsome's family now. And we're starting a new lineage.' Sage stroked his girlfriend's belly, and as he did Mae's phone beeped. Savitri leaned over and read it with her friend.

Happy birthday, beautiful, please call.

A few seconds later there was another message, this time on her phone. *Please wish Mae from me. It's her birthday today.*

They both pushed their little red buttons without saying a word and put away the devices that kept their flying van tethered to bumpy clouds. Savitri lay back on the mattress where the moon goddess must have conceived the child who was starting the new lineage and a new religion that didn't require believers: a religion as pure and irrefutable and consistent as moonlight. Her body was shimmering with the illicit urges that must have driven everyone who had ever eloped from the beginning of time. And she could imagine Winsome and Sage making love in that van with soul-conjuring intensity. 'Lucky baby,' she said wistfully, as the story van flew past the layer of clouds.

There was a knock on the van, even though it was clearly in the sky.

'Can you fit in an extra?'

It was Nitin, the boy she'd met on the beach, returning like a tide on a full moon — perhaps by magic? He climbed into the bedroom the size of a mattress, where everyone huddled closely around Savitri, who lay in the middle, looking up at the stars painted on the roof, feeling her skin's sensory capacity extending out towards the boy who had arrived in their van as effortlessly as a wave. Nitin took the joint, and with it joined the story.

'If Sage had wanted to convert, I would still be a Witness now,' Winsome continued, 'and we may even have been allowed to get married in the Kingdom Hall, but the elders were really upset about the yoga.'

'I went to a meeting with them,' Sage said. 'And I was told that it was a practice in the worship of false gods.' Mae giggled and Sage continued. 'Yeah, right, they went on and on about the fact that these were physical and mental exercises aimed at gaining unity with an impersonal god and somehow that was the wrong thing to, like ... connect with. They told me that one Witness who'd done yoga experienced forces trying to take over his body for months afterwards.' Everyone laughed. 'And they told Winsome she'd be better off jogging or swimming — like it was all about working out.'

'That's so tripped out,' Nitin said. 'Poor Savitri. According to these people, her religion is full of evils like yoga and false idols and demons who curse you.'

Savitri was enjoying the conversation, and loving the fact that Nitin was trying to defend her faith, but the lucid moon was prompting her to tell them exactly how far the superstitions in her religion could go.

'Yes, and maybe they're right! Maybe we should all become Jehovah's Witnesses. Who's to say it isn't the right path? And yes, they're right about us Hindus. We have three hundred and thirty million gods and goddesses, as well as the one god because we believe in totality!'

'But that's different. You've also got one of the oldest religious traditions in the world.'

'Yes, and somewhere in that ancient tradition there's a belief that the man I marry will die because I was born under a *Manglik* star. Is that any more rational than the other stuff?'

'Fuck off!' Nitin was clearly shocked. He took another toke on the third joint going around.

'No, this is also Hinduism, believe me. And this belief was dragged into the twenty-first century. And did you know, I have to marry a Peepal tree before my real wedding takes place so that I don't taint my husband and kill him by accident.' She was giggling at her own predicament, such was the distance from it she now enjoyed, courtesy of the Mullumbimby Madness.

'What the hell? You can't just accept that. We have to test out the theory.'

'You mean the belief?' Sage interrupted.

'No, theory. I'm a scientist, don't forget.'

'So how are we going to test it, Einstein?' Mae asked.

'Well, if someone is telling Savitri that anyone who marries her is going to die, then we should put that thought out of her head once and for all. We have to test the theory.'

'Put that thought out of my head? You'll have to pull out the whole plant that took root at my birth. And then you'd take my brain with it.'

'Don't you think there's something ridiculous about having to marry a tree?' Nitin asked.

'Yes. Totally.' Savitri had never mentioned her astrological affliction to anyone in India; however, telling people over here, it sounded utterly ridiculous yet also somehow fitting. It seemed appropriate for this revelation to join the air in a smoky, semi-lit van crammed with a pregnant moon goddess, a white sadhu, a scientist and the woman who never became her sister-in-law. Besides, the scientist was half priest, a gorgeous boy hearing her confession. Just being near him seemed to draw out her affliction. 'But maybe it's worth marrying a tree, just to get it over and done with.' She echoed the 'logical' thinking instilled in families who still couldn't stop themselves from consulting superstitions.

'No, that's not the point,' said the determined and deterministic scientist, dragging on the fourth joint that was now circulating. 'You need to marry a man without marrying the tree first — you've gotta, like ... have sex without the condoms.' He looked Savitri's way and found her smiling. 'Otherwise, how will you know whether you've just killed your husband or not?' They all laughed.

'Right, then. We just need to organise the wedding.' Sage seemed ready for the mission as he seeded this suggestion. He'd clearly smoked enough of his greens and had a great feast. The only thing left to do tonight was conduct one of those Mullumbimby-style weddings that required you to jump over a broomstick and chant a mantra or two.

'It's a wonderful night for a moondance, with the stars up above in the sky ...' Mae sang.

Savitri laughed. 'But who will I marry?'

'I'm taken.' Sage looked over at Nitin.

'I'm not,' Nitin replied.

'We'll drive to Mount Chincogan and do it there.'

'But how can I get married? Nobody has come with a proposal.'

She was still lying down between them all when Nitin crouched on top of her on all fours (and even bended knee) and said with a wicked stoned grin: 'Savitri, let's get married.'

She was loving this. What would her mother say, after trying for all these years? After enlisting their cousins' friends' wives' uncles and pulling every string on every cord they could find, here was a marriage proposal being made in a passion wagon! The thought of her mother just made her giggle. They wouldn't need to hire a single dance master or flower seller or caterer or light bearer or musician or whatnot.

'And tonight,' Sage added.

Savitri thought of her mother's friend's son Himanchu, who'd hardly looked her in the eye when they were introduced, and she thought of Ramachandra, who'd come all the way from Coimbatore to meet her, on account of a great friendship between Savitri's grandmother and his great-aunt. Then she thought of the life she could have had with Mohan, which she'd almost agreed to just so that her father would learn to meditate. No, none of it was meant to be, because how could she have arrived at this perfect seaside proposal if she had taken any of these other paths in the yellow woods?

'Okay, then. Let's get married.' It was the only answer she could give on a night like this.

So Sage started the engine and everyone else sat in the back as he drove the van down the road towards Tyagarah. Nitin slid the curtain back along the wire rail to look at the hills moving around their flying van. He opened the window to let some of the smoke out, and the warm wind made Savitri's face glow. Mae began laughing in the wind.

'If your parents disapproved of me, they're going to hate Nitin.'

'You just didn't give them enough time.' It was the first time Savitri had talked openly with Mae about the broken engagement. 'My father, in fact, wanted me to persuade you to return. He said he'd fly you back first-class and come himself as your escort if you agreed to it — and I was meant to tell you that ...' She trailed off, knowing she'd been instructed not to talk about any of this, by Mae and also by Arunji. And they must have been right, because even mentioning the separation brought a serious tone to the evening, and to what seemed to be her own impending marriage, fast becoming a lunar experiment to challenge the power of the sky and the beliefs of generations of people who had lived on the Gangetic plains, staring at ancient stars and monitoring the corresponding fortunes on earth.

They turned onto the perfectly straight road to Mullumbimby, where all this madness came from, and there, awaiting them like a pyramid, erect, dark and promising against the night sky, was Mount Chincogan. Mae had pointed out Chincogan when Savitri first arrived and told her it was a much revered fertility site for Indigenous Australians.

'Are you sure we're okay to be doing this on ground that's sacred to the Aboriginal people?' Savitri asked.

'It's okay if we're doing a sacred ceremony. It's respectful,' Nitin replied, quite the scientist — and then added with a smile: 'We used to come here on bikes as a dare when we were kids.'

At the base of the mountain was a dark forest, with a Moreton Bay fig tree reaching out to touch all the other trees in its circle. While some of its thin branches trailed down, its giant roots were raised high above the ground like dragons' tails. 'If I had to marry a tree I'd marry this one,' Mae said wistfully. She lifted her sarong a little and straddled one of its tails, lying down to stroke it, her blonde hair falling to one side as it took her up into the sky.

From out of nowhere, Sage managed to manifest a didgeridoo, as his tribute to any elders past, and as apology for finding cause to use the land in any way that might be offensive to the rightful owners.

'This is magic,' Nitin said.

Sage brought the cushions out of his van and created a circle next to the Moreton Bay fig, making it a witness to the wedding.

'Shall we use a torch?' he asked.

'Let the moon light up the church,' Nitin replied.

Savitri and Mae were instructed to arrive from some trees in the distance, so they disappeared further into the forest, where they sat down out of sight in a small clearing in the moonlight.

'You need a veil,' Mae said, taking off her sarong. It meant that Mae was now going to attend the wedding in a bikini, but it made no difference — none of it did. The veil seemed to fit with Eastern and Western traditions, even though they were breaking with both. Mae pulled the veil entirely over Savitri's head, blocking out the moon beams, making Savitri sway with nuptial blindness. And once her sight had been completely dismissed as a useful aid in this dramatic leap of faith, the solemnity of the occasion struck her for the first time. She was in blindfolded solitude now, as if for her own birth, the sarong trapping her giddy thoughts in a makeshift tent.

'Let's make them wait,' Mae said, so Savitri sat there, not knowing whether there was still a world out there anymore, or a moon hanging in the sky, or an enchanted tree nearby where she would be taken. The only connection she had to the bewitching story that involved her and this night was a warm, moist hand. She squeezed Mae's hand and Mae leaned over and kissed her. 'We're going to stay here until they're aching for us to arrive.'

Sage's didgeridoo stopped playing and the silence beckoned them. Mae helped her blind sister stand up and led her down a path through the ferns and the creepers and the trees to where the others sat, before lifting the veil.

Savitri saw Winsome first, sitting in lotus position, a smiling witness to the wedding they were inventing. Then Nitin, who was looking at her with such intensity she felt herself stumble. So she was now actually getting married without any notice, having avoided engagements all her life, and to the sexiest-looking boy who could ever be chosen.

'How are you feeling?' He seemed to care. He hadn't run away. It seemed he was utterly ready to risk his life now, for her, to lift the power of *Manglik*.

'Happy.'

Sage seated Nitin and Savitri together, with Winsome next to the groom and Mae as the sister to give the girl away. He clearly hadn't planned what to say, and he didn't know anything about Savitri's traditions, so he seemed to reach for Western convention to begin his ritual.

'Does anyone present know any reason why these two should not be wed?'

Silence. It was a powerful question to ask, given that they were conducting this moonlit ceremony outside any law of any land, while trespassing on an Aboriginal sacred site and flouting the ancient suspicions of *Manglik* that had thrived along the banks of the Indus for generations. Yet neither the excommunicated Jehovah's Witness nor the bikini-clad daughter of a homebirth doctor whispered a single objection, even in their thoughts.

'Could you please hold hands?' There was no ring, and the words that Sage must have heard in countless movies now sounded empty and repetitive and incongruous with the moon and the Moreton Bay fig and this moment that invited new future worlds and possibilities to manifest before their eyes. Savitri began doing exactly as they were told, but holding hands seemed like something for good friends, not lovers for life and lovers of life. Sage must have noticed. He cocked his head to one side. 'Actually, Savitri, could you please sit on Nitin's lap?'

She was aching to get closer to Nitin, and utterly willing to abide by the new strange rules of this country's arranged marriages if they involved such delicious intimacy. Mae got up and helped her onto Nitin's lap and he held her, kissing the back of her neck, shifting her slightly so that she wasn't sitting quite so directly on his erect penis.

That looked more comfortable. She smiled as she saw Sage assessing the situation with a druid's discernment, ready to invent, confident that a new tradition could be summoned to suit the

purposes of the future, not the past. But what would the sermon of
the future sound like? She couldn't wait to hear it. What principles
and values would the new world require? And what would be
worth taking into that great future, of all the traditions the world
had held sacred for centuries? Perhaps it wasn't even a sermon
that was required, just an invitation. It was as if he'd picked up
on her thoughts.

'You are invited guests to the wedding of Savitri and Nitin.
Many have not been invited ... We did not invite the customs of
the past that blind us into submission without letting us question
or resist. We did not invite the people from our past who want us
to repeat their mistakes. We did not invite the people who do not
share our hope and our trust. We invite the future ...'

Savitri was loving this ceremony. It sounded so righteous. A
powerful antidote for the damning star that had hung over her
since she was a baby in a cradle.

'We invite a future where Savitri and Nitin and their children
will begin to solve the problems that the previous generations have
created through their greed, through their disrespect, through
their inability to see the world afresh or to respect the earth.'

This speech may as well have been translated into *shlokas*
and sung in Sanskrit for all Savitri cared, it felt so perfectly
harmonious. There was absolutely no need for any sacred fire,
except the one between Nitin's chest and her back, which burned
with anticipation ... and the one between his arms and her body.
Everybody should do it this way, she thought. *No time to freak out like
Mae and Neel. The right moon and the right people at the right time and
place. Pure righteousness.* Every fear she'd ever had about marriage
felt misplaced in that forest clearing.

'We invite this future to arrive with all its risks and uncertainties and promise and passion. We conjure this future to bring with it great hope and humanity. And courage to help us make the rules that will truly serve us ...'

Savitri heard these words as sacred — the perfect words to express the uncertain future Sage had just invoked. The future had to be about more than just the two of them, or the five of them present, and it had to be about more than the odd billion in India, or the paltry millions that inhabited Australia beyond the shire. It had to be about humanity, about a kind of cosmic contribution ... and once again he read her intentions with a druid's perception.

'Do you both agree to serve the world and the people in it, through your minds, bodies and hearts ... through your marriage and your lives together, in deed and in spirit ... and ... and even if the past collapses, do you agree to keep faith in the future?'

'I do.' Nitin responded almost before Sage had finished his sentence.

'Yes.' Savitri responded. If that was the only commitment she needed to make to have Nitin, she was happy to break with every tradition she had ever been taught and agree to the moon's rules.

'And one more thing,' Sage continued, 'do you promise to never doubt the power of this wedding? The power of this union as sacred? The power of tonight? Do you promise never to falter on this commitment you have made with the moon watching, in the presence of an unborn child, and in the presence of all of us here as your witnesses?'

If there was a moment when the seriousness of this night arrived, along with a chasm that they as initiates would have to jump over, it was now. Savitri was speechless.

'I promise.' How had the words come so easily to Nitin?

'I promise.' It was the only fit response.

Sensing that this was the moment that the two of them were married, the others gathered round and hugged the newlyweds, Winsome hugging sideways.

'The baby's kicking,' she said. 'Feel it.' And they all reached out as she lifted her top.

Savitri stroked the happy belly. The future was joyful. *How did that just happen? I'm married. Shit.* It seemed so perfectly unreal that this ritual she had artfully avoided for years now seemed complete. She had married a boy she had met only a few days earlier, as her grandmother had done. Only she had touched him in the curling wave and known that their bodies were suited to each other, without consulting a single astrologer. She had just known.

In the van on the way back home to the nature strip outside Mae's house, Sage chose a song to put on for the newlyweds: 'Changes' by David Bowie. Savitri had never heard the words before, but they seemed to touch on all the valiant sentiments of the evening and the newness of every second that had elapsed since she sat on Nitin's lap in the forest.

When they arrived back at Mae's house, a different world greeted them. Mae's birthday dinner had turned into an impromptu wedding. The feast that had started off as a celebration of Mae's birth had turned into an event that celebrated the birth of a new world. So much in one evening. Sage and Winsome, the two strangers who had walked in to join the dinner party, had been transformed into a hierophant and his wife.

After they had said their goodnights, Nitin took Savitri's hand and they walked through the Garden of Eden in Terry and Patti's courtyard, and the python didn't even lift his head as they passed. Tonight there was a wedding gift to give. He took off her clothes singly, purposefully, laying them to rest like pieces of art on the rattan rug. Then he took off his clothes and opened the mosquito net that hung on bamboo poles, to welcome Savitri to the new world inside.

If she'd been in India the bed would have been decorated with marigolds and rose petals that they would have had to crush; there must be invisible flowers they were pressing now. The sacred fire that had burned between them in the evening could now burn the room down, for all Savitri cared, because they were alone. Consummation. The word sounded so rightly delicious.

It was a first proper kiss and she felt like a truly Indian bride, kissing for the first time when they were naked. From the time she had reached for that joint, she had wanted only this, and now her body was able to focus on the One Thing with pure intention.

Whenever Savitri had thought of weddings before, they had been acts of duty, to please the parents of groom and bride. Now her duty was to her body first, and to his, which somehow served the same purpose. This was a blissful duty, pushing them closer together. Before, weddings had been an act of finality, a way of quashing the anxiety of an unwed daughter — dismissing spinsterhood — but this was a new seeking of finality that pushed towards rapture, not resolution. She thought of the forest clearing and the enormous tree that had somehow played its part at her wedding, and the kind of moonlight on a fertile, erect mountain that she would never forget. Before, weddings had meant the giving of courteous gifts in measured quantities, but this gift had none of that containment. She pushed herself closer to Nitin and felt gifted.

She didn't want it to stop. She could be forever in the service of that moon and the mystery it spanned if that was what was required of a married woman.

Outside, on the nature strip next to the house, a van rocked gently on rubber wheels freshly returned from paying homage to Chincogan, the sacred mountain of fertility. And Mae, alone in her room, felt the cries of consummation like an encounter with an ultimacy that eluded and excluded her.

She picked up the phone and called the one person she knew who could give her that much insuppressible pleasure.

GOLDEN TICKET

ROM THE TIME Neel was born and Siddharth went to see
Arunji in his DDA flat, it had been expected that this
firstborn son would work in the family business. Like the
plate set for a guest yet to arrive, his place had been laid in the very
name of the company, Neelkanth Enterprises. Only when Neel
was ready would the doors to the company be flung open. Then,
the darling, most precious son in the world would stride in with
dynastic rights — with an understanding of entrepreneurship
that favoured the longevity of blood lines over the occasional,
disruptive, fly-by-night innovator.

When Neel was a kid he'd played *dukan*, setting up a shop on
one of the balconies of their old apartment in Golf Links. Back then,
Siddharth had seen this as the birth of his young entrepreneur, and
made sure that the shop was always stocked with useless things:
trinkets and souvenirs from trips overseas, a few toys that had
lost their lustre, some paper flowers, old cutlery, bottle openers
decorated with European leprechauns. And every time a family
friend or relative came to visit, they'd be taken to Neel's *dukan* and

forced to make a purchase, going home with a doll that was missing an arm or a box of tissues for ten times the price they would pay for it at the market. The theory was that the love of trading knick-knacks would grow into a love of trading stocks and shares, and then a love of the well-considered risk, combined with an eye for opportunity and a hunger for the game — the bigger stakes of a large enterprise. Siddharth was ready to fund every dream his son had, if it was within his means, but nothing was closer to his heart than the idea of having his son sit in the office next door to his. Perhaps he could even put in a door to link the two rooms directly?

However, within a year or two the *dukan* was left like a deserted zoo enclosure. Nobody went to that part of the house, so it was some years before it was finally cleaned up and the enterprise considered bankrupt. Meanwhile, Neel's next business was an in-house cinema, where he screened movies from his father's laptop to lined-up chairs in a darkened room, charging the servants for the tickets he'd hand-drawn. *Resourceful*, Siddharth thought. He used to pay the servants to buy tickets from his son and didn't mind when Neel got the equation of exchange muddled and began paying them to watch movies instead. What was worrying, however, was the filmy layer through which Neel now saw his future: as a Bollywood actor, always with a gun in his back pocket and *goondas* for henchmen ready to back up his crimes. Of course, he would never have considered such a career for his son — who would? But he knew that desires need to be exhausted before they can be forgotten, so he talked to a friend who had an uncle in Mumbai, and his son was asked to perform in a film.

When Neel first heard about this he felt as if he'd won quite the golden ticket. He was flown down for two days of filming and dressed in matching shorts and shirt, and given glasses to wear, which he didn't like. Then he was made to stand in a crowd for five hours while some minor characters he'd never seen before danced with each other — again and again and again and again and again and again. This foray into film was a huge success, because Neel's contribution to the world of masala films began and ended with a single credit on a forgettable B-grade movie. The only problem was that Neel was now without an ambition in the world. Having grown up on a diet of aspiration and enterprise, he had remained rudderless ever since he had returned from his economics degree at Sydney University.

'How about coming to work with me today?' Siddharth asked Neel casually as he was leaving the hotel room.

'Yah, yah.' Siddharth knew this meant no. He'd asked him every day for a week now and the answer had always been no.

'Just come, yah. Keep me company.'

'You want me to come and twiddle my thumbs?'

'No, I can teach you. We'll find some work.' The truth was he'd been building projects for Neel to step into for the past month. The path was paved: one call and the red carpet would be laid out. Something to do would be better than staying in a hotel room all day doing goodness knows what. Thinking of the most meaningful transactions that could possibly take place in Neel's life now, Siddharth came up with an idea that went well beyond the confines of his usual business operations.

'If you come into the office with me today — just for one day, just to see if you like it — then I will call Mae's parents and ask if we can set up a conference call.'

'They're not Indians, Papa. You can't ... just, like ... call them up and arrange the wedding.' Yet the minute Neel said this, he felt that his father might have struck on an idea. Terry and Patti were very Indian in some ways. They'd liked him. They were very supportive of their daughter — and he'd done his best to be the perfect son-in-law. When he and Mae had announced that they were going to have an Indian wedding, they'd talked long into the night about what clothes they could bring and where they would travel after the three days of feasting and dancing were over. Terry had even planned meetings with professors of obstetrics at Delhi University — goodness knows, they would have been devastated that the wedding was cancelled.

Like a fish caught by a tide, Neel had elegantly switched directions, and this flick of silver wasn't lost on his father.

'We haven't even spoken to Mae's parents since the wedding was called off,' Siddharth continued. 'It's only right that we should call them ... and what with Savitri staying with them.' Siddharth had always been good at negotiations. He knew how to reel in the fish, and now that he could sense a large, sultry one swimming in the darkest, deepest ocean, he knew exactly how much more line to release.

'But I can't come in and do nothing ...'

He needed the weight to sink a little deeper.

'I wouldn't want you there if you were going to do nothing. I'd prefer you to stay here and watch rubbish.'

'I suppose I could come along if you have something for me to do.'

Yes! He'd bitten. Now he had to reel in the line imperceptibly slowly. Hiding his delight, Siddharth went to the bathroom to brush his teeth. Neel hadn't dressed yet, so he took his time, but the catch was assured: you could almost see the hook in the side of Neel's mouth.

'You're not wearing that. You have to dress up smarter.' Siddharth knew the deal was his and he could state his price.

'I don't have any smarter clothes. They're all at home.'

'Then we'll go home.' Siddharth said this with utter self-assurance, pulling an empty suitcase onto the bed and reaching for his clothes in the wardrobe.

Cool.

Siddharth could feel his son summon Mae. She was so close now he could smell patchouli oil. He had cast his line in a last-ditch attempt and he would be going home with the fish. Why, they'd probably even make it out of the hotel before check-out at 10 a.m.

❧

The car pulled in to the farmhouse, and even in his moment of triumph, Siddharth felt a little nervous about what kind of reception they would receive. He'd come home with quite the prize, complete with their son joining the family firm that very same day.

Yet Tota could be unpredictable.

He watched.

Tota embraced their son, then self-consciously gave Siddharth a hug.

'Neel's coming to the office with me — we're just here for him to get dressed.'

Tota looked at Siddharth with conspiratorial curiosity, as if to ask, *How in this terrestrial realm did you organise that?* Perhaps she could even begin introducing him to some nice girls next.

MAKING THE CALL

WHEN THE CUSHIONS arrived from Brisbane by truck, Mae opened up each and every package and laid them out in piles until the entire living room was covered with the handywork of a thousand village women, turning their home into a riotous Indian bazaar: embroidered, layered and dazzling. There were cushions lining the hallway; cushions stacked up in the laundry and on the benchtops.

'It's like being in a bloody camel fair without the camels,' Sage commented when he came in to check out Mae's delivery. Winsome chose a couple and insisted on paying for them to help kickstart her friend's business. Terry brought his patients through the house to look at them and a few left clutching purchases.

Dolly had come out of her room to sit in the middle of the chaos and admire the incredible industry. She began to pull some of the cushions to her nose to smell them and Mae did the same. They could both smell the unmistakable musky fragrances of hessian bags stored in the heat, the dust and oil of a thousand sewing machines, godowns in remote Indian villages, combined with smells from the hold of an Indian vessel on the high seas — what an aroma! And what adventure lay ahead! As she swooned the phone rang and Mae rushed over to pick up the receiver at the end of the corridor, near the Buddha.

'Hello?'

'Hello, Mae. I am so happy to hear your voice.'

She was stunned. She recognised Siddharth. 'Er ... hello.' She'd never been able to call him Papa or Dad, as Neel had requested.

'I have Neel with me.'

'That's nice.'

'Are your parents in? I'd like to have a word with them.'

'No.'

'Then can I speak to Savitri, please?'

Mae felt awkward. *Hadn't Savitri told them?*

'She's moved out to live with her husband.'

There was silence at the other end of the line, and Mae could hear Siddharth struggling to believe her.

'Sorry, Mae. Can you repeat that, please?'

'She's moved out to live with her husband.' She spoke louder now, which meant that Dolly could hear her, and a strange three-way conversation ensued.

'Mae, did you say that Savitri has a husband?'

'She didn't tell you?' Mae felt somehow satisfied as she spoke these words.

'She didn't need to tell him — he should have known anyway,' Dolly joined in.

'Who has she ... married?'

'Nitin.'

'Oh, did she marry the lovely man in the van?' Dolly interrupted.

'No, Dolly — that's Sage.' Speaking back into the receiver, Mae said, 'She hasn't told you yet?'

'No ...'

Hearing Siddharth's hesitation, Mae couldn't help but be provocative. 'Aren't you happy about it?'

Dolly interrupted again. 'Tell him we're all very happy over here.'

'No ... no ... I mean yes ... I am happy ... yes, I'm happy ... but surprised.'

Mae felt indignant on her friend's behalf. *Savitri's got every right to get married. Who are you to stop her?*

'I'd like to congratulate the two of them. Could you please give me her ... husband's phone number, please? She hasn't been picking up her cell phone.'

'I'm afraid I don't have his number.'

'It's okay to tell him the number, darling,' Dolly interjected.

'You can't stop them — they're already married,' Mae continued.

'I don't want to stop anything. I'm just interested in who ... encouraged her to get married.'

He's trying to blame me ...

'I mean, who was so kind as to organise the wedding for her ... because I would have been more than happy to give our assistance ... and provide the necessary funds.'

'She didn't need any money for it. You don't need money to get married, you know. We don't live in India.'

Unstoppable regret was exhaled in the vapour it took to voice these words, which were unfitting for the magic of the wedding she'd witnessed — the charged air in that forest clearing under Mount Chincogan ... the dragon tree ... the moon.

'Oh, I see ... how glorious. I so miss my Savitri.'

'She's really happy about it, you know.'

'I know. I know ... thank you, Mae. Thank you. I am so grateful you came into our lives.'

'That's very kind of you.'

'And I would so love to be there with you and Savitri,' Siddharth continued. 'I feel we have failed you and Neel so terribly, and if there is anything I can do to secure your happiness in the future, you must tell me ... you really must.'

Listening to Siddharth, Mae lost a tear to one of the cushions below.

'Can you get Neel on the line?' Dolly piped up. 'I have something I really need to tell him.'

'I'm sorry. Can you call back later?' Mae said in a cracked voice. 'It's not a good time ...' And she hung up.

༚

Siddharth hadn't succeeded in talking to Mae's parents, as he'd promised, but Neel clearly understood that the call had been more profound than either of them had anticipated.

'Did you meet Nitin?' Siddharth asked his son.

Neel knew what his father really wanted to hear. 'If there is one person in this world who will be honourable and kind to Savitri, it is Nitin. I'd trust him with my life.'

That was all Siddharth needed to be convinced. The rest had been confirmed by Mae's voice. Savitri was going to be happy. And it seemed impossible that Mae — the person who had been painted as a shrew, a virago, a siren, an *asura* — had achieved the Herculean challenge that so many had failed to achieve: the marriage of Savitri to ... well, just about anyone.

'But we shouldn't tell Mama about this ... right yet,' Neel suggested. 'She'd hate him as much as she hated Mae.'

Siddharth knew that even if Nitin came from a 'good' family, it wouldn't constitute the right kind of good for Tota. They would have to break the news to her at some stage and hope that no cups, saucers, hearts or anything else broke in the process. Siddharth couldn't think when this right time might be for breaking the news. And he had no idea how he would answer the million questions that would then be showered upon them all, like confetti at a Western wedding.

'We must find out *what-all* we can about him later — after work, perhaps.'

Siddharth was well aware that there was work to be done in the office: unpleasant work, starting with a meeting with Manish in ten minutes. He wanted Neel to be present at that meeting, not only as the CEO's shadow, but with his full faculties alert, leaving his hormones at the door, together with his dreams of Australia.

'Remember I told you about Manish ...' he started. And then he began thinking about the discourse that Lord Krishna had with Arjuna on the battlefield of Kurukshetra. 'You're going to have to go into battle like the Pandavas against the Kauravas ...'

The words of the Bhagavad Gita were framed on the walls all around Neelkanth Enterprises, courtesy of Dadi.

Whenever dharma declines and the purpose of life is forgotten, I manifest myself on earth. I am born in every age to protect the good, to destroy evil, and to reestablish dharma or righteousness.

But how did Krishna approach the Kaurava army — with its thousands of chariots all filled with people that Arjuna had grown up with? What do you do when the world crumbles around you and the people you most love are doing that which is most incorrect? What to do when the actions of a few can destroy the future of us all? When the wisdom and faith in that future are threatened by copious greed and the short-sightedness that can emerge in a single self-centred lifetime?

Behind Siddharth's desk, etched in copper, were the words: *There is nothing in the three worlds for me to gain, Arjuna, nor is there anything I do not have; I continue to act, but I am not driven by any need of my own.*

'Will you be able to tell Manish that he has to go, Neel?'

Siddharth was handing the bow to someone who had never held one — but how long can you remain innocent when you are swinging a sword with every action you take? Better to remove the notion that you're free to act without bearing the brunt of your consequences.

'But Papa, I don't know him.'

'That'll make it even easier.'

Siddharth explained Manish's entire backstory to his son so he could go into battle armed with knowledge before they heard a knock on the door.

Manish sat down, a twitch in his eye revealing his anxiety. He was so polite, as always, so respectful. Neel began by asking some questions about Janmashtami Enterprises. Manish answered them like he always did, talking fast, with a firm sense that he was helping them to find information, not helping himself to any of the profits of Neelkanth Enterprises.

'I am absolutely certain that Janmashtami Enterprises will turn a profit in the next year.'

Neel, having never held the bow, still had the advantage.

'Did you know that your son-in-law never had the capability to deliver the software we paid him to develop? Did you know that he doesn't have a single staff member or that he failed his degree in IT?'

Siddharth watched without any pleasure, seeing the story unfold. He watched as his son drew the bow back further still, until it was almost ready to release.

'He is a very capable young man and would be an asset to the company if we were to employ him.'

'If you wanted him to join this company, why didn't you ask if he could come for an interview? Why did you pay five crores to him first? And if you really wanted him to work for us, then why are you helping him and your daughter to get visas for the US right now?'

'How did you know this?' Manish had all but stabbed himself with this question. Neel needn't have released that bow.

'Manish, can you please go to your desk right now, pack up your things and leave the premises within fifteen minutes. Anything you don't take with you now, we'll send with a peon to your house.'

Siddharth, who hadn't said a word while his son took on this battle, extended his hand towards Manish, who watched for a second in shock. Then he took Siddharth's unshakable hand, simply to hold, without moving it in any direction of automatic formality.

'Thank you for your years of service, and for the good work you did. No matter what, I will always consider you to be a friend and teacher.'

If Manish was shocked before, then this final salute came at him like a kick in the stomach: a recognition that his fallibility wasn't the sum total of who he was or what he could be in the future. He thanked Siddharth and left to pick up the perfunctory remains of his job at Neelkanth Enterprises, his heart counting out the allocated seconds with flagellations of guilt.

After Manish had left, Siddharth switched his mobile phone back on and was welcomed with this message. *Yr mother is v sick. Pls come home.* It was the ultimate lesson in a day devoted to self-conquest.

Somehow, without the inclusion of a single telecommunications network and without the missing vowels, Mae was informed of the same news, via Dolly, on the other side of the world.

'That lovely girl needs to go home and say goodbye to her grandmother,' Dolly told Mae. 'She needs to go very quickly, because the dear lady is waiting for her.'

On hearing this, Mae began to weep, remembering the gentle way that Dadi had stroked her hair, sweetened her mouth and held her hand as they sat on the bed together after the incident with the servants' children. She knew that her grandmother was probably right, and that she was the only person who knew where Savitri lived, set away from the rest of the world up in the hills of Main Arm. She got into her car and began the journey up to the hippie hills where Nitin and Savitri were having their honeymoon.

UNEXPECTED JOURNEY

SAVITRI HAD BEEN living in something she would describe as a handmade jungle hermitage: a single hexagonal room that made up a house, with a kitchen on the edge of a bedroom on the edge of walls that sloped outwards, removed from the world, hidden from the small winding road cut out of the tropical overgrowth. Their love nest had wooden floorboards, an old Kookaburra stove and a queen-size bed draped with lace and mosquito netting, beside a window with a king-size view of the valley below them. Outside the single room was a shack for the toilet, with a moon-planting guide posted on the door and an Indian-style hose next to the cistern.

The hut was surrounded by an orchard, and if Mae's garden had seemed like Eden, the overgrown profusion of trees here seemed to precede even the original myths of creation. Any seed that had the good fortune of falling on this soil would surely be granted the right to flourish. Papayas shot up like random declarations of fertility; unfamiliar fruit grew here, with names like tree strawberries, candle fruit and rose apples, which Savitri had never tasted before.

Then there were banana palms, avocados, guavas, lychees and mangoes, as well as a giant macadamia tree that shot nuts down as if there were monkeys up in its branches taking aim.

This had been their island and they had remained here willingly, only occasionally walking down to the small store twenty minutes down the road. Savitri was happily stranded, feeling no need to send any kind of message to worried parents — and what could she possibly tell them, anyway? How could she ever share the secrets of their honeymoon? They were castaways, with no one but the lyrebirds to overhear and mimic the sound of their lovemaking, and nobody to observe them walking naked to go and pick fruit whenever they grew hungry for anything more than each other.

It was here that Savitri learned a little more about the man she had married. He was the son of a father who worked as an engineer for the Northern Rivers Regional Organisation of Councils, and a mother who worked as a nurse. Savitri could understand how Nitin had grown up with an interest in science, but he'd also lived a childhood up in Byron, where you had to learn to smoke your greens as well as eat them. And so she understood that in this man the scientific principles of objectivity, observability and repeatability were tempered with an openness to mystery and spirit. A perfect match for her in every way.

They were dancing to music on the balcony when Mae's car pulled up, and Savitri heard the screech of the wheels as if they were an omen. She went inside the hermitage to reach for some clothes and Nitin threw a sarong around his waist and went down to greet Mae, neither of them quite prepared for this interruption.

Mae walked up to the balcony with him, took off her sandals, sat down on a sun-bleached wicker chair and put her bare feet up on the rails.

'You guys been having some fun?'

'Yeah, it's not bad,' Nitin replied. 'I'll get you a beer.'

Savitri could tell that Nitin wasn't going to reveal anything and wanted to share just a little more with her friend.

'I've never been so happy in all my life,' she replied.

'Look, I wouldn't have come up here to interrupt anything, but your father called ...'

Savitri felt herself stiffen. 'Is everything all right?'

'Actually, I'm not sure it is — Dolly thinks you should get home and see your grandmother.'

Of course. The marriage. Savitri knew what this meant and she knew exactly why she should be getting this news now. She knew the part she'd played in this turn of events and she knew that the time had come for her grandmother. There might never be another moment that could replace the happiness of the past week up in Main Arm, but she would have to leave that same day and try to get home.

'Do you want to come to Delhi with me and meet my parents?' she asked Nitin when he came back holding a beer.

It didn't surprise Savitri at all that he said yes, without flinching, just as he had on their wedding night. Over the past week she had got to know the person the heavenly bodies had assigned to be her husband, and she couldn't imagine anyone more suitable. He was utterly trustworthy and good to the core. But would any of this matter to her mother? *How much does he earn?* Well, he doesn't — at least not yet — and how would she explain that to them? *When will he cut his hair?* Actually, she quite liked it this way.

As for Dadi — this was just what her grandmother had waited for all these years. She would do her grandmother the honour of defending Nitin against every evil eye that might be set upon him by others ... And this she would do to her last breath.

LAST RITES

THE MINUTE SOME bars appeared on her phone, just past Durrumbul Hall, Savitri rang her grandmother's Bakelite phone.

Neel picked up. 'Good God, where have you been? Everyone has been trying to get hold of you.'

It was true that since Dolly had picked up on the message, several other phone calls had come through to confirm that Dadi wanted to see her granddaughter. Now the bliss of the hermitage in the hills was banished, and all Savitri could feel was the pressure to get back home. A lifetime of love and fondness needed to be consecrated with a timely sacred duty: a return.

'I've been with Nitin. How's Dadi?'

'Not well. She can't speak, but last time she did, she asked how you were. She's going, Savitri.'

'Tell her to wait. Tell her I'm coming home and I'm going to bring my husband.'

'Yes.'

'Yes. Tell her I'm married now.'

'Yes, yes, we know — congratulations, yah.'

A lifetime had come and gone since she'd last spoken to her brother, and even though he'd studied in Australia, she couldn't expect him to understand what had happened the night the moon had swelled. He hadn't been there. What would he know?

'Please tell Dadi to wait for me.' Even as she said these words she knew they were cruel. Dadi's wait had been excruciating. Her years had been measured out in Savitri's refusals of all the decent boys who were ever presented.

'Are you bringing Nitin with you?'

'Yes.'

'That's great. He's so cool, yah — I really like him.'

Neel was talking around the obstacles. Both siblings knew that this was the way to have such a conversation, casually parting the veil around this intensely private elopement, dismissing the naysayers, the centuries of soothsayers, the family history of bigotry and possessiveness.

He could be saying this to a casual acquaintance. He doesn't understand. How could he?

Savitri didn't take all of her clothes from Mae's house, wanting a reason to come back to this place, which could soon disappear as if it were just a temporary lapse of reason. She packed only a small bag before she and Nitin caught the bus to Ballina airport to catch a plane that would connect with the next Air India Dreamliner from Sydney to Delhi.

A WEDDING ANNOUNCEMENT

ARUNJI VERY RARELY came to the big house since his family's patron had moved out of central Delhi, but when he heard that Dadi was seriously unwell he came at once. He was ushered into Dadi's room by Buddhi Ayah, who wiped tears with the end of her soft white sari as she led the way for this momentous visit, because when the family astrologer came, it was surely time.

In Dadi's room were Siddharth, Tota and Neel, sitting on the chairs that usually remained ceremonially empty. Arunji did *salaam* to the family, then went straight to Dadi, sat on the floor next to the bed and held her hand.

'Mataji, I have come to take your blessings.'

Haven't you already taken enough of these? Siddharth could hear his wife's impoverished response in thought form.

'Savitri will be here tomorrow, Ma.' Siddharth took his mother's other hand.

So much for the blessed granddaughter being married before your passing, Tota offered as her unspoken contribution to the conversation.

Hearing her thoughts, Siddharth was stung with guilt that he hadn't told his own wife that their daughter was married.

'And everything has come to pass,' Arunji continued in his reassurance to Dadi that she could finally meet her 'date with destiny'. 'You can rest now that Savitri has her husband.'

Tota looked at Siddharth with questioning eyes, and then winked, as if she'd understood that this was how they had all agreed to play the game. This was how they must allow the old lady to leave her body, her family and a century she hadn't particularly wanted to enter. 'Everything has been settled,' Tota piped up, in support of the collusion. 'And this time Savitri has even agreed to the match.'

If ever there was a moment to let his wife know, it was now.

'No, she has already married,' Siddharth added with certitude, staring down his wife.

Siddharth saw Tota shrug and read her thoughts. *If you're prepared to take the deception this far, then who am I to disagree with a story told to your dying mother? So be it. We are doing our duty in telling her all of this.*

Dadi who struggled against the heavy eyelids that had willed her soul to shut out the light these past few years. 'I am so happy for her ... and so happy that Neel made a good choice for his sister ... I ... I so ... wanted to meet him ...'

'You will meet him, Mataji, you will,' Arunji said, and squeezed Dadi's hand lightly. 'This is your wish, and I can promise you it will be so.'

Siddharth could hear his wife's thoughts loud and clear now. Being the only person who had no clue that her daughter was married, Tota had begun wondering how on earth they were going to conjure up a groom to stand next to Savitri as her devoted consort tomorrow. For a second moment he heard her wonder about the dishonesty of putting on the charade but dismiss the thought immediately. *Of course, it must be done. The poor woman has been told by the idiot astrologer that Savitri would have to be married before she can leave this world in peace, after all …*

'Mama, we will put the two of them in front of you and you can bless them both to have a long and happy married life,' she added. *Maybe we can persuade Mohan to come over. We could put some mehndi on Savitri's hands and wedding bangles up to her elbows, and Dadi wouldn't know the difference in her state.*

'It's so good you sent her to Australia or she would never have found Nitin,' Dadi continued, squeezing Arunji's hand with the little strength she had.

As the name of their new son-in-law was announced, Tota stared at Siddharth, mouthing the name 'Nitin' and shrugging.

Again, the guilt of it.

Why, Tota was the only person in the room who didn't know that her own daughter was married. What on earth had taken place in their lives for such concealment and duplicity to emerge between mother and daughter, husband and wife?

It was only later that Siddharth was able to sit down with Tota quietly and tell her the truth about what had happened to Savitri — or at least the truth as he had heard it, through the impoverished, dry, yeastless version of the story that had percolated through the interpretations of thought forms and memories across a crackling international mobile call.

There was a long pause.

'You cannot be serious. You're telling me that *youall* knew *thisthing* and *youall* thought that I might not want to know? You didn't tell me about my own daughter's marriage?'

Siddharth offered silence rather than reason or excuses, to allow his wife some space to contemplate exactly why this might be the case. To allow her to feel her part in the way things were.

'You're telling me that you were lying to me in front of your mother. You're saying that everybody in this house knew that Savitri was married *except* for me — even the bloody astrologer?'

'Of course the astrologer knew. Arunji was the first to know, probably. Even I found out by accident.'

And so the outpouring began — full, guttural, heaving howling, and Siddharth held her as she shuddered while clutching the edge of the bed. *I have destroyed my family single-handedly. I have pushed every single one of them away. My own daughter ... my own daughter ... I couldn't do a thing to help her.*

'Savitri would never have married anyone that we chose for her — and she probably would never have married an Indian boy because of the *Manglik* thing,' Siddharth interrupted. 'Arunji always said that Neel would have to choose Savitri's husband.'

'And what exactly do we know about this boy that Neel has so kindly chosen for our daughter?'

'Very little,' Siddharth confessed, 'except that he's a lovely boy. A scientist.'

'Do you have a picture of the wedding?' Tota needed some kind of proof to assuage the shock and disbelief.

'I have nothing, except some ... information from Mae — something about a wedding under the moon.'

'*Hai Ram.*' The mention of Mae sent every suspicion in Tota's body into high alert. 'That girl has gone and set up this mischief as revenge!'

'*Chup!* Isn't the marriage of your daughter something you have always wanted? Why curse it? She has a good boy — and happiness that neither of us was able to organise or buy or arrange for her. Think about it, darling ... think about how hard it has been for you and I to do this thing for her. Arunji always said ...'

'It has nothing to do with Arunji. She found a boy because over there these things happen like this. People mate like animals ...'

Siddharth pulled away from his wife. '*Chup!* Your daughter has just been blessed in marriage — something you have wanted for years — and you can talk only of mating! What is wrong with you, woman? What do you want? Do you want them to divorce? Already? Is this your plan? No, no, no — you must accept her happiness as something that has nothing to do with yours and let her be.'

All the worries of the world. Siddharth could feel the proprietorial nature of worries, and how it might be possible for someone to own absolutely all of them, probably in their shoulders, making them rise and knot with each additional concern. It was an urge that came from thinking that one could control the universe, and what a risky endeavour to take on — guaranteed to fail, given the enormousness and eternity of the task. How much easier it would have been to let the natural, more experienced cosmic mechanisms turn planets and galaxies into an effortless spiral rhythm and forget about trying to rule the rotating world and all those who cling to it.

'She didn't even tell us — she didn't *care* about what we might think ...'

'She does care. She's coming home tomorrow, and you'll see her, and you'll see that she's happy. This much I know. But more than this ... *matlab* ... you will see that she is given a proper welcome and that her husband has the respect we should give anybody who has taken on the responsibility of our daughter's happiness.'

Ensuring a proper welcome was a weighty request given the supposedly preposterous nature of Savitri's insult, and Tota wasn't certain that she should entertain it, lest her indignation and self-righteousness give way, but somewhere she knew, too, that her hands had been taken off the wheel, forcibly. She could offer her love and support or she could fester in disdain and disgust. But how could she decide which she would offer when she hadn't even met the boy — or seen Savitri to know the full consequences of this decision? How could she *know*? How could any one of us *know* anything?

DADI'S HEAVENLY ABODE

NITIN FLICKED THROUGH the offering of films on his
Air India entertainment screen. He had the choice
between old classics like *Gone with the Wind*, a few
B-grade Hollywood movies or a solid curation of Bollywood
blockbusters. He decided to go fearlessly Indian — as either
acclimatisation or initiation for the journey ahead. He was nervous.
He'd heard stories from Mae about his future in-laws that he would
never be so unkind as to repeat to Savitri.

He flicked and swiped some more. Next he had the choice
between subtitles or *Desi* view, and he decided to watch without
being propped up by foreign words. *No subtitles.* Click. No chance
of learning Hindi, just the language of those dramatic eyes. They
paraded before him, one minute coy, enquiring about what he
was doing going over to India. The next moment, he was meeting
the gaze of an Indian elder: eyes deflecting light, eyebrows raised.
Conservative and critical. Then there was the circus medley of
colours, all saturated; then an outpouring of emotion to shrill
music, made shriller still with frenetic drumming and horn-
blowing, together with the unlikely sound of whinnying horses,

all amplified through cheap rattling earphones. *Click*. Off with the jaunty sounds. Now there was no sound of music, just some dancers, and a silent dancing diva, her back curving multi-orgasmically over her lover's arms, fully clothed in swooping silks (so suggestive she may as well have been naked).

Nitin switched off his screen, thinking that sleep might be his best preparation for the real-life drama ahead of him, if Mae was to be believed. He took Savitri's hand. 'What was it about Mae that your mother didn't like?' He had so many questions that he didn't know how to ask. *And what if she doesn't believe in ... well ... the religious nature of our marriage?* He himself knew that there was courage in what he'd done — but how would this translate?

'It doesn't matter what my mother thought about Mae,' Savitri replied. 'And I don't care what she thinks about you, either. I'm the one who has married you. Not her.'

Savitri knew that this trip wasn't about her mother, her husband or her brother. It was about Dadi. She thought about her grandmother, wondering if she was still alive in the hours they'd spent up in the sky speeding towards her wavering soul. Her beautiful Dadi — she of all the people who would want to see her 'settled'. Even the word all the elders used was right. 'Settled'. If one thing had transformed in the past two weeks, it was the fact that she was free of her restlessness. She really had surrendered to a kind of happiness she'd never suspected could be associated with marriage — not the word as she had known it until now. That word was to be avoided like the channa bhatura she shunned whenever it was served up in her house, which was as regularly as the offers of marriage came in. Now the matchmakers could go take a siesta and some Calmpose — and *they* could settle down. No reason for anyone to bother her about this again. She had arrived miraculously on the other side of marriage and avoided the ugly business of it. And now ... well, even the word 'marriage' sounded strangely lyrical from this side of the conjugal divide. It could have been a word to describe one of those perfect balanced states on the way to cosmic consciousness. There was none of the subjugation she'd grown up to imagine: nothing but blushing exaltation. (Too privately satisfying to even confess to Nitin.) She lay her head on his shoulder and the two of them fell asleep, the unlikely heroes of their own Bollywood drama, unfolding slowly now as the picture of the aeroplane (flying in slow motion across the flight path screens in front of them) started drawing closer to its destination of Indira Gandhi Airport.

Only Neel and the driver were at the airport when Nitin and Savitri arrived home as newlyweds, but her brother had brought two garlands of marigolds and roses to honour this moment. Neel touched the necklace he had given Nitin. 'Good on you, mate, for coming over. And welcome to India and your new family.'

Savitri didn't know quite what sort of a welcome it would be or how familial the family would be, but she was hopeful as she hugged her brother.

'How is Dadi?' Savitri asked.

'Waiting.'

'Thank God!' *But oh, the guilt of making her wait!*

'You won't recognise her. She's gone so thin.'

'I'd recognise her if I saw her in another lifetime,' Savitri replied, then added, 'Was she happy about our marriage?'

'Everyone is happy,' Neel confirmed.

Savitri knew that he wasn't really speaking for everyone — but generally, there must have been enough happy people in the world for there to be some truth in this statement, and he at least was happy.

The car pulled in at the farmhouse and Siddharth could hear three internal conversations, without any kind of harmony, approaching as if from a distance.

My God, what's a bloody gunman doing at the gates?

Dadi, please be awake ... please, please like Nitin ...

Mae and I should have got married like they did — there would have been none of this tamasha ...

No, you're joking — is that Savitri's palace? My God ...

We have to see Dadi first. First I'll take Nitin to her room, then ...

In Australia, Mae could have worn a bikini to our wedding — nobody would have said anything ...

I wish I'd had a chance to brush my teeth ... oh shit...

Then we could have arrived here and been given a marital suite like Savitri and Nitin ...

Why am I feeling guilty? Stop feeling guilty ...

The car pulled up beside a long porch that stretched around the house, with fans and cane chairs strewn around, some inside a netted cage. Multicoloured bejewelled chandeliers hung from the ochre ceilings.

Savitri opened the door of the car while it was still moving. The driver braked swiftly so he wouldn't lose his job on account of the fact that the daughter of the house had accidentally fallen to her death on her arrival back at the family home as a newlywed. Savitri didn't wait for Nitin, or even stop to admire the exquisite welcoming *rangoli* floor decorations that Buddhi Ayah had sprinkled for her to step over as she crossed the threshold. Proceeding with the focus of a missionary, she flung open the heavy wooden doors to the farmhouse and walked straight around to the right, to her grandmother's room.

Savitri wasn't prepared. She'd wanted to see her grandmother so badly, but she'd expected to see her awake and ready to greet her, for some obscure reason. Not in a deathly sleep. And absolutely unrecognisable.

Dadi lay there, head back on the pillow, mouth wide open, her skin a sallow, powdery, deathly tone. Was she, indeed, dead? If not, then she would have to leave that body soon, as it was clearly not going to serve her for much longer. In all the years she'd watched Dadi's deterioration, she'd never seen the moment so close. She closed her eyes and wept for the death of her grandmother, even though she was still alive. Seeing her weep, Buddhi Ayah, who was almost as old as Dadi, and who was sitting on the hard ground next to Dadi's bed, levered herself up to hug Savitri and catch some of those tears on her sari *palla* — the same swatch of cloth, no doubt, that had caught Baby's tears when she was a child. Savitri looked at her ayah, her skin like a husky coconut and a smile that was crooked and radiant. *How can Buddhi Ayah sustain such joy while keeping company with the Angel of Death?*

Nitin came in and held her hand, and Neel followed.

'Come, she's sleeping. Mama and Papa want to see you both.'

'I'm not leaving until she wakes up,' Savitri replied.

'Fine, I'll take Nitin up to meet them.'

She couldn't have planned for this. Was it right to let Nitin face them without her? *Who knows, it could be for the best.* What could her presence add to this inevitable encounter except more anxiety?

'Tell them to come down if they want to see me.'

Siddharth began to hear Nitin's and Neel's thoughts as they climbed the stairs.

Here goes ...

The door opened.

'Papa, Mama. This is Nitin.'

Both Tota and he stood up.

Tota turned off the super-sized television with a remote and got up to shake Nitin's hand. 'So nice to meet you at long last.' (Had the wedding taken place a few years earlier, not simply two weeks ago, Siddharth might have been less surprised by this statement. Nonetheless, it did feel as if this moment had the inevitability and destiny of the words 'at long last'.)

'Welcome, welcome,' Siddharth said as he reached out to hug his new son-in-law, trying to counterbalance the boy's discomfort with warmth. 'We've heard such wonderful things about you.'

'Yes, yes. Welcome to India. Where's Savitri?' Tota added, extending her slightly more circumspect hand.

'She's with Dadi,' Neel replied.

'Oh, I see.'

Siddharth could hear her thoughts.

What for did she send him up alone?

Tota continued. 'I must get you something — *what-all* would you like to drink?'

'Nothing, thank you.'

'*Beta*, do one thing and ask Ram Lal to bring some Rooh Afza for us all, and some mithai,' Tota instructed Neel.

Neel left the room and Nitin took a deep breath. Siddharth could tell that his new son-in-law had now been deserted by both the crutches he'd expected to cling to — yet he could hear Nitin's bravery. *They're lovely. What was all the fuss about? I just have to come straight out with it.*

'I've been so wanting to meet you, because in Australia it's customary to ask for a girl's hand in marriage ...'

'And in India, too,' Tota responded quickly, but not unkindly.

Siddharth intervened. 'But this is a love marriage, yah? Even in India, *thisthing* happens like it has ...' He was making his most sincere attempt to bring out the beauty of this encounter.

'So I know it's a bit late to ask for Savitri's hand in marriage, but I'd still like to ask for your blessings, and I'd like to assure you that I'll look after her ...'

Siddharth could hear that Nitin was going to say 'like a princess', but the words trailed off. He wanted to interrupt these financial considerations: they'd all been taken care of well before Savitri was even born. 'Of course you have our blessings. We're so happy for you both.'

I can do this. They didn't set up the firing squad. They're chill ...

Ram Lal arrived with the Rooh Afza. 'Please, try this drink. It's typically North Indian. A sherbet, with white lilies and lotus roots and herbs in it. We all grew up on this.'

Nitin took the saccharine red liquid, and as he took a sip, Siddharth leaned in to listen.

They're absolutely lovely. Of course Savitri and Neel couldn't possibly have horrible parents ... But what a revolting drink. I'll down it and they'll think I love it as much as they do.

'Have you been married before?' Tota's question came from the far left field of her consciousness, utterly undetectable, and with no time for Siddharth to intercept it.

Okay, here we go ... 'No, absolutely not. And I only intend to be married once.'

'And you have no children?'

'None.'

'That you know of ...'

'Darling, what for to ask Nitin all of these things? He's just come off a long flight ... And he is a guest in our country.' Siddharth was trying his utmost to invoke the image of the guest as God, his eyes widening in a warning as he looked in his wife's direction, beseeching her to be polite. Even if Tota was too modern to have the ancient suspicion that God could come disguised as a visitor, she should at least respect the sanctity of their son-in-law meeting them for the first time. Why, they should be showering him with gifts and sweetening his mouth if they cared about how he would look after their daughter.

'I just want to know why the marriage has gone on like this, without anybody knowing anything. Why did you have to keep this big secret? Why no invitations? Why not even a phone call to tell us? We are her parents, *hey nah*.' The words flushed out as an authentic demand. 'Do you have the wedding certificate, even?'

Siddharth found himself interrupting again. 'Can you produce *our* wedding certificate, darling? Whoall can show one of these in India?'

And then Savitri walked in and saw the three of them standing together in ceremonial awkwardness, not knowing how to conduct the formalities and not knowing which cultural observances should be privileged. Siddharth observed her closely as she did a quick audit of the room, noticing that Nitin was avoiding her gaze. She clearly needed to deflect the attention onto herself. And fast.

'And why haven't you come down to greet me after we've come all this way and after all the big changes in my life?'

'My darling *beti*!' Siddharth was the first to hug his daughter. He so wanted this to be easy for everyone. 'We have all been desperately waiting for your arrival!'

Tota reached out and hugged her daughter, offering no words of greeting or consolation.

'Your mother has just been asking me why we didn't tell them about our marriage, Savitri.' Nitin was looking over at his wife, pleadingly.

Her response was instinctively indignant: searching out her only option. 'I wasn't going to go and have a big wedding while Dadi was dying. What were you all thinking? What kind of person do you think I am?'

'And I'm not much in favour of the big white wedding either,' Nitin added. 'We wanted it to be a low-key affair. We didn't want anyone to have to fly over or give gifts.'

There was a silence while Tota considered all of this.

'You must tell us all about this later once you have settled. Have you seen your room? You'll love all the work that Buddhi Ayah has done on it.'

ॐ

When Savitri walked into their nuptial chamber she didn't see the bedroom of her childhood or the dreaming place of her stubbornly single college years but a shrine to her new status as wife and goddess. Marigold flowers and dusty rose petals were laid out in decorative circles that spiralled out to the very edges of the room, and the bedcovers had so many flowers and auspicious patterns of rice laid out on the silk that it seemed almost sacrilegious to destroy such a devoted offering to love. And heavy in the air, like a nuptial aphrodisiac, was the smell of tuberoses and Raat ki Rani, with its feminine promise. If the reception committee was a little dismissive, the flowers recognised the sanctity of their marriage with perfumed grace and tantalising welcome: if ever there was a wedding certificate, it was laid out in blossoms, validated in patterns of tuberose, marigolds and roses spread on the bed and the floor before them.

Savitri took off her shoes and took the hand of her lover and husband. Nitin took off his shoes and their feet pushed down the buds on the hard terrazzo floor. By the time they reached the bed the door was closed behind them. For the first time ever in her family home, she felt like the goddess she was named after — and she knew with great certitude that there was nothing that anybody could say or do to take Nitin away from her.

POEMS IN A TOMB

THE NEXT DAY Savitri watched her grandmother wavering in fluid conversation between two worlds — as if Dadi was swayed between the thesis and antithesis of life, awaiting the final synthesis. Somehow her grandmother's life was more miraculous and meaningful in its final flames of manifestation than in the times they would lie together for a 'chatting siesta'. *What were we thinking? That 'warm days will never cease'?*

Precious. Sacred.

She had the foresight to know that these moments would be recorded in etheric memory, wrapped in silk in her personal Akashic records of all time.

Dadi was just arriving into something resembling a waking state when Guruji walked into the room to quietly stand alongside Savitri in her bedside vigil. It took her a moment to notice him, so focused was she on committing the features of Dadi's face to memory. *Can the dying be disturbed if they know how keenly they are being observed?*

'You have arrived here like a daughter of light.'

Savitri touched Guruji's feet, just as Dadi seemed to heave in response. He was the right person to have arrived at the correct time. They watched her as she lifted her hands, her quavering eyelids attempting that strange threshold between light and shade.

'Savitri, you of all people — even named Savitri — must know that death has to be conquered.'

'Beti, you came ...' Dadi's voice was weak but clear, with an intentional force as articulate as a temple bell.

'I wanted to spend some time together.' She held Dadi's hand. 'Is it hard for you to talk?'

Dadi didn't say anything more.

Guruji spoke. 'Ask of her anything you like. Anything.' He could sense the moment. A boon could be granted. Time was scored, split — offering an open liminal space in mystery's presence for a most uncommon type of emergence to occur. If Savitri had a request it was to keep her grandmother with her, somehow — to keep something about her, even a single strand of her hair.

'Dadi, I want you to come back ... I mean, let me know, somehow, that you're not gone ... I want you to stay with me ... somehow ...'

Guruji smiled. 'What did I say? Mother of all goddesses!'

Dadi smiled. 'My darling beti, Savitri. I love you and I've always loved you ...' Who knows if this was an agreement to the request, or whether love could conquer death? She struggled to breathe and Guruji gestured to Savitri to leave the room to talk.

Outside they went together to the living room and sat on Dadi's familiar Art Deco sofa, the sofa she had always loved, with its teak arms bent like elephant tusks — bought when Dadi was just married, starting a new life and furnishing a house of hope and future dreams back in Kolkata. Savitri took a deep breath as if compensating for the lungful of air that Dadi couldn't attain.

'Guruji. Something to drink?'

'Chai is fine. Just ask Ram Lal to bring it — we need to talk.'
He knew that Savitri always made the tea personally when he came
to visit, but today she did as she was instructed.

'Now do one thing,' Guruji continued. 'You must absolutely be
sure you are with your grandmother when she leaves her body, and
only you, because of your request. It is integral that you are alone
and by her side.'

Savitri felt the gravitas of this request with the alertness of a deer
with its ear to the wind; her eyes were so large they bordered on a
state of mild panic.

'Do you think she will go tonight, Guruji?'

'I am not Arunji — you will know.'

'I didn't mean to put Dadi under any pressure ...'

'All you asked was to be shown the truth.'

'The truth?'

'That we are more than this.' Guruji was grabbing at his arm
under his shirt. 'More than just flesh. You asked to be shown that
we withstand the passing of these forms.' Guruji sensed that Savitri
was a little nervous of the boon she had asked for, at his request,
so he knew he had to reassure her, to ennoble her with the ability
that she had yet to find in herself. 'You were born — and named —
to ask this question, Savitri, but you are going to have to be ready
for the moment.'

'Meaning?'

'You will need to be there, like I said, and be ready.'

'But how to be ready, Guruji?'

'Being ready means being alert to your own psychic, invincible
presence, and your own transformation. You will need to be alert to
your witness self because you will be shown absolutely everything.'

Guruji spoke as someone who had been shown the secrets of the three worlds and beyond, who could predict much more than the mathematical calculations that simply restricted themselves to forecasts of earthly events. After she saw him to the door, she went straight down the marble hall back to Dadi's bedroom and told Buddhi Ayah to fold up her bed and take it to her own quarters. She would be the one to look after her grandmother's spiritual and physical requirements from that moment onwards.

Then Savitri went back to the silence of two souls in one large room and a fan that rotated gently above them. Dadi was quiet except for the occasional laboured breath, so the only communication Savitri had was a series of text messages with Nitin.

What you up to? she wrote, feeling slightly guilty that she'd brought her beloved new husband to India but was unable to spend any time looking after him.

Just bin speaking w yr rents

All OK?

Ur mum knows my dad

WTF?

She asked me what your new surname was

And?

I told her you didn't take my name coz you didn't like Portendorfer

Cool

She asked if I knew the Brit poet Rohan Portendorfer

She studied literature + law. That's why she knows him

No, they've MET.

WTF — come down w Neel!

❦

228

Savitri would never know the full implications of what had just happened in an upstairs living room of the Ghitorni farmhouse while she was downstairs in a semi-lit room with her dying grandmother, but she sensed a shift in both Neel and Nitin, even from the way Neel knocked on the door and entered, beaming rainbows at her. He hadn't looked so fresh and happy since he'd been in the company of Mae some months back.

'Tell me. *What-all* have you been talking about with Mama?'

'Just listen to this ...'

'I've sent an email to Dad — I'm trying to set up a time for them to chat. Apparently, they met when she was at college and he was travelling around India.'

Dadi groaned.

'Shhh. Speak softly. She's sleeping.'

Neel went around to the other side of the bed and lay down next to Dadi, just as he had when they were children and she was trying to soothe him at siesta time.

'So she really liked his work? Is it any good?'

'It was so weird, Savitri. I've never seen her be so nice to anyone,' Neel interrupted. 'She was all over Nitin, wanting to know every-thing about him. Just imagine! As if she'd just been introduced to a goddamn prince or something — like, he's the son of a poet and suddenly he's so important, yah ...'

'I thought your dad was an engineer?' Savitri asked.

'Well, he is ... and a poet. Who survives just as a poet nowadays? Who ever survived as a poet?'

Dadi was smiling and tried to say something, but gasped instead.

'Shhh. Go upstairs. Bring me some dinner, Neel.'

'You're not joining us?'

'Not tonight. I'm sleeping here, Nitin — just for a night or two. Neel will look after you.'

'Cool.' He kissed her, charged with the newfound blessings and approval of his mother-in-law.

It had been a most unexpected turnaround in events. The anxiety he'd developed about answering Tota's questions over the past couple of days had miraculously lifted, together with the growing peptic ulcer in his stomach; he had the sense that he had no more tests to face. Now he felt he could truly relax in India as he grew to know his wife's family a little better, and be the grateful, charming, impressive son-in-law he'd always intended to be before his arrival.

Later that night, Siddharth was lying next to Tota in their bed and he started to see and hear stories from the last century of an unwed girl he could hardly recognise: Tota before she became his wife. He could even feel the pleasure of her heartbeat as she thought about her encounter with Rohan Portendorfer in the Full Circle Bookshop in Delhi all those years ago, before a single line marked her forehead with anxiety over the marriage of her son, or any proposal for her own marriage had been declared.

Through her conjured sepia film, he saw it screened as if it were still happening. *The two of them walking from Khan Market, Rohan offering to carry her bag, Tota trying to carry it herself. A playful fight over the bag ensues. She grabs the hand of this young man and holds it confidently.*

They carry on walking, with determination.

Siddharth could tell that she wasn't screening this film for the first time in their married life.

They stroll slowly over to the Lodhi Gardens: she is now leading him into one of the domed, columned tombs, the Lodhi dynasty's gift to the future young lovers of this city. There's shade inside. They're kissing now, leaning against the column, and she's gripping his hands, cold hard stone against her spine. The poems he's written for her are in a scrapbook, in a cloth bag, now cast aside ...

She's anxious: they cannot take too long. She pulls up her lehenga. She does not want to stop, even if they're in a public place, in a tomb — it's getting dark enough now and mosquitoes are biting, just like they did when they went to his rooms in Paharganj ...

Siddharth suddenly felt the screen burn out like an ancient film on an overheated projector.

But I'm married. Siddharth is here.

'Don't stop just because of me.' Siddharth felt like an intruder, a little guilty even to be able to observe such private business.

'What?'

'You were in the Lodhi Gardens with someone.' He wasn't prepared to say 'Savitri's father-in-law'. That would have been a little unkind. But he knew.

'What nonsense!'

She would have dismissed anyone who'd caught them in the act all those years ago, but being caught out now by her husband, was utterly, utterly shocking.

'Okay.'

'What makes you say this?'

'Because I can read thoughts.'

Seriously, he can see me copulating in a tomb from so long ago? Tota looked at her husband like he'd been possessed by jinns, and perhaps she was even right.

'Who taught you *thisthing*?'

'It's not taught. It's a gift.' He wasn't sure anymore whether it should be called a curse. 'It was given to me by Guruji.'

'Well, it's nonsense and you know it. Stop talking such nonsense.'

'It's all right to have loved someone before me — or even slept with someone before me, even in the Lodhi tombs.' He was aware that he might be considered a voyeur of her most private moments, but his only other option was to continue to be a voyeur without her even knowing, and perhaps that was even worse.

'Don't be ridiculous.' *What is he doing to me? He's eating my brains. He's spying on me!*

'I know that it's very hard to believe, but I wanted to tell you about *thisthing* that's gone on. *Thisthing* that Guruji gave me, when I learned to meditate. Every day after that it's been happening.'

'So you can actually know ... what I'm thinking?'

'Yes.' *She's not going to believe me.* 'I have for a long time.'

He could sense that Tota was trying to make her mind blank as self-consciously as she could, so that she wouldn't reveal another fragment of an image or any words that could be used as evidence against her, but the very act of supressing thoughts brought the most private moment back — that moment when she'd gone back to that tomb and burned the poems he had left in India for her in a hardback school textbook. She had burned them on the exact spot where they had made love, right down to the ashes, to end it all: to kill even the memories.

'Why did you burn the poems?' *This is the fairest thing to do,* he thought, *otherwise I'll be the one withholding information, not her.*

Realising that her mind was spilling out beyond her control, she began her full confession. 'Well, I was about to get married ... and how would you have liked me to bring a book of poetry written for me by another man, and left it beside our bed ... to share with you? How would you have felt?'

Siddharth thought about how the world might be if everyone had his gift. *Perhaps a better place.* As he considered this prospect, he distinctly overheard her thinking about Guruji. *Maybe he can teach me something like this too?*

'Guruji was here earlier today. We can both go and visit him if you like.'

Tota looked closely at her husband, with her mind on display like a temple that hadn't been cleaned for years, the deities fingerstained with beseeching prayers till they were black with petitions. The doors were open now, and if this was going to be a marriage, it would have to be an honest one. She moved closer to Siddharth until they were entwined in each other's arms, as they had been in the earlier days. The rest of their conversation took place without any words.

I wish you hadn't left me that time and gone to the hotel. I was so lonely ...
He stroked her head.

I wanted to call you up and ask you to come home ... and I wanted my baby back, too ... and I felt so bad that I couldn't do it nicely. I didn't want to be nice — I hated you ... She started sobbing.

'It's all right. It's all right.' Siddharth felt closer to his wife than he had in years. *So strange. This is the gift of that poet, Nitin's father — it's the gift of poetry.*

I want it to be like it was ... I want our family like it was ...

'Everything can be perfect,' Siddharth said. 'We just need to aspire to perfection and it will happen.'

THE LANGUAGE OF BUTTERFLIES

SAVITRI STOOD STILL, holding her grandmother's head in her hands — a head full of the last century's stories and secrets and tragedies; that century slipping through her fingers — a head all the more precious for the fact that soon it would no longer be hers to hold.

It would have taken about twenty minutes for the family's oldest living member to leave her body, she guessed. Savitri could still feel some energy coursing under the skin of her fingertips after her grandmother's last breath. She held her grandmother's head until that had stilled entirely and the body was like a soft, inanimate object that looked like someone she used to know. During that twenty minutes she also sensed the presence in the room of some women who inhabited the past as well as the unknown future: women she had never met. They would have stayed for around twenty minutes, no longer, and her grandmother appeared to welcome them as they laid their hands on her body during those minutes she stepped out of it. Perhaps these women were angels she'd read about, who helped the dying arrive on the other side of life: the gentle midwives of death who had been waiting in white spirals to attend this time of passing — the point where the future meets the past in the most dramatically finite point of reckoning. And yet there was nothing dramatic about that moment.

She had personally made her grandmother her usual cup of Horlicks before going to bed. When she asked Dadi how she was feeling before she closed her eyes, she replied, 'Perfect.' It was precisely the word 'perfect' that made Savitri draw closer. Of course: the soul's return to perfection. It had to be. If not now, then when?

After Dadi had finished her Horlicks there was something about her breathing that gave the game away — this death game, that is. She was breathing as if she were in labour. Her rasping seemed to push out a new life with it, as if she were forcing her soul out with her lungs, and this soul of hers rattled. Hearing this, Savitri thought about whether she should call for the doctor or wake up her parents.

But why?

There didn't seem to be any pain or complications. If this was Dadi's moment, she thought, she would feel so disappointed should the doctor attempt to resurrect her. No, this exit strategy had to work, and it had to take place through the night while everyone slept, oblivious to Dadi's mission — there was no way her grandmother would be permitted to leave her body and this place in broad daylight. Some family member would fumble to call Dr Isha, and he would use his medicine as a glue to stick body and soul together as alienated, compromised companions. And then Dadi — poor Dadi — would be forced to open her eyes again to a new sun in the old world, caged still as a bed bird, powerless to fly.

The best way forward was to remain silent and be present and simply observe the process, without letting any of her awareness that these were the final moments sully the magical disappearance of her grandmother in the dark of night. Silence was required. One word and she could bring her Dadi back to language, with its concrete feet in the world. And what would she have said, anyway? 'It's all right — you'll be all right' or 'You can do it, Dadi', as if she were coaching a football team? No, of course not. In that moment there was a job to be done that required full consciousness and, strangely, full presence of the body.

It was clear that Dadi needed no distraction or encouragement from her granddaughter. Besides, before too long the etheric women were present; with far more experience of the process, they seemed perfectly aligned to the moment and able to assist in a way that Savitri never could, with the blunt instrument of her physical body, unable to do anything but witness the mystery of this soul as it unbolted itself from form and gathered up ethereal presence, while she looked on, transfixed in space and time.

The women didn't seem to mind that she was there, heavy in physicality, with arms, legs, torso of matter, simply witnessing this etheric reunion. These midwives of departure, unlike the midwives that managed birth, at first went about their business oblivious of Savitri, until one of them looked at her and smiled. It was a smile that spoke of their family's history: a smile that could have been taken from the family album, clicked in sepia tones and eaten by silverfish. This would have to be her grandmother's mother, who had died in childbirth after delivering her eighth child; the great-grandmother she had never met, except through stories. And the smile? It was sweet and plump and concerned, confirming to Savitri in a flash that our forebears have an affection for and an interest in everything that they have left behind. That we, the living, have significance as experimental beings who are cast into this world to live out our consequences — we are their legacy.

As Savitri thought about her grandmother's imminent departure, she wondered how impossible it would be to leave behind the world without kissing each blade of grass on the lawn goodbye — without looking at the setting sun and trying to remember the majesty of each layer of orange in the sky forever. But how often had Dadi been out in the past years to love this life as she used to? She hadn't so much as plucked a flower in recent times, let alone gone up to the hills to breathe pure Himalayan air. She had only witnessed the stubborn four walls that enclosed her.

Dadi isn't leaving, she is arriving, Savitri told herself, and continued her silent vigil, trying not to think about herself or her needs or her love or the bewitching miracles of the earth that Dadi was leaving behind. She tried to focus only on this moment, which was probably the last time she'd hold any part of her grandmother's body as a form that was still inhabited. She watched the still flesh, moved only by the struggling chest, the eyes that were closed to the world, hopefully one last time, and she felt the final traces of currents below the skin's surface searching for an exit point as they coursed the body. *How can I be of assistance?* she thought. And then the idea came to her: perhaps her best option was to die a little herself — to go part of the way with Dadi, as far as her body would let her go, hinged as it was to physical reality. She closed her eyes and in a moment of meditative grace she travelled some of the way, finding herself living the fear of the most remote star in the known universe, its light quivering only slightly as its rays shone into the furthest reaches of darkness.

There was no awareness of her body as such. No awareness except the surface of her palms and the head they held. It was only a thin veil of contact with flesh and within a few seconds even that was gone, leaving her fingertips dipped holding her grandmother's head — fingertips in an ocean of love that rocks its waves down the aeons. And together with the sensation in her hands came a subtle awareness of the path of a tear that rolled down her cheek.

With her closed eyes and distant flickering starlight illuminating the worlds of inner sight, she caught a glimpse once more of the others in the room, who were invisibly traceable in presence. Who were the two other women with them on this auspicious midnight vigil? There was no way of knowing unless she asked, but how? The method came to her at once. *You ask, not in the way that you do when you have a mouth to shape the words, but in the way you do when your thoughts mouth words.*

She let her question go like a butterfly, and one of the two women turned her head as if surprised that Savitri could speak their language — this language of butterflies. And with the precise conveyance of pure thought, she answered in thought form. *You don't know me, but you will. I am your great-grandmother's mother, your great-great-grandmother.*

But how? You're older than she is?

You can't understand when you count in years. Count in ... the word was not there. *Count in ...* the word was still lost on the wings of a butterfly. *We are here now ...* the voice trailed off towards the meeting point of past and future. *Of course.*

Will you be there for me, too? Savitri asked. *Will I meet you again?*

Of course, came the thought. And once again with great affirmation. OF COURSE.

A THOUSAND MARIGOLDS

DADI WAS LAID out on the marble floor of her room in a crisp white sari, surrounded by a thousand marigolds, her head facing south. Five flames from clay *diyas* flickered light on a photograph of her healthy, vibrant younger self: a photograph garlanded with sandlewood shavings with a smudge of vermilion dust pressed into the centre of her forehead. A local Brahmin priest was reciting the required *shlokas* and the room filled with chants to expel evil spirits and expedite Dadi's soul on its journey.

Under the photograph, on the floor, Dadi's physical body (without its escapee soul) looked positively relieved — the strains of life that had lined her face were barely visible now. Savitri stared at the body she'd helped bathe in rosewater earlier. It was so clearly not her grandmother — she had walked freely away without looking back — and yet it was so familiar, this body, representing a lifetime of service.

Sitting around the body on the floor of Dadi's bedroom were her many final visitors — family and friends who appeared from all corners of her life to pay their last respects. Among these were employees from Siddharth's company; they'd known Dadi as the caretaker of hearts, who had come to supervise prayers and install the framed posters from the Bhagavad Gita around the workplace. Unexpected drinking companions of Siddharth's from the Gymkhana Club arrived; they had known Dadi as the mother who took the whisky away from her son after only two glasses. There were friends from the local Farm Association, who knew Dadi as the revered elder who had insisted on building the health centre down the road for the villagers, and also helped commission one of the tarmac roads. A couple of childhood friends from her convent school arrived too. And there were a fair few of Guruji's followers from number thirty-three, who had followed the decline of this noble soul through various encounters on the roads between the farmhouses where gossip was exchanged. There were relatives with relationships so distant that explaining the connection would have been too complicated. And later in the afternoon, just before the crematorium sent the ambulance to take the body, even Joyce from the Women's Chamber of Commerce came, as did a few parents of failed suitors of Savitri's, together with the parents of a possible new girl for Neel. (Although, naturally, this death in the family would do nothing to facilitate any such matchmaking.)

The most constant vigil, however, was conducted by the immediate family and their closest companions. Siddharth sat next to Dadi's body and heard a chorus of blessings, reminiscences, regrets and thoughts — some of which didn't seem to belong at a funeral — mixed together with Vedic *shlokas* and the odd Nokia ringtone. The office *chaprasi* was wondering how long he should stay to pay his respects; Hari, who sat next to Siddharth, was missing his own mother so badly he could almost see her in Dadi's corpse; Savitri was assuring herself that her grandmother was still present, replaying the miracle of the night before; Arunji, who sat on the other side of Siddharth, was weeping tears of gratitude for the woman who had all but saved his life, remembering her from the days he had washed clothes for the big family; Neel was weeping tears of loss for everyone and everything, as if the earth had lost its sky, and its crust and mantle had crumbled; and Tota was staring at Dadi's lifeless form, thinking about her own death and how it would feel to be in a white sari on the ground, not now, but well ... sometime.

Nitin sat at the back of the room. He wanted to enclose Savitri in his arms to show her that his love would never die, but it didn't seem appropriate to touch her in public, not here, not now, so he sat still with his back against the wall, observing the barefoot rites, inhaling the incense until he was giddy. The thing that most surprised him about these rites was the way that people answered their phones, as if their work was part of their religious life. His vibrated gently in his pocket. He wasn't going to look, but he found himself unable to stop his hand reaching in so he could read the message. It was a few lines from Mae, telling him to pass on the news that her grandmother, Dolly Morrows, had died the day before. It felt strange to get the news of a death at a funeral — and stranger, too, to see how closely the two families seemed to be linked.

After a few hours on the floor, Dadi's body was picked up and placed in an ambulance to go to the crematorium — to leave her house and family. The finality of this act created a sombre, heightened disquiet as the body was carried out by Siddharth, Neel and Nitin, heads covered; the *shlokas* that were sung to keep away the evil spirits had stopped, and in their place came the profound realisation that this was a final departure from the family home, and the only thing the living could do was be silent witnesses to the moment. Tota, who in the shrunken form of her mother-in-law saw herself being taken out of this same house, started weeping loudly. As she did she caught sight of a holy man looking at her, and recognised him from Savitri's pictures as their guru — the two-hundred-year-old-man who had given Siddharth the special powers. *I need to talk to him*, she told herself, and invited him to sit next to her in the car. So while Savitri, Neel, Nitin and Buddhi Ayah accompanied the body in the shabby white ambulance, Siddharth, Tota, Guruji and Arunji followed behind in the Mercedes.

They drove past the fountain, through the gates, along the tarmac road that Dadi had commissioned and onto the MG Road towards the crematorium, in silence at first. Tota was rehearsing how she might ask Guruji to teach her how to meditate, when Siddharth seemed to intercede on her behalf.

'Guruji, we must come and visit you soon because my wife would like to receive your blessings.' He straightened his back. 'She'd also like to learn to meditate.'

'Yes, yes, she must come ... and we have been waiting to see you again, too.'

And so it was that the death of Dadi brought about the biggest transformation in the family — a transformation that Dadi herself would never witness except through her psychic being, immersed as it was in the hope for the world she'd left behind.

'Of course she must come. The Mother has gone, so it is necessary to find another who will do her work.'

'I'll ask Savitri to organise something,' Siddharth said. 'Mama would have been so happy to know that you would bring us together like this.'

'She knew she was going to bring you together, but she could only do so by leaving you,' Arunji replied. 'She knew you would all rise to the occasion on her passing. This much confidence she had.'

A silence followed, filled with the noise of thoughts.

Mataji made miracles happen ... so quietly ... nobody even realised she was doing it, such was her Shakti ...

That's settled, then ... we'll fix a day to go to see this fellow sometime after the chautha ... maybe before we go to the Ganga for the ashes ...

She wanted nothing but the happiness of others ... who will do her work now?

The Mercedes arrived at the crematorium and they were welcomed by an oversized Shiva, God of Destruction, standing with legs apart, his two feet planted defiantly on the gate, his trident pointing towards the heavens, a moon and a star hanging from his unruly dreadlocks. They parked the car and joined the chaos at the edge of the world, where the mourning population of a city bulging with life queued up to settle the sacred duties of death.

'I'm sorry. You'll have to wait your turn,' said one of the orderlies. 'Please be standing over on that side.' He directed Dadi's funeral party to one side of the funeral grounds. A three-legged stray dog roamed at their feet, sniffing old coconut husks. Siddharth found himself wondering why on earth they couldn't modernise the procedure, make it a little less grim. What-all was this twenty-first century? He tried to pass a small bribe to the man who ran the facility, but he wouldn't accept it — there was another body to be burned before Dadi's, an order in this line to heaven that had been ordained, and why were they in a rush, anyway?

'Dadi was so used to waiting. She waited and waited for this day!' Savitri said.

'And we will wait with her,' Tota added. 'It's the least we can do.'

THE PINING

MAE HADN'T PLANNED to sell cushions at the market that Saturday, but she needed the distraction before Dolly's funeral, otherwise she'd have been like a pin cushion made out of a water balloon before she even arrived at the hall. Better to chill out and take it as it came.

She was laying her cushions down, exhausted from the events of the two days since her grandmother's death, when she was approached by a girl with a young baby clinging to her chest in a papoose. She'd grown up with women and babies thanks to her father's practice, and no doubt there was something in the water that made everyone within a few miles of Mount Chincogan fall pregnant. Either that, or the geolocation on every girl's mobile phone switched to an invisible 'fertile mode' when they came to the shire.

The girl bent over and unravelled her suckling package. She squatted with her baby on her knee, sifting through the cushion covers, stroking the embroidered surfaces. Mae watched, flooded with the familiar pining for a child that had only amplified since she'd split up with Neel. Now it felt almost necessary to have a child — to compensate for the loss in her family. To help with her grieving.

'Where do these cushions come from?' the girl asked Mae. It was the question that absolutely everyone asked.

'From India.'

'I love India. I went there to get pregnant.'

It was an odd comment. Mae noticed the baby, with its skin slightly darker than its mother's, and those extra-large Indian eyes with lashes so long they could have been painted on.

'I was going to get married to an Indian fella,' Mae said. 'Could have had one of these cuties.' She'd lost interest in making the sale now — she just wanted the story. Why India? Why leave the shire of fertility?

'Where in India is your partner from?'

'He's not Indian, he's true blue Aussie, but he's a paraplegic — he can't have kids.'

'Wow!'

Mae didn't have to enquire too much further: the story unfolded like a Persian carpet, filled with intricate, intimate details. The young woman, Gail, lived on a farm with her husband, Jerome. They'd bought it together with the settlement from his motorbike accident, which had immobilised him from the waist down. They grew avocados, and now they were raising their son, Rudra, together. 'We're really happy and we really love each other.' (And no, her husband didn't mind when she announced that she was going travelling for a while to get pregnant.) 'He understood completely — and he wanted to be a father.'

Now Mae couldn't stop her questions; she was onto a potboiler and she needed to know absolutely everything. 'What about the biological father? Does he know that he had a child?'

It turned out that one of the young sadhus who lived in the hills above all the ashrams in Rishikesh was the father. Gail pulled out her phone and produced a picture of him. He had long, thick, dark hair and a charming smile and was dressed in the white robes of an ascetic. 'Wasn't it against his religion or something?' Mae was thinking of the conservative values of Neel's family. What would Tota have said?

'He knew he was giving me a child. It was fully conscious ... and loving.'

And then Mae asked the question she was begging to ask. 'How did it feel to leave him?'

'I knew I was going to leave him. Everything was done intentionally — especially the conception. And then I had all the support I needed from Jerome ... and I have my memories.'

Yes. The memories. *Tell me about those.* Would it have helped to have left India with a baby to remember Neel by, now that she felt so alone? Would it have be easier to lose her grandmother if she knew she had a life growing inside her?

Mae asked if she could help with the baby while Gail looked at the cushion covers.

As soon as she lifted Rudra to her chest he tried to suckle, and the infant's reflex made her nipples harden with love and loss, and a tear fell down on baby Rudra's face. He simply shut his eye to exclude the alien tear and kept rooting for a mother's breast — any mother's breast.

Gail chose one of the covers with two horseshoe shapes next to a river, the symbol of two women sitting in conversation in Dream Time — sacred women's business.

'Take it,' Mae said. 'It's a gift.'

She packed up her stall early, loaded her gear into the van and headed back to the community hall in Mullumbimby to have some time alone before everyone arrived for her grandmother's funeral.

EQUALITY

'**D**o you have any strange sensations in your ears?' Siddharth asked his wife, as they made their way back to the farmhouse from the ashram after she'd learned to meditate.

'What for? Why are you asking about my ears?'

'I had this thing before.'

'No.'

'Nothing different? You don't notice something in your hearing?'

'No difference,' Tota repeated, firmly, sanely.

Siddharth was disappointed: he'd hoped that they'd be able to share identical experiences. Never mind.

At her initiation, she'd asked for the same gift as her husband had been given.

'It seems a little unfair to give such an advantage to one person in a marriage and not the other,' she'd told Guruji, and he'd smiled.

'So what you're really asking for is equality?'

Tota had nodded.

Siddharth, a little embarrassed by his wife's demands, had said, by way of apology, 'My wife's a feminist, Guruji. She works at the Women's Chamber of Commerce.'

He didn't know what else had gone on in that meditation room, but when Tota strode out she'd simply said, 'Let's go. Work is done.'

Only later did he find out that Tota been given some other 'gifts' — together with equality she had also been given the boons of goodness and generosity. These were virtues that percolated slowly, filtering like water through gravel, sand, mud and clay; they were feminine forces with an ability to persistently and persuasively shape new realities. His gift had been quite the thunderbolt, and somehow he'd expected that all blessings or curses would come with the same shocking force.

But Siddharth's disappointment was unfounded. Slowly, after they'd returned to normal life after the death of his mother, he noticed a phenomenal change in Tota — a trickle-down effect following direct contact with cosmic forces.

'We should continue supporting the village health centre,' Tota told him one day. 'That way we can continue your mother's work, in her good name.'

'Yes, of course.' He tried not to act surprised.

Then, of all the things, she suggested that they should go together to see Arunji, whom she had scorned all these years. 'He has had such an interest in the family. He's your brother, no? We must not distance him now.'

She wants to see Arunji, really? If only we could bottle these gifts she's received and distribute them as homeopathic tinctures on everyone's tongues!

The two of them paid Arunji an unexpected visit at his DDA flat on the way back from the Gymkhana Club. At least, an 'unexpected visit' was what Siddharth and Tota felt it might be. Nonetheless, the family astrologer didn't show even a flicker of surprise, which was strange, considering that they'd given him no notice, and Siddharth had brought his wife, who had never been to the apartment before, had never sought insight from celestial bodies and had never been one iota interested in Arunji's relationship with the family. Yet here they were, at the auspicious time that had been fixed without being fixed.

Arunji's calm anticipation was reassuring for Siddharth, even though the loud banging on the roof was distracting, as always.

'Oh my goodness, I was going to send my man to sort out your problem,' Siddharth remembered.

'What problem?' Tota asked.

'Arunji has someone building illegally above his flat. The *goonda* is paying the bribes and getting the work done without DMC permission. I was going to send Kapil to sort it out.'

'I can sort it out. Just give me his address,' Tota replied.

Siddharth knew that Tota now had more power than she'd ever had before in her life: the power of Kali, mixed up with the thrust and heft of the law — that imperious, utterly worldly force. She was a female lawyer with a red tongue hanging out!

Arunji took them both to his table, covered with vinyl and sheets of paper, to show the prepared charts.

'It seems that you have been called upon to do some very important work,' he told Tota. 'And I'm not talking about the work you'll be doing for me — no, this work is much larger. It is a job that is delegated to the Shakti energy of the universe, the female power.

Siddharth was impressed. His wife — and with such a task! He looked at her stoic face and read the lips that didn't speak.

Is he talking about me? Hai Ram! Does he tell this to everyone?

'Can you tell her what this task might be, exactly?' Siddharth asked. 'You're asking for something quite, err ... unusual.'

'She's been given certain powers for this stage in her life ... *matlab* ... how to say this ... if this is to be an era of the goddess rising, then ladies will have to be kind to other ladies — not, *matlab* ... hinder them — and that way they can all rise together.'

None of this made sense to Siddharth, but as it happened, Tota had been thinking of the fourth wave of feminism that very morning. It seemed obvious. The first wave involved the suffragette movement, basic bloody rights; the second wave was all about gender politics, us against them; and the third wave was what she described as girlie feminism, defined by individualism and individual rights. And now it was time for the obvious step — for a collective spiritual movement — a fourth wave of kindness — for feminists to support other women. They'd be leading a new collaborative force that the world had never before witnessed. Savitri had given her a copy of *A Room of One's Own*, and just a few hours ago she'd read Virginia Woolf's words: 'Women are hard on women. Women dislike women.' And reading this had made her think of the young intern at the Chamber of Commerce who had done so very well ... and how she had organised for her to be moved on at the end of the month.

But the intern was simply a reflection of another problem, as Arunji revealed.

'In particular, you must be kind to your Australian daughter-in-law, who is going to marry into your family, like it or not — and bring your grandchildren into the world.'

Both Siddharth and Tota sat in shocked silence. Here was a

prediction in the blazing light of day, utterly unfiltered. *Arunji is a brave man, much braver than I*, Siddharth thought.

Tota still didn't speak — she simply wiped away a tear. And nobody said anything to comfort her, lest they dilute the power of that moment.

'Arunji, please give us the best date for the wedding and I will adjust accordingly,' she said.

Arunji scribbled some dates, and as he did his eyes widened. The date for the wedding was outstanding for Neel and Mae, yet it was a date that signalled the end of the world for Savitri and Nitin.

He handed Tota the piece of paper as he tucked his comb-over back into place, coughing.

On the way home Tota kept thinking about all the other things she hadn't done for other women — even Savitri, her own daughter. Why, she'd kept Savitri's dowry locked up in the bank. Lying in the dark were jewels that should have gained more power through gifting — the solid gold *mala* that had adorned the neck of her own grandmother, and the one she had worn to her own wedding. Then there were the gold wedding bangles from Kolkata, imprinted with flowers and paisleys, not to mention her emerald ring surrounded with Golconda diamonds.

'How did we forget to give Savitri her jewellery? And how did we manage to give absolutely nothing to Nitin for their wedding?'

Siddharth didn't know how to answer. These were not his concerns, as he had never been in charge of the lockers — they were securely and steadfastly in Tota's female domain. *Was I even consulted about what-all would be given to her?*

As for Nitin and Savitri's marriage, everything felt so complete, so perfect ... except for one thing.

'They want to travel together. We should give them a honeymoon as a wedding present.'

A few days later Tota arrived home like a bank robber from the family locker, with a sack of jewels the size of her handbag. As she locked the jewellery up in her special Godrej safe at the farmhouse she realised there was one more very important gift she had failed to give: her own wedding sari. She'd always dreamed that Savitri would wear this to her wedding when the great day came, and she'd kept those dreams preserved safely in camphor all these years, along with the taffeta silk and 22-carat gold threads.

She opened up the box and laid out the sari with its blouse and petticoat, like maharani's treasure. How long had it been since she had dressed like a goddess? *It's still perfect: so unconditionally beautiful.* She locked her bedroom door and put on the blouse. *One last time.* The hooks no longer contained her breasts, so she took off the blouse and decided to wear the sari topless, just like the tribal women did. Then she tucked the sari into her petticoat, deftly made the folds and placed them in elegant rows, moving in front of her dressing table mirror to straighten each fold and adjust the length so that the extravagant gold trim perfectly framed the entire length of her body.

Tota looked at the woman in the mirror. There had been a time when that woman was a young girl in love — not with the person she was going to marry but with herself, and with her dreams and fantasies. The garment that circled her body so elegantly and luxuriously now in six yards of entitled silk was enough to bankrupt a family in a dowry demand, and yet it had sat in its complacent folds for years. Tota knew it wasn't hers. It made her feel like Sleeping Beauty's wicked stepmother. And it made her even more acutely aware of the fact that her flesh-and-blood daughter, now a married woman, had not been given a single diamond or millimetre of silk on account of her new life status. How had she and Siddharth managed to miss giving Savitri what had always been hers? How had they managed to seclude a dowry that had sat in bottom drawers and bank closets for years, waiting for the auspicious moment of her marriage?

That same evening, Tota gave her daughter all the jewels and the sari, and took Savitri, Nitin and Neel out to eat Chindian food at the Gymkhana Club.

There, she decided to come out with what she'd been planning to say to Neel ever since she visited the family astrologer.

'Neel, I have spoken to Arunji and he has given me the most auspicious date for your wedding to Mae, which I can share with you if you like.'

On the other side of life, Dolly and Dadi were cheering Tota on. On this side, in the Gymkhana Club, Neel found himself running to the bathroom to spew up his favourite dish — veg Manchurian. So unexpected was the swing of events in his direction that it knocked him in the gut and brought him to his knees before a porcelain bowl. Whatever else had happened to make his world spin he couldn't even consider in that moment. It was all so perfectly beyond comprehension.

27TH OF OCTOBER

I T WAS THE morning of the 27th of October — the date being significant because Winsome had had a dream some days earlier where she looked at a number 2 for half the night and a number 7 for the other half. She woke up thinking, *Well, that was bizarre. Why would I be dreaming up numbers?* Then she put 2 and 7 together and arrived at 27, then the 27th. Of course! This was the day Winsome's baby was going to arrive! How logical. And what dreams a pregnancy can cook up!

Winsome and Sage had been parked outside the doctor's house all these days in anticipation of this day dreamed up for the birth. The kerb was supplied by the council, but the real hospitality was the offer of a bathtub and a home where the new soul could arrive on planet earth. They'd been living in Kuranda, in a place called Rainbow Valley, when they first heard from locals about the best homebirth doctor in Australia. The children Terry delivered were called 'Terrors', and the parents of these kids from all over the region seemed to have a secret cosmic link.

And so they'd climbed into their truck, revved up the engine and gone in search of the man who had started Australia's homebirth movement so that he could help them deliver their unborn child.

‎

Terry met a line of big-bellied women and their barefoot partners on a daily basis, all of them insisting on homebirths, but Winsome and Sage were different: they wanted to have a homebirth but didn't have a home.

'I could help you deliver the baby in the birth centre,' he'd offered.

'No. We've decided that we want a homebirth,' Sage insisted.

'What about our van?' Winsome suggested.

Terry could tell that they'd never been anywhere near a birth. Never before had he offered one of his patients his own home for a homebirth, but in his many years of practice as a country doctor, he knew that he encountered more 'first times' than most medicos. Like the first time there was an emergency transfer in Main Arm and he had to help carry a woman in second-stage delivery through a flash flood up in the hills. Or the first time he delivered a woman with two uteruses. Or the first time he delivered a baby in a field.

And so it came to Winsome's first time as she strolled into the house on the 27th of October and announced that she was going to be having her baby that day.

'Are you having any contractions?' Terry asked.

'No.'

He said nothing. For him, labour had a shape, a sound, a presence and a command. She wasn't in any kind of labour that he knew of — why, she could even talk! But on the other hand, he knew that he could never understand everything about this state of mystery — there was always a story that had yet to be told: a story to be coaxed out. And from the moment Terry first began attending births in the shire, he was wise enough to know that labour was a state of spiritual contact — a mystery that defied the hubris of any medical textbook. And as for labouring women in the shire, you could never tell any of them that you knew more about their bodies than they did! How would you dare?

'Have your waters broken?'

'No. Nothing.'

'Okay.' He didn't know how to suggest to Winsome that this was not labour, what with her prediction and everything. However, he knew that his connection with this child was momentary, but that Winsome could have had a connection that lasted millennia. Of course she would know more than he.

'How about going for a walk to see if you can bring on some contractions to help with the labour?'

Mae, who had been listening to the conversation from the breakfast table, offered Winsome some fruit.

'No. There isn't room for another thing in there. I can't tell my baby to make room for even a seed of passionfruit.'

'Take some water with you,' Terry suggested. 'You should keep your fluids up.' *How do I tell her that this is going to be a lot longer than she thinks?*

'Yeah, first births can be long,' Mae said. Spoken like the true daughter of a baby-catcher. Terry was grateful.

Mae had been a doula for a few lonely single mums at her father's request, so when Winsome asked her to be the doula for hers she was honoured. She knew that she could remain unruffled when women quavered; she knew how to reassure them that it was possible to get through the next contraction without dying, so she offered to go on that walk with Winsome and Sage to bring on the birth.

The three of them strolled barefoot down to the beach, where they could see the bays stretching out to the white lighthouse on the hill beyond. *Bliss*. It made her think about the day Savitri arrived, an innocent, unmarried Indian girl.

'This is where I introduced Nitin and Savitri,' she told Winsome. 'It's a magic love spot.'

'Let's sit here for a bit then,' Winsome replied.

Sage helped her sink down slowly onto the sand, where she spread her crimped yellow skirt around her like an unbroken egg.

'You're doing so well. I hope I'm as healthy and pain-free as you are when I'm in labour!'

'Will you get your awesome father to deliver your child when you have one?' Winsome asked.

'I'm going to have my first baby in India,' Mae replied.

'How do you know that?' Sage asked.

'The same way that Winsome knows she's going to have her baby today.'

Actually, it was different. Mae had pulled some tarot cards on Neel recently, after her mother had mentioned that both Dadi and Dolly had 'visited' to tell her that Mae would be marrying him. And she had taken to waiting for the invitation, just like Winsome was waiting for her due date.

'Cool.'

Neither of them wanted to break the trance of the fertile moment by asking whether she would have that baby with Neel, so Winsome changed the subject. 'Tell me about this magic love spot. Tell me what happened to Savitri when she met Nitin.'

'Goodness, let me remember. She wanted some help with swimming ...'

'Was she trying it on?'

'No, it was more perfect than that. She wasn't confident in the water. I think it was a pretty rough day for the surf.'

'Seriously?'

'They're not really into swimming in the surf in India. Nobody does it over there. Neel was a hopeless swimmer too. And she was wearing this really modest little number that somehow made her more attractive.'

'I can see how that would work.'

'And I don't think she'd ever had a boyfriend before — at least, not that I know of.'

'My goodness, I don't think I can bear it. Too romantic. Just like their wedding.'

'That's where they went into the water.' Mae pointed. 'Just around there, holding hands — complete strangers. About to be married but not knowing it.'

'Oh my God. Oh my God.'

Sage and Mae looked at Winsome.

'There's water coming out.'

Sage lifted Winsome up off the sand, and when she stood they could all see there was fluid running down her pale legs and her yellow maternity skirt was wet.

'An offering to the ocean!'

'Yeah, bring it on. Let's walk some more.'

'Oh my God. This is so exciting. It's really happening to me.'

'Let's walk. Let's get it going some more ...'

Winsome began walking so swiftly it was hard to keep up with her, and she was showing absolutely no sign of an imminent labour, except for the neonatal lump that hung deep in her pelvis, making her walk like John Wayne after a long ride on a stallion. Mae was impressed, and that familiar physical craving somewhere between her heart and her uterus started pulsing — that desire to be on the precipice of an unknown adventure, an aching for the future, for mystery, for love, for a creature in her arms she would know till the day she died — so perfectly small, and miraculously incubated, appearing out of nothing in those cosmic oceans, without so much as an account of its origins.

'Let's go home and see what Dad thinks you should do,' Mae suggested.

They went back to the surgery waiting room and they sat down with the small crowd of patients, next to another woman with a swollen belly.

'Do you mind if we jump the queue?' Mae asked. 'We have a woman in labour.'

But when Terry came out of the surgery he confirmed that Winsome wasn't actually in labour. Besides, he had too many patients to see. 'Go to the birth suite in Byron and see if they can help.'

When they arrived at the birth suite they sat in the waiting room and received the same response.

'Darl, you're not in labour. You can try bouncing on one of our gym balls to see if you can bring it on before going back to Terry's, if you like, but he's probably right. We don't need to do an internal examination yet.'

And so Winsome sat on the ball and bounced like a child, but it gave her pains in her pelvis — just not the kind that any Mullumbimby midwife worth her Rescue Remedy would ever call a contraction. Despondent, she closed her eyes and began to meditate in the corridor, enviously peeping over at a woman who paraded in front of them, arms draped around the shoulders of her husband and birth support person. *They have rooms at the inn for such women, with befitting swoons and groans.*

'It's going to happen,' Sage reassured her.

And it did.

Winsome was still meditating when the woman's cries from the other side of the wall turned to shrieks, and then groans and gasps. Mae could tell that she was starting her contractions by the way Winsome's face changed. Subtle but real. This was it. Nobody could tell her now that this wasn't labour.

'It's happening.'

'Of course it is.'

The quavering, seething, primordial sounds from the other woman crescendoed behind the closed doors, triggering even more contractions for Winsome. The waves returned more frequently, in harmony. Then, after half an hour, the noise from the birth suite stopped entirely and a midwife emerged to announce that a little boy had just been born.

It was all that was needed.

Winsome's pains shifted to a different pace and rhythm. This was it. The 27th would be the day that Winsome's baby was born, just as she'd predicted.

'Let's go back to yours, Mae, and see if Terry will take us more seriously now.'

Sage lay down with Winsome in the back of the truck and Mae drove them rapidly down the straight, narrow road that seemed to emerge from Mount Chincogan. She was breaking the speed limit and the cows in the fields rushed past: it was the only indication she gave that she was a little nervous.

It was around 5 p.m. when they returned home and Winsome was finally ready to struggle into Terry's surgery, deserving an examination. Terry was calm, as always. *He's waiting for this story to be told*, Mae thought. Her father was always so confident in the unknowing — and she loved working with him. 'Not bad. Nine centimetres. You're in transition.'

Transition.

That step between one state and the next. The moment of transformation of such intense pain — the only kind of pain that can lead to its total and utter opposite, the rush of pleasure at holding your own child in your arms, releasing rivers of love that will last a lifetime. The evolution into motherhood. And it seemed to Mae, who had seen a few births now, that Winsome was having just about the most terrifying transition she'd ever witnessed. It was so rapid that there was no time between contractions.

'You could try filling up the bathtub,' Terry suggested to his daughter.

'No. No ... I don't want to move ...'

'Well, then, bring a couple of yoga mats.' Mae was familiar with some women's need to remain earthbound. The idea of a water birth, so appealing in pregnancy, could seem like a form of torture to a woman who wanted to feel the weight of her body and the force of gravity catching her baby.

'It's not going to be long,' Terry told Winsome. 'I'm willing to place a bet that you'll have your baby in your arms by seven-thirty.'

Winsome must have heard the words 'baby in your arms' because Mae could see something alter in her friend. It seemed as if that moment of openness had come.

'The head's crowning. Reach down and feel it, if you like.'

Mae saw Winsome reach down to that gate of motherhood and touch her baby's head, and then she witnessed yet another major shift, as if Winsome's pain had been replaced with unstoppable, ultimate power.

And then she pushed, with a long groan.

'Hold your breath as you push. It'll give you more strength. Mae, hold her feet, it will help keep her grounded. Sage, you come round here. You're going to catch the baby.'

And so the baby slithered out onto Sage's hands, on a yoga mat, on a wave of blood on the doctor's surgery floor. Sage had tears in his eyes and couldn't speak, immediately bringing the baby up to Winsome's breast — and she looked more winsome than ever as she looked down and saw that the child of their new lineage was a girl.

'It's not over yet.' Mae had noticed other women look as if they'd finished the job when they'd pushed out the baby, but she also knew that pushing out a placenta was no major ordeal. Once the final task was done, Terry instructed Mae and Sage to get Winsome to take a leak and have a shower and settle herself down to get some rest. 'Let them have your bedroom, Mae. Change the sheets and put a yoga mat underneath in case there's any bleeding.'

In the quiet hours of the morning Mae was lying down in the van, still too charged to sleep, thinking about Winsome, now on the other side of a chasm, with her story known and a miracle in her arms. She was remembering the primal urgency of those sounds on the other side of the wall at the birth suite — reliving the power women had to create change for each other, feeling that potency in her own body.

It came as no surprise to her when Neel's call came through before the birds had awoken for the new day. It was the proposal she'd been told about several days earlier.

'So ... what do you say?'

She could almost hear his heart beating through his voice.

'Yes.' *Of course. But why are we both so nervous if this is meant to be?*

'So can I book you on a flight out tomorrow?'

'No. I want to wait until my bridesmaid recovers. We just delivered her baby a few hours ago.'

Mae didn't expect Neel to understand what she meant and didn't want to explain. And she knew that they didn't have bridesmaids in India, either, but what the hell. She was feeling lucky.

'Bring your maidservant,' he replied.

Mae decided not to get furious about their bizarre cultural differences. Not now. Not this time round. But she did want to test him just that little bit further.

'I'd also like to invite the two kids who live in your servants' quarters to be a flower girl and a pageboy.'

Whether Neel could agree to this request without consulting with his mother was going to be her final test.

'Of course,' he replied.

INDIA, AGAIN

W HEN NEEL THOUGHT deeply about the miraculous
and mysterious changes that had taken place in his
life, and the way the world had bent to conspire
with his wishes, he couldn't help but think that Savitri must
have had a hand in these unexpected boons. Why, Savitri hadn't
waited for permission to enter the future — she'd thrown herself
through the birth canal of time and space to arrive there before
anyone else. And ever since she'd arranged her own marriage,
without any hesitation, at the moment of marriage itself, aided
by the principles of synchronic time, she'd laid out a path for
his future too.

And it was clear to him that his future would not be aided by
a family wedding.

All he had received from his mother and Arunji was a date, and
there was simplicity and clarity in that. There certainly wasn't any
divine clarification about whether this should be a Hindu wedding
or a Christian wedding, or whether there should be a religious
ceremony at all. Besides, what would he do with all of those

bridesmaids and pageboys that Mae had dreamed up as attendants? Would they invent a new syncretic tradition by walking around the fire seven times carrying posies behind the bride and groom? Or could he put the pageboy on top of a white horse, like the *sarbala*, and give a few pieces of jewellery to the bridesmaids to sit quietly and not steal his shoes, as per Punjabi tradition?

Tota had begun asking Neel about the guests he would like to invite and the venue they should book and whether or not they should serve pure veg or non-veg. Even though these enquiries were kind and patient, he was reminded of the preparations they'd made for the last, ill-fated wedding, and like regurgitated food from a toxic nuptial feast that never took place, such talk tasted sour in his mouth.

'I'd like to get married quietly, without a fuss, like Savitri did,' he said, and like his sister, added his grandmother as an excuse. 'How can we have a grand celebration the year that Dadi left, anyway? What will people think?'

Tota didn't need the explanation. What's more, she already knew that she wouldn't be required to attend the event, and perhaps it would be better if she didn't.

'So how about this — you book the wedding, do *what-all* you'd like to do, and just let us know how we can help. We don't need to come. We can share your joy on the day, knowing that you're happy. Knowing that it's the right day.'

This wouldn't have been possible unless Savitri had done thisthing first, hey nah?

'Actually, I've already been thinking, and I'd like to go somewhere in Rajasthan.'

'Maybe we could send you off on the Orient Express?'

Neel had done a lot more than just think about this wedding: he'd made many enquiries, and none of them involved such first-class extravagance, because he knew that Mae would prefer to do it village style, so he'd asked about whether they could get married in the desert, on safari, under the moonlight — and yes, it was possible. This had been his dream wedding all along, ever since he'd first heard about Savitri's moonstruck affair. It would be on the dunes — far from any interference by the world, with hardly any luggage and certainly no baggage from the past. The heaviest item would be the pandit's metal hearth, which they'd use to light a sacred fire.

'I'll find out who's coming from Savitri's side and then we will book some first-class sleeper train tickets to Jaisalmer,' he replied. He'd actually planned second-class sleeper for a more authentic experience, but if there was one concession he could give, it was an upgrade on their train tickets.

And so it was a budget holiday, as far as Tota was concerned. Savitri and Nitin had decided on taking just Neel, Mae, Sage and Winsome on their honeymoon, and rolled into that honeymoon was Neel's wedding, booked under the stars.

'So long as you're happy,' Tota said. 'It's your marriage.'

When Mae arrived at Indira Gandhi Airport for the second time, they brought two cars to wait for the entourage of Sage, Winsome and their baby girl. Tota could remember the last time she'd lined up to see her new daughter-in-law and remembered her own superiority with more than a touch of shame. She remembered the way she'd almost refused to look in the direction of 'that influence', hoping to wish her away. This time she couldn't wait to welcome a new daughter into the family. She remembered how she had expected a compliant Indian daughter-in-law, albeit with blonde hair. This time she was expecting a feisty, disagreeable, antagonistic young woman, and was even looking forward to it.

And so they waited alongside the drivers with placards boasting hotel logos and unfamiliar names. When Mae, Sage, Winsome and their baby walked past the guard and into the arrivals hall, it was Tota who was waving furiously and charging towards them.

She waited for Neel to embrace his fiancée before opening her arms out to Mae.

'Welcome back to India,' she said, and realising that this time she had no garland of marigolds, without hesitating she took off the long, thick, gold chain that was double-looped around her neck and put it over Mae's head.

'What's this for?' Mae asked, surprised at the weight of generosity around her neck.

'It's my apology and it's my blessing, and it's my way of welcoming you back to India, most sincerely, as my daughter.'

Mae was so taken aback that she was hijacked by tears and put her head on Tota's shoulder. Tota embraced her, wiped her tears and added her own. Neel embraced the two of them and added his own tears to the marble floor of the arrivals hall. None of them wanted to say anything to break the spell. Mae didn't even say thank you, except by squeezing her mother-in-law, and Tota certainly didn't say what came to her mind, which amused her too much to articulate. *I don't even care if you sell it. The money will bring you just as much luck as the necklace because you cannot escape your blessings!*

Next, she welcomed the young family: the pretty Chinese girl who was smiling and clutching her baby in a pouch and waiting her turn to be welcomed, and the earnest young man whose hair was so long and knotted he could have been Lord Shiva if he'd been given a trident and received the Ganga in his dreadlocks. There was a time Tota would have gone out of her way to avoid such people, but there was simply no fathomable reason to be anything but happy in that moment.

'You must be Sage and Winsome.'

She'd asked Savitri the names of these friends again and again, because even though she understood their meaning, they were adjectives not Proper Nouns according to her education, and a little too unusual to simply trip off the end of her tongue.

'And what's the name of this cute little *bacha*?'

'We're waiting to see what suits her,' Sage said. 'We'll know it when we hear it.'

'Thank you for inviting us to India and for being so generous,' Winsome added, taking Tota's hand and warming it in hers.

'It's nothing. You are guests in our country and we're delighted that you can travel with the children for Neel and Mae's wedding.'

If Neel had known that the reunion between his mother and his fiancée was going to go so well, he would have organised for the party to stay a night or two in Delhi, but having anticipated awkwardness, he'd booked the train tickets for the same night. It gave the guests hardly enough time to have anything more than some light snacks at home before they had to get on the train to the future, starting from New Delhi Railway Station.

That night, Tota and Siddharth came to the station to see them off. Tota had brought a box in a canvas bag that she had always intended to give to Savitri: the wedding sari she had worn herself years earlier.

'Just take it,' she said to her daughter, passing it unceremoniously through the filthy bars on the window of the first-class carriage of the Delhi Jaisalmer Express. 'I saved this for you. Maybe you can wear it at Neel's wedding — you decide.' *And take with it all my hopes for your future and a better, freer world, my darling ...*

It was a world that she hadn't dared think might come of age.

UNSHELTERING SKY

THE WEDDING PARTY of six arrived in the remote city of Jaisalmer, which rose like a crown out of the Thar Desert, each building a jewel, and all the jewels enclosed by an ancient stone wall, sinking under its ambition to contain the design frenzy of an almost imaginary city. When Nitin first saw it, he thought they would all be honeymooning in a fairy sandcastle. Their hotel had the feeling of a domed underground cavern, filled with treasures collected by Aladdin over several lifetimes: crossed spears, portraits of coy Rajasthani princesses wearing large nose rings, a wooden swing suspended from an intricately carved wooden stand. Dark red velvet curtains and illuminated sandstone corridors gave way to graceful pillared halls that looked like temples, each stage set giving way to another.

Neel was busy organising the final touches of his desert wedding trip. Having been given the options of 'touristic route' or 'non-touristic route' when booking the camel trek, he'd naturally chosen the latter, and he'd even organised for all the camels to be garlanded, with colourful cloth rags on the saddles and pompoms hanging from their halters. Next, he had to make arrangements for the pandit, who would ride with another cameleer and be taken back to Jaisalmer immediately after the wedding ceremony.

Everything was ready, but on the morning of the day prescribed for the wedding, Nitin lay in his bed, incredibly sick yet unable to vomit — absolutely unable to move. Savitri stayed with him in that palace underworld, sitting next to him on the four-poster bed, staring at the latticed alcoves that surrounded them. He could tell that she was willing him to get better and he couldn't help but feel the pressure of her unspoken wishes.

'Don't worry, I'm coming with you,' he assured her. 'I wouldn't miss this for the world.'

Yet he could see she was worried.

'We can stay and you can get better. We can celebrate when they return. We don't need to be there when they get married.'

'No. I'll be okay.'

But when they met the cameleers at the edge of the desert, the trip took a surreal turn. The others hopped happily onto their camels, but the man in charge of Nitin's camel couldn't get enough control over it to get it to sit down. Even the camel looked unwell. It made a loud, gurgling, belching sound until it vomited out its stomach and hung the putrid stinking thing out of the left side of its mouth, to air the red veins just beyond its rotting teeth. Nitin stared at the camel, and at the cameleer in a huge bright green turban, welcoming him with an echoing laugh. Then he vomited up the contents of his own stomach alongside the beast.

'Okay, that's it. We're going back to the hotel,' Savitri insisted.

'No, no. I'm feeling better now. Better out than in.'

Nitin's camel finally went down on arthritic bended knee for him to get on. It lurched forward and up with a fart, and then the cameleer hit the creature's hump and it trotted after the others to form a single line that trailed out under the blue unsheltering sky. And he followed at the end of the line, looking back to see the Jeep driving away and endless dunes ahead of them, which they paced along aimlessly.

He managed to stay upright. He managed a smile. Good. The dunes kept their promise — there wasn't a single tourist in sight, just wave after wave of curved, swaying sand. Nitin tried to distract himself from the hallucinations that appeared in the dunes, looking up instead at the impermanent blue, then at the toxic-green turban ahead of him. He vomited skilfully, this time a projectile that missed the side of his camel. He was at the end of the camel queue, so nobody would notice, except perhaps a camel trek later on that day along this same non-touristic trail.

When they stopped for lunch the others were so caught up recounting tales about camel behaviour he could only attempt to listen.

'Feeling a little better?' Neel asked.

'Yeah, mate. Much better.'

'We'll stop before too long to prepare for the ceremony.'

When the time came to get back onto his farting, grunting, stinking ship, Nitin climbed aboard and followed the line once more, thankfully from the rear, leaning forward on a writhing hump, his sweat pouring into a red rug and joining the smell of camel sweat.

When they stopped at dusk, the cameleers constructed a simple tent for Mae to get changed in. Savitri tied on her mother's wedding sari before showing Mae how to tie hers and helping tie a sari on Winsome. The magnificence of it all was wasted on Nitin.

'Nitin, you're next. You'll need to wear a *pagri*.'

He went into the tent with Neel and Sage to get their Rajasthani wedding clothes on. They seemed to fit well, but the coils of fabric Neel twisted around Nitin's head never seemed to stop. The *pagri* pressed his thoughts tighter into his painful cranium and the weight of the cloth trapped them there, crushing and sealing fears of death inside metres of pink cotton fabric.

'You're sweating lots. Did you get a bit hot up on that camel?'

'Yeah. Not used to it, I guess.'

When they came out, the girls commented on how handsome the three boys looked, but once again Nitin couldn't summon any enthusiasm to respond as a handsome man might.

'What's wrong?' Sage asked.

Did it show? Nitin laughed. 'Nothing wrong, mate. The moon's coming up. I can't believe Neel and Mae are actually getting married this time.'

The moon had risen a little higher than the sands by the time the pujari got to work organising the wedding party into two ritual circles around the *havan* fire. The inner circle looked like an upmarket version of the turbaned cameleers in the outer circle. The camels, thankfully, were left to smooch and burp at each other a suitable distance away from the nuptial ceremony.

Then the Vedic *shlokas* began, interrupted only by the sound of bells and bangles whenever one of the girls moved an inch. The hypnotic rhythm seemed to match the waves of the desert and Nitin tried not to sway. He wanted the whole affair to be over. He wanted to be able to press himself into the sand and imagine it was a bed.

But the wedding went on. And on. And on.

More prayers. Then the couple were tied to each other — his *pagri* to her *palla*. They walked seven times around the fire. The fire ... the fire was burning hotter than his forehead. He felt himself sinking, knocked out by the prayers. The sand. Under him. His head was against it.

'Quick, make him a bed.'

'I should have stayed with him at the hotel.'

'Just let him rest, yah. He's not used to the food, that's all.'

Nitin heard the voices. He heard the discussions about which dune would be best suited for the 'honeymoon suite'.

'The furthest from the camels!'

He heard the tinkling of bells as Mae walked with Neel over to their nuptial dune, and he heard the cry of an unnamed baby seeking milk and sleep, and he looked up at the moon as Savitri's hand soothed his aching forehead.

'Tomorrow we'll leave the others on their honeymoon and see if some of these guys can take us home.'

'No worries, sweetheart. I'm so sorry ...'

Nitin sank into his dreams as his body sank into the sand, and he found himself converting the strange Vedic words and sounds from earlier into Christian epiphanies. He dreamed of Joseph in the desert, with angels going up and down the ladder to heaven. (Wasn't Moses in the desert too, when he saw the burning bush?) Then he saw Indian gods and goddesses emerge from behind the dunes. Savitri appeared in her mother's beautiful red and gold sari as a goddess holding a lotus flower, then Mae as Mary, but an Indian Mary, in a red sari. He was sweating. More epiphanies. *There is no single religion. In this desert. No God to claim here, just souls ... and bodies, ripe for harvesting under the full moon.*

THE SEER'S DILEMMA

ARUNJI HAD ALWAYS been one of those astrologers who believed that a prediction about the date of death should be hidden from the person seeking his services. He resisted the argument that there was any benefit in knowing. Even when Mataji had been desperate to know about her 'date with destiny', as she so euphemistically called it, he could have given her the exact numbers for when numbers would cease to exist, but he'd refused to give her such knowledge. Instead, he gave her reassurances around other events, such as Savitri's marriage — meaningful occasions he knew would make her happy; he'd given her something she could look forward to as she lay trapped in her body in that room.

But just as Winsome had known the date of the birth of her baby, when Arunji was given Nitin's date of birth to create his chart, he knew that Savitri's husband would expire the day after Neel's wedding. The date and time were that precise. A clear-cut case, astrologers would say. Yet what caution could he give? Tell the young couples to drink only bottled water? Avoid salads?

Eat only food cooked in front of them? Avoid death wherever possible, at all costs?

So the phone call he received from Neel in the middle of the night was perhaps the hardest consultation he would ever have to give.

'Arunji, Nitin is extremely sick,' Neel began, without even saying who was on the line. 'I'm thinking — could it be the curse of your *thisthing, Manglik?*'

If Savitri was struck by the curse of *Manglik*, then Arunji, in that moment, was struck by the curse of knowledge. Far too much knowledge.

'... and Savitri is beside herself ... she's worried she might lose him ... is there any prayer ... or something?'

The family astrologer could hear that familiar voice of helplessness.

'Savitri will be all right ...' Even as he said these words he knew they were pathetic, because Neel wasn't seeking advice on his sister, even though he feared she might soon be a widow. What they wanted was a prayer, a potion. A petition with the god of death.

He started again, thinking this time beyond what he knew, into the current moment and how he could offer some kind of intervention. 'There is a ceremony we do for *Manglik* people before marriage, you know. You can try it after the event and see *how-all* it might help, but you must consult a doctor for Nitin. Really, this is so important.' What else could he do from his apartment in Delhi but balance magic with medicine?

'We've called a doctor. He's staying the night with them.'

'Good. Good. You must do the needful ... And have you told your parents?'

'No. We don't want to worry them.'

Arunji finished the call mid-sentence, like he always did. So many times he'd had news for Siddharth, Tota or Mataji but hadn't wanted to worry them — hadn't wanted them to have that same curse of knowledge. What could he say, anyway? All he could do was to send Neel off into the desert with a plan: with the eternal hope of humankind that death could be conquered.

He rang Neel back on his mobile.

'Make sure Savitri listens to the doctor — none of those homeopathics that people are using. She has to do everything he is wanting.' *Or she may have to live with regrets.*

Neel sat with Savitri, Nitin and the doctor they'd summoned in that underground room until their food was delivered, but Nitin couldn't manage the smell, so brother and sister took it in turns to eat outside in the corridor. When they were all together, Neel approached the idea of a belated *Manglik* ceremony.

'It's just a suggestion. Arunji said it might help.'

The doctor said nothing.

'No.' It was a weak no, from Nitin.

'Over here, Nitin, you'll see trees with saris on them. The villagers worship them. Down south in Tamil Nadu they paint them red — they even hang the placentas of their cows in plastic bags on the banyan trees to increase the milk the cows give ...'

Nitin's mind, when confronted with an image of a cow's placenta, transformed it immediately into his camel's hanging, stenching stomach.

He vomited.

'It doesn't have to take that long, yah? We just tie the sari and go,' Neel continued, as if he were describing a mechanical act, as Savitri went to empty the vomit bowl.

'And how, exactly, is me marrying a tree going to make Nitin better?'

Even Nitin managed to voice the words 'not necessary' as a half-hearted intervention, making Neel feel as if he'd uttered the most superstitious nonsense to have entered the twenty-first century.

'I'm not leaving this room,' Savitri said firmly. 'I'm going to stay until he feels better. Forget it.'

'Then maybe we should airlift him to Delhi?' Neel was trying to sound responsible but was finding it hard to hide the panic.

'No,' Nitin whispered. A fresh hallucination appeared now: a sky made of flying camels, chanting strange hymns, smeared in the scent of nauseating green curry. One of them spat at him and the spit landed in his mouth. The spit of death. He exhaled deeply.

'Shhh. Let him get some sleep.'

Savitri slept next to Nitin and the doctor slept on the chaise longue opposite their four-poster bed, while Nitin's soul hovered above them all, wakeful, walking alone down a sandy tunnel with minarets carved out of its peaks.

In her dream, neither Savitri nor the doctor were asleep — and perhaps they were both awake, and none of it was a dream. Either way, in that transcendent state between worlds and time she remembered only a few things ... like when the doctor spoke to her about the broken thermometer and repeated the words he'd told her earlier. 'It is not possible to have a temperature of 108.'

'But he has it.' She found herself conversing with this doctor, in her non-sleep, all-seeing consciousness, surprised that he now had the exact same voice as Arunji.

'He doesn't have a temperature anymore.'

'Good.'

'He's cold.' She could hear the doctor telling her something more. 'His time has come.'

'Nonsense.'

'We've lost him.'

'I will never lose him.' Yet even as she said this she could see him walking down that turreted sandy gully. She bent over the physical body he'd left behind and touched his forehead. It was cold, just as the doctor-astrologer had told her. The same unearthly cold as her grandmother when she'd touched her for the last time, before she was taken away on the bier.

She walked after the moving, transcendent form of Nitin, down that gully, but even as she did she could hear the doctor's voice telling her to stay.

'You cannot follow him.'

'I can.' She had followed her grandmother some of the way, hadn't she? *The doctor has the voice of Arunji — it's a mirage. I can't believe him.*

Turn back while you can. There will be others.

'Others?' There was only one person ahead of her, walking swiftly into the transparency of air. 'I have not chosen any others.' *I can't listen to him. He's distracting me. I'm losing sight of Nitin ...*

ॐ

Neel had borrowed a torch to conduct the *Manglik* ceremony he had no idea how to conduct, but the moon was so low and bright that he could see everything without help. The tree they'd chosen to stand in for Nitin in the 'marriage' was an elegant mature one on the outskirts of Jaisalmer. None of them knew the names of trees, but perhaps it could have given a little shade to travellers who'd awaited the right of admission to the fortress city in earlier times.

Winsome had her sleeping baby strapped to her chest as she took one end of the ornate, red brocade sari with its 24-carat gold threads and wound it around the sacred tree until it looked as if it had two legs reaching upwards, wrapped in a silk far more elegant than had been draped around any sacred tree in history, no doubt.

'Who's gonna stand in for Savitri?' Mae asked, looking at Winsome. 'Would you mind?'

Winsome agreed. She'd never intended to be married — a failure in her imagination, perhaps, or a firm intention to break with the past — but she knew that she would be able to act the part of her friend if the ritual demanded such a substitution.

Neel felt the discomfort of his sister and Nitin as he continued dressing the tree ready for the wedding, draping the luxurious *palla* with its fine gold threadwork over a final branch.

'I feel as if I'm making this up as I go along, it's crazy.' With one hand on his mother's prized wedding sari and the other on his phone, he decided to call Arunji.

'We have the sari all wrapped around the tree now, yah. What-all to do next?'

Arunji was woken from his own dreams, which had released

him from his worries about events in a distant desert, and now he was forced to return to the world, an astrologer turned unofficial hierophant for a make-believe ritual that would achieve nothing — absolutely nothing. Nitin had already gone. It had been quick, and fairly painless according to his accounts.

'You need a pandit to conduct the marriage.'

'Fuck, do you know what you're asking? It's the middle of the night, yah? Where the hell am I going to find a pandit?'

The heirloom sari had already sustained a nasty tear from the place where the tree split its trunk. Neel took his hand to the silk and slashed it further in frustration.

'Maybe you can just say a few prayers and finish off,' Arunji replied. *Why not let the young ones feel some hope? Nitin is already dead. What harm can they do?*

'I can say some prayers,' Sage offered hopefully. 'I married Savitri and Nitin.'

And so Sage closed his eyes, but the words that came out were strangely Christian for such a voodoo act. 'Do you, Winsome, acting as Savitri, take this tree, acting as Nitin, to be your faithfully wedded husband?'

'Fuck, that's hopeless.' Neel hadn't meant his words to come out that way, but his helplessness in the face of these religious rules was insurmountable. 'I'm so sorry. It's not your fault. It's ours. It's the whole bloody, stupid, shit that we've swallowed for far too many years.'

The baby started crying and Winsome pulled out her breast, sitting down in the sand next to the solitary tree, which looked well overdressed for a night out.

'Why are we even doing this?'

The wedding party began walking back to the hotel inside the fortress ramparts, leaving the tree lonely on the outskirts of Jaisalmer — its only sacred purpose now to convert carbon dioxide into breathable oxygenated air: a selfless act that would go unnoticed, except for the fact that an heirloom sari from the last century lay draped far too elegantly around its forked trunk.

The women in front of Savitri in her dream were the familiar strangers from that long night she'd spent with her grandmother — that last night they'd had together. They were her past, as well as her future. Not angels of death but angels of birth — mothers in her lineage and beyond: a line of women that receded into white light in the distance, beyond recognition, but still pulsing with familial familiarity. Closest to her was her grandmother, transcendent and resplendent, the one she knew best in this feminine line. Behind her more faces, smiling with encouragement, but this time many more than could be possible in a single lineage. And more of them kept arriving: a multitude. They arrived as supporters from distant times and places, with features that bore no resemblance to hers, except she felt that she was of their line: all of them. Women born of women, born of women. The sacred feminine incarnate in its once-worldly multiplicity.

There was a light in the distance, which drew her in, as if her soul had soft moth wings growing from unfathomable corners.

'Who is that light?' she asked her grandmother.

Dadi replied with a word she had never heard before, which seemed filled with life and song, and Savitri asked her to say the word again. When it was repeated, whispered in that tongue of butterflies, it was uttered as a single syllable that sounded like 'you'. *Could that be right?*

Her grandmother stood before her, with the same transcendent spirit she'd felt that long night — the last they had spent together. Savitri took her hand, and reached out for more hands, some of them jewelled, with bracelets, bangles, soft skin reaching out for her, lifting her up to a greater height where she could see further up; a coolish wind streamed across her face.

Then the most bizarre unexpected music began to play. The song that Mae had sung after their wedding: 'Losing My Religion'. Not a song that any of these women would have ever heard. She laughed. The rising sensation continued, until all of those women merged into a single manifestation of light. It began at her toes, that light, and then it rose, further and further through her body, until the form she felt as her own was consumed by the weightless intensity of its godly glow.

A NEW WORLD

ARUNJI COULD NO longer rely on the noise of construction to wake him in the mornings, so he set his alarm clock for 6 a.m. to wait for the call. He knew it would come soon. And that he would be one of the first to be informed of Nitin's passing.

But 10 a.m. came and went, and then lunch, and still there had been no call. *Neel was angry on the phone last night. Maybe because I could be no help to them.*

He decided to call Siddharth instead.

'What news of the wedding party?' he asked.

'Not good,' Siddharth replied. Arunji waited for the announcement ...

'Nitin nearly passed away last night.'

'Nearly?'

'Yes.'

'But he's better?'

'Good God, why do you think he wouldn't be?'

Of course. Siddharth has the power.

Arunji's surprise was loud for all its missing utterances.

'You told them that he was going to pass away last night?' Siddharth was concerned now.

'No. I would never have done such a thing — that's not how I do my work. But Neel did call ...' Arunji tried to blank out his thoughts so there would be no trail that led to any kind of prediction. No hint of shameful shock or relief to give away the fact that Nitin's survival past his mathematical deadline was unimaginable.

'Something he ate, that's all. Savitri had been taking him out to eat on the streets and to Old Delhi from the day he arrived.'

'My God.' He adjusted his words. 'Thank God.'

Siddharth immediately read the backstory to Arunji's tangible relief.

'So you really predicted that Nitin was going to die last night?'

'Yes.' There was no point lying now.

'Then we are very lucky that our old rules no longer hold true.'

'Perhaps some of them do ...'

Siddharth realised he might have sounded cruel. 'At least we should be grateful that mystery will always remain mysterious.'

'Yes.'

I checked my calculations. I rechecked them.

Siddharth continued, 'You're finding it hard to believe this, no?'

'It's impossible.'

'Many things that we believe are impossible are going to come about.' It was the futurist, not the astrologer, making predictions now.

Siddharth could feel his brother's grip on the world failing, and it reminded him of his persistent cosmic dream about taking his hands off the wheel of that driverless car. He thought about all the convincing numbers that would have to cohere to create such an unimaginable feat: a car that actually drove itself, with all the sensors and data and satellites at work. And yet the real mystery remained in that moment of lifting one's hands from the wheel — lifting them and observing the survival of the self.

'We must always continue to believe in greater miracles,' Siddharth went on. He was thinking about what must have taken place for his children in Rajasthan. If Arunji was correct — if they really had just turned a corner at the edge of the world — then they had engaged with that future mystery, with all its natural elegance and timeliness and promise. So simple. And yet complex beyond the imaginings of numbers.

Seven days after Neel and Mae's wedding, when the moon had shed a quarter of its fullness, Nitin was well enough to sit up and eat rice and yoghurt and sugar with the others for breakfast. They were all in a beautiful place once more, sitting on the roof of their hotel under a friendly sun, near the ramparts of the fortress in an entirely new world.

'Do you remember anything?' Neel asked.

'Nah, sorry, mate. Nothing except Savitri's presence — that's all.'

'Do you remember talking to the man on a black buffalo?'

'What the hell?'

'Because you were talking to him, you know. You were having a fantastic negotiation for your soul.'

'Sorry, mate. Don't remember having any yarn with any fellas on black buffalos.'

'You should have heard yourself raving ...'

'It was worse when we heard you'd stopped raving,' Winsome said. 'So scary.'

'Could you hear the doctor say we'd lost you?'

'Did you see a tunnel, like they say you do?' Neel asked.

'Maybe ... dunno ... I just remember Savitri. I had to come back because I saw her pregnant.' He tried to change the subject in case he was taken back to that moment. 'Anyway, how was your wedding?' It came out wrong. As if he hadn't really attended.

'You were there,' Mae replied. 'You tell us. What was your favourite bit of it?'

Winsome laughed. 'That's not fair. That's like asking Gayatri.' She was practising the sound of her baby's name. The word emerged as more beautiful and suitable every time she said it.

'Oh, is that her name?'

Nitin tried to remember something nice to say about the wedding but couldn't conjure up anything that was pleasant.

'I'm glad it really happened this time round.'

Yet even as he said these words, he couldn't be sure that the wedding had been anything more than a hallucination. He couldn't know for a fact that he had even attended, as if the sickness had created in him a parallel persona that would never be fully remembered or recovered in the state of consciousness he now held.

❦

Arunji kept calling Siddharth for confirmation that Nitin's recovery was sustained. (Yes, he has had food many times now. He's asking for more. His bowel movements have returned — yes, thank you for asking — and he's walking, too. And for the further calls: yes, yes and yes.)

Absolutely unfathomable. It was as if the new world had no place for an astrologer. As if he'd been asked to evacuate the premises of the present to make way for the new, haphazard construction of an unpredictable future.

He thought about what could be worth dying for and what might be worth protecting forever in this new century. The hopes of the worthiest ancestors. Memories of the Golden Age. He had no wife and no children, so his line was finished — there was no caste of *dhobis* to continue slapping wet clothes against rocks with soap. The washing machine had reforged lives.

He rang Siddharth once more. Yes, Nitin was still alive. The two parents had flown out to Jaisalmer to be with the children and their friends.

Irrefutable.

Why, I too have survived to witness the birth of the new India.

When the survival was indisputably confirmed, he began to wonder about the dozens of other predictions he'd banked on for the future, and pondered what might have survived among those as he navigated this new country with its ancient stories and rules and temples for landmarks, its castes and creeds and primordial music. What, among all the wreckage ... the liberalisation and deregulation ... the corruption ... the new money ... and even more new money, and the lavish farmhouses in Delhi's food bowls and the new empires beyond in Gurgaon — what about those? What might be immortal ... what might be worth saving in this new India? This new world? What scraps of sentiment? What beauty in the forgotten lore? What fragments of cloth, or vermilion dust from the rituals performed daily for millennia past? What, if anything, should be preserved like a flower worth keeping, and pressed between the pages of an eternal book?

ACKNOWLEDGEMENTS

This novel is a belated offering, taking many years to surface in the world, because life is like that.

It was started with many other works as part of a course I ran at the NSW Writers' Centre — The Year of the Novel — back in 2012. I decided that I shouldn't set my students the challenge of writing a novel in a year without going through the same struggles myself. I thank every one of those students for the rich conversations and their beautiful stories — a year where we 'murdered our darlings and kept some of the remains ... carved symbols out of fire and discovered that you can, actually, learn to fly a helicopter using visualisation.' We published an anthology together that we titled *Dandelions and Helicopters* as 'an airborne metaphor' for the flight we took together.

The other students and staff I'd like to thank have worked with me in my role as founding Course Director for the Bachelor of Creative Intelligence and Innovation (BCII). All ideas have heritage and lineage, and many of the concepts in this novel come from discoveries into new worlds that we've opened up together. Leading this world-first transdisciplinary degree was a creative project like no other, keeping my imagination constantly seeking new territory. I thank every one of my students and staff for signing up for the adventure and for teaching me so much.

Thank you to my publisher, Barry Scott, for taking risks and helping to turn them into gold — for championing the more ephemeral, spiritual literary works that speak to the meaning and purpose that the world's most abiding stories have always been tasked to address. And to my cover designer, Josh Durham and typesetter, Patrick Cannon.

And of course, I have to thank the hours of time that my editors have spent working with me as my secondary senses.

They say that authors 'write drunk and edit sober.' Seeing flaws can be a punishing process, with no end, so I thank my first editor, Linda Funnell, for flooding light on the big tasks that needed to be done. Thank you, Linda, for the talent and care you put into this novel and for your work on the others that you championed through HarperCollins. I am so grateful for your support. And thank you Penelope Goodes, my second editor, for painstaking attention to details — for helping me stand back and see this work as 'Finished.'

Niki Zubrzycki, one of my first readers and dear friend, thank you for always being the first to read my books and for being so thoughtful in your responses. Sue Woolfe — thank you, too, for being a long-term supporter and for being a partner in organising literary soirées and other offerings for our literary community.

My family are my world and I thank them all for being the joy at the centre of my life. My sons, Tally, Rishi and Kashi for being my hope. Thank you Jan Golembiewski (if thanks could ever be enough) for being my fellow explorer of the miraculous. For being so present, so adoring and such an active co-creator of beauty, love and happiness in our lives. (Jan is also the author of 'Magic,' and a brilliant storyteller, so his reading of my work was incredibly valuable.)

I should mention that this novel has journeyed through many transitions, taking the time it did, and one turning point was a sabbatical I was generously offered through the University of

Technology Sydney, when I went to Auroville to complete this book. I am so grateful for being given time to write in India's utopian community that celebrates the lived experience of human unity — one of the themes in this book. The founders of Auroville were invisible contributors to this story and their legacy is found in its future-facing concerns. My protagonist was named in response to Sri Aurobindo's poem, *Savitri*, about the transformative power of consciousness — a tale from the *Upanishads* that deserves re-telling. Thank you to all of my friends in Auroville who provoked me to think deeply about how we could live — especially Aster Patel.

Sabrina Lipovic — thank you for my title. How easy it was when you pointed out to me that my elephant wearing a headlight in the streets of New Delhi was a simple metaphor for the challenges inherent in an era of driverless cars!

In the time it took to write this novel I also suffered many losses, some of which are reflected in this book. None more significant than the loss of my father, William Le Hunte, who rang me up from the other side of the world to tell me that he was dying and that he loved me, the night before he left us. I share this in my acknowledgements because those so dear remain present, no matter where they go. I love him back, just as much as I ever did — perhaps even more so, if that's even possible.

Then, there's the subject of birth. Thank you David Miller for cropping up as someone worth acknowledging in all my books! Your work delivering babies in the shire is an inspiration.

Thank you to all the people who move in and out of our home, share meals and become part of our lives — as well as my mother-in-law, writer and artist, Kathy Golski, and our extended families.

I feel so blessed for these many relationships, and I offer blessings to my readers, who make writing worthwhile.

Love and wishes,

Bem Le Hunte, 2020